£ (

– MARK S

Masel

Taranis Books
1992

Printed in Scotland by Bell & Bain, Glasgow

ISBN 1-873899-35-1

About the Author

Mark Smith was born in Los Angeles, California, in 1960. He attended Stirling University, in Scotland, and studied Political Science, Economics and English Literature before graduating in 1983. He has travelled extensively, and has worked as a journalist throughout Europe and parts of South America, Asia and the Middle East. He is currently living in Glasgow and working with the Scottish Daily Record. He is also working on his second novel.

ACKNOWLEDGEMENTS

The songs sung by Masel are *Lay Lady Lay* (Music Sales (MS)), *Maggie's Farm* (Blossom) and *The Gates Of Eden* (MS), Bob Dylan; *Truckin'* (Peter Maurice Co.), Garcia/Lesh/Weir/Hunter; *Casey Jones* (Ice Nine), Garcia/Hunter; *When The Music's Over* (MS), The Doors; *Voodoo Chil'* (Schroeder) and *Purple Haze* (MS), Hendrix; *Fool To Cry*, Jagger/Richard; *Cry Baby*, Ragovoy/Berns; *Imagine* (MS), Lennon; *Help* (MS), Lennon/McCartney; *Rolling Hills*, Morrison; *I-Feel-Like-I'm-Fixin'-To-Die Rag*, Country Joe McDonald; *White Rabbit* (Rondor Music), Slick; *My Generation* (MS), Townsend; *Love In Mind*, Young; *Oy Gevalt Blues*, E. Masel. I'm particularly indebted to the works of Leo Rosten, whose various gems of Yiddish wisdom I quote frequently, usually in altered form. I have borrowed good lines and ideas from other writers, past and present, noteably Friedrich Nietzche, some of the rabbis of the Kabalah, Bernard Malamud and Chaim Potok, and from numerous aquaintances, friends and loved ones, especially Cath Conlon. The industrious may discover other sources, more than I know myself - among them the works of John Gardner, Franz Kafka and Saul Bellow. I am also indebted to Scott McMeekin, who helped me devise the hologram ideas used in this book, and to Susan Conlon and other friends for their kindness and assistance. I would like to express special gratitude to Cath (once again), who gave me friendship and inspiration, as well as a place to write when I had none. She also gave me advice and encouragement, read the manuscript in its umpteen stages, helped me see my mistakes and coaxed me to remove stupidities, errors and improbabilites. Thanks also to Vicky Smart, who produced the excellent cover for this book at extremely short notice.

Though based on real places, the Glasgow of this novel is fictitious, as are the characters. I've moved many of the city's streets and districts around for plot convenience. As far as I know, there are no caves in the city's Botanic Gardens (although there might be), nor is there a concert venue called the Glasgow Baroque Hall (GBH) or anything resembling it.

Finally, Glasgow 'culture' is not in reality the contrived, shallow notion I've made it. The slogan "See Glasgow, see culture" cited throughout this book gives good advice. Take it whatever way you wish. If any Glaswegian still feels put upon, let him blame the novel's hero, Elliot Masel. I tried to help him, but he's a desperate man.

I ask my family, with heart-felt affection and gratitude, to divide the dedication of this book evenly between my father, my mother, my sister and my grandmother, who between them taught me the beauty of life and how to be nobody's fool.

Life's but a walking shadow, a poor player
That struts and frets his hour upon the stage
And then is heard no more.
                        - WILLIAM SHAKESPEARE

A human being must either climb up or climb down.
                        - TALMUD

Only a shlemasel believes in masel.
                        - YIDDISH FOLK SAYING

And if you gaze long enough into the abyss, the abyss gazes also into you.
                        - FRIEDRICH NIETZSCHE

■ The Arrival
■ One

ELLIOT MASEL, an American folk music expert and self-confessed failure as a performing musician, arrived in Glasgow, Scotland amid violent April storms. An ominous portent or just a beginning, he wondered. He knew he must be out of his mind. At the exact moment he cautiously poked his nose from the jet's rear exit, a massive column of sheet lightning flashed. It surged out like a wild flush of fire, bathing and ripping the puffy, black sky over his head. Masel, conscious of quaking limbs, shuddered. Was that for me? He allowed himself a small smile, felt the thrill of adventure in his gut. Zelda would laugh if she could see me now. He thought of her fondly. Elliot Masel doing what? Get serious. Yet here he was descending the portable metal staircase, not without difficulty. Ah, the new world, he sighed. In one perspiring palm, he gripped the hard, black case of his beloved Gizmo guitar; in the other was jammed a half-empty, imitation-leather travel bag. As he stepped on to the oily, grey-black runway, a low, thick cloud emptied its belly. Thunder clapped and the lumpy rain soaked him. Fatigued, dripping, he looked around in a foreign land for a welcome. Who can a man like me expect to find on an airport runway?

The last passenger to leave the plane, Masel jogged through the downpour in search of passport control, his body turned this way and that like a shadow boxer, his bright-white soggy sneakers squeaking too loudly. From somewhere in the back of his mind - or was it his belly? - a small but anxious state was taking hold of him. He cautioned himself to behave. The rain dirtied the green sweep of hills in the distance and muddied the rumbling asphalt under his feet. When he caught sight of the dense cloud that darkly wreathed the head of the navigation tower, he became convinced that only his concentration had brought that big, silver son of a bitch to roost safely.

He thought for a moment what the word for passport might be, but then remembered they spoke English in Scotland. Another boom of thunder went off, like the blast of a cannon, and the storm grew frenzied, gushing. Masel, making a dash for cover, his forearms loosely raised, spoke only American. He had the smell of water in his nose. Hope was a scary business. He spoke passionately to himself: "Dear God, I'm sick and tired of being in this hole that I'm in. Let me extend beyond myself." Who knows what will happen? he thought. He was, in the same breath, fearful, amazed, that he had managed to muster the confidence in himself. Imagine, me in Scotland, the northern land of Celts, purple heather, Bonnie Prince Charlie, Scotch whisky, passionate folk songs ... and rain, all this rain. Now that this was the point of no return, what now? He shuddered.

* * *

He stood at the tail-end of the passport-check line, slightly disorientated. The transcontinental flight had been long and exhausting, the transatlantic leg worse. Now, standing in line, he was abruptly at the point of dropping. He experienced mild hallucinations when his concentration waned: a wall twitched beneath the weight of the yellow fluorescent light, the chequer-board floor momentarily moved like a sea under him. His heart bumped. He blinked rapidly to snap out of it.

"Holy Moses," Masel breathed out loud. "That's a weird day out there."

He shook the water from his head and his blue flannel suit like a wet dog, a little self-conscious of the action, his ponytail dripping. The man in front of him, broad-shouldered and sharply dressed in a charcoal-grey business suit, pink silk shirt and black leather shoes, turned quickly. He appeared horrified.

"Moses?"

The American grinned lamely, took a step backward. "It's just an expression."

He felt himself drawn into a gaze. The man stared deeply into Masel's eyes, as though he were looking into a mirror for the first time in twenty years. His eyebrows were like a tangled thicket of hawthorn. Masel, gulping, observed something vaguely Asiatic about him, perhaps in the roughness of his skin, a windswept nomad from the steppe lands, a Mesopotamian. His eyelids were profoundly wrinkled. There was also something familiar - this was strange to Masel, a little creepy; maybe he had noticed him on the plane or at San Francisco International Airport. He thought the man looked a little drunk. His nose was like a rock avalanche, his eyes like two caves. Masel felt an icy chill run down his spine.

The two men gazed at each other, searching, as if they could be twins separated at birth. Masel wondered if he had anything to do with his ex-wife, but then discarded the theory. What if he's a spymaster or a terrorist? I'm a paranoiac. Suddenly, the man's pink shirt burst forth into shining fire, its flames licking out in every direction, consuming all that it touched: the slab ceiling, electrical wires, a red-roped line cordon, the imitation-leather travel bag. Masel jumped back, protecting his Gizmo. What the hell is going on? I must be hallucinating again. Wake up, for God's sake. He took a deep breath, closed his eyes and snapped them open again.

"So can I help you with something?" He was relieved to find the fire was out, his travel bag unscathed.

The man grinned widely, an imbroglio of silver hair ascending from his tanned dome. "Don't malign the weather, my friend. It keeps the grass green and the tourists out. Besides, this is God's country."

Although the man's voice had a tendency to boom, Masel strained his hearing, his brow lowered, to understand the harsh, lilting accent. Nervously, he checked himself. He could feel his heart pound against his rib-cage.

"How do you mean exactly?"

The man laughed heartily, almost cackling, then stopped mock-seriously. He rolled up his red-rimmed eyes, his face suddenly twisted. "I mean being in Scotland is in itself an atonement for your sins."

Masel looked at him suspiciously, then laughed hoarsely,

relieved. His little ponytail hung now like a drowned animal from the back of his head. "I'm a little jumpy," he apologized. "This is my first trip to Scotland."

The man let out a snort. "See Glasgow, see culture."

Masel had no idea what he was talking about. Although he fought it, nervousness rose like a flame within him. It was caused by everything, and now this.

"Very nice," he said. He remembered, with trepidation, what an airport official had said to him at San Francisco International before embarking: "Are you in possession of any marijuana or cocaine?" Why me? thought the folk expert. Masel had said, "No way", his heart beating wildly at the recollection, even though he had given up drugs ten years ago. It's my over-active imagination working against me again.

The passport-check line advanced, leaving a lengthy gap between the possible spymaster and terrorist and the remainder of the line. The American abruptly noticed two security guards, large men, advancing toward him from the left. He didn't think this was his imagination; rather, he knew this was the end, the bubble bursting before it got off the ground, the dream, so long and painful in conception, still-born. His one shot at getting his act together lay in ruins before him, as did the rest of his pitiful life. He knew any moment now he would be refused entry into the country, sent home in shame, humiliation and embarrassment: perhaps an invalid passport, the wrong visa, a marijuana conviction, the wrong face, the wrong religion, his failure as a performer, his failure at marriage, the death of his father, the death of his mother, any number of these could be brought against him to seal his fate. Acid filled his stomach. He closed his eyes and, thinking of San Francisco fog, waited to be arrested. From within deep silence, he heard the booming voice of the possible spymaster and terrorist echo loudly around him.

"What charge? You must tell me the charge."

Masel's back sizzled with hot sweat against his wet tee-shirt. He snapped open his eyelids. A small crowd of jet-lagged commercial travellers and tourists had gathered. Masel, raising one eyebrow, bit his lip. The two guards flanked the possible spymaster and terrorist, tenaciously grasping a forearm apiece.

"Come along quietly," one of them grunted, a thin-faced man with depthless eyes.

"I demand you tell me the charge."

"Keep it shut," said the other guard, pink-faced, his voice adenoidal.

Masel watched in disbelief, stood immobilized, his arm resting stiffly on his upright guitar case, his testicles shrinking. Spymaster? Terrorist? The American shuddered. The man's jaw was clenched, and his gaze shifted sharply back and forth between the two guards. He let out a brief snorting laugh.

"The henchmen are always worse than their masters."

Masel pushed his eyes away, forcing himself not to stare. Dizziness assailed him. He abruptly sneezed.

"AH-CHOO!"

The guard with the depthless eyes swivelled around. He looked Masel up and down, at the guitar case and his imitation leather travel bag.

"Aren't you that American who does all that psychedelic stuff?"

The self-confessed failure as a performing musician, labouring to clear his mind, sniffed and glanced at the case of his beloved Gizmo guitar. He felt exposed.

"Er - I've given lectures on that subject, and, I suppose, the odd show."

The guard cocked his head, eyeing Masel warily. He nodded slowly, as if he were quietly praying. "I thought I knew your face." He jerked his head in the direction of the suspected spymaster and terrorist. "Do you know this man?"

Masel denied it, his heart pounding. He felt blood rising through his neck. "I think I recognize him from the plane. But before that, never."

His arms laden, Masel awkwardly pulled a wet handkerchief from the breast pocket of his blue flannel jacket and blew his nose. He couldn't believe what was happening. It was madness. I should never have come here. Look what's happening already. Already I'm in trouble. I can't look.

The American looked. The suspected spymaster and terrorist jerked free and pushed his frame close up to Masel, his eyes wide and fiery. "Those who cannot control themselves become absurd when they attempt to control others."

The guard with depthless eyes grabbed him, and held him bent in a headlock; the other gripped him by his jacket. The suspected spymaster and terrorist, his tongue thick and bent back on itself, struggled modestly, throwing his arms out like pallid wings in resistance. In the confusion of bodies, an elbow smashed into his cheek, a knuckle struck his eye. Blood fell from his nose to his mouth, and he shook his head, as if he were trying to break free from a spell. Both guards held him by his armpits now and they were nearly lifting him.

"Remember life, my friends, and remember death," he called, his head shifting between them. "Bless you. Bless you."

The guards dragged him violently into a side room and shut the door. Masel checked himself against the impulse to run. He became aware that he was shaking. He closed his eyes in an attempt to calm himself. When he opened them, he found he was alone, the line ahead of him, gone. A female passport official was standing in a glass box, eyeing him, her arms folded impatiently. He embarrassedly walked toward her, his semi-liquid stomach heaving. What am I doing here? He had hoped this trip would bring him a change of luck. Gevalt, he thought, God help me, luck like this I can do without.

* * *

Masel shakily relaxed his grip on his passport, surrendering it cautiously to a youngish, blonde woman, who he thought wasn't at all bad looking, save a festering herpes simplex on her lower lip.

"I'm sorry," he offered awkwardly. "It was a long trip."

There was a look of smiling efficiency about her that let you know she could keep you standing there for as long as she felt like it. To hand it over, he had to clasp the travel bag awkwardly between his legs, his guitar case precariously propped against his elbow. The intensity of his clenched thighs caused his testicles to meet in nauseating discomfort. His stomach swished as he caught the sour odour of whisky on the woman's breath. Masel groaned faintly. She stared at him as though in alarm. The American, dripping, was making a puddle wherever he spent more than a few seconds. Where was it all coming from? He handed the woman a wet letter.

She read with thick concentration. Glasgow District Council had invited Elliot Masel, musician and recent, though mature, PhD graduate in American Folk Science, to the city's Culture Festival. He was to perform three of his "extraordinary" stage shows on the 1960s youth revolution and, to supplement his income, he might if necessary give a series of lectures at the university.

"I see you're to perform at the Glasgow Baroque Hall."

Masel stood a moment, his groin grieving faintly, a nerve from somewhere down there catching him somewhere up here. "That's correct."

The woman said nothing, nodded, her lips faintly curled.

"A George MacGregor from the district council is supposed to meet me," he said, through a constricted throat. "He's in charge of the culture committee. It's all there, isn't it?" He paused in hope of a response, grinning. She gave him a pitying, superior smile. His adam's apple bobbing as he gulped.

The woman returned his wet letter and, licking her forefinger, flipped to a British Embassy visa in his passport entitling Masel to stay in the country for up to a year.

"And how long do you actually intend being here?"

"It depends on how things go. A few months, I guess." Unable to resist, he admitted, "I'm looking for a little change."

Smirking momentarily, she stared at him to confirm his identity and checked her big book. She looked him up again and then down, striking his passport hard with a rubber stamp.

"See Glasgow, Dr Masel," she said, "see culture."

Masel thought that he heard a snigger when he was permitted to pass. He sniggered himself, at his good fortune.

* * *

He found himself in the middle of a crowded airport, a giant vortex of tourists and travellers, lost, inching ahead, his body cocked forward, as if he were pitched against a very high wind. Exhaustedly, he pulled behind him his little two-wheeled valise affair, like a child's toy wagon. The case embarrassed him.

He imagined he was running in circles. Masel, sucking in his unshaven cheeks, pooped, looked through the mass of people. Where the hell is George MacGregor already? What if he has come and gone and left me here? What if he's forgotten about me? or decided he doesn't need me anymore? It occurred to him he had absolutely no possibility of recognizing George MacGregor, even if the Culture King were to run up and bite him on the ass. That MacGregor would recognise him was also doubtful; he had sent only one passport-size photograph of himself. A renewed wave of panic flushed through him. I'll never find him and he'll never find me; nor was the American wearing a red carnation. Here he was, stranded at a strange airport in a strange country, sick of being fate's football. He wanted to go home.

Instead, he caught a short breath and murmured, "God help me. Please don't make me endure all You know I can."

With a start, Masel felt a limp tap on his shoulder. Despite the weight of his luggage, he jumped a foot in the air. What now? He turned around and, to his surprise, glimpsed a pair of skinny, black-stockinged legs.

"Holy shit," he whispered, blinking rapidly. "George MacGregor?"

 Two

Although she had a quick, energetic way in her demeanour, she seemed to come at Masel in slow motion. His eyes climbed upward on her nimble legs in surprise - give chair legs a couple of knees and feet, he thought - to a black mini-skirt, an almost gaunt waist, a vermilion blouse to which was pinned a badge, stating GLASGOW CULTURE VULTURE, and a silver glittering bow tie. She had a smooth, soft smile, distracted green eyes, and thick, brown-reddish hair that curled to the bottom of her freckled neck. Masel changed his mind; now he wanted to stay. The girl was very attractive, if not beautiful. Longer hair and she could be a Druid queen, he thought. The American folk expert, always falling for exotic beauty, melted. Oh, no, not the apple of my eye, not my dream girl. In truth, she was perhaps the most perfect creature he had ever seen. Be on your guard, he warned himself, these things never work out. Don't even think what you're thinking, he thought. It was too late. Masel's heart was already aching at the sight of her.

She spoke enthusiastically. "Dr Elliot Masel?"

He admitted it, blushing badly.

"Welcome to Glasgow, Dr Masel, See Glasgow, see culture. I'm Katy McArthur." She automatically smoothed her skirt. She was a bursting wild flower on a long, thin stem, a bright, blossoming orchid in a wide, open field of green. "I work for council public relations," she said. "I'm your host for a day or two, until you get settled in."

Hesitantly, Masel said, "Hi." He closed his eyes, took a breath and, for one wishful second, tried to seal his fate to hers. He struggled with his luggage; with his left arm, he hugged the Gizmo guitar case closely to his chest, with the other he grappled with his travel bag and the little valise. The bright airport lights assailed him. He was painfully aware that the girl was standing only inches from him.

In response, she gave the first warm smile he had had in months.

"Sorry, I got held up," he said, hoarsely, breathing heavily. She was a rake of a woman, apple-cheeked, with thin buttocks and sharp, braless breasts. Masel smiled back and felt his own cheeks flame. When his glance again fell on her bust, he immediately looked up into her lit eyes. She seemed startled. Over her outfit, she wore an open, brown duffel coat, with a twisted hood that flopped awkwardly at the back.

"Unfortunately, we've had quite a few terrorist threats recently," she said, her dark red hair bobbing on her shoulders as she spoke. Her breasts seemed to be pointing at him. "It's the same on all the flights nowadays"

The idea of terrorists panicked Masel. "So, what happened to MacGregor?" he asked, quickly instead. "I thought he was supposed to meet me."

Masel was immediately sorry he had said this. Was he appearing ungrateful for this beautiful young woman with pronging breasts? May my insides churn like a music box for a crack like that. What am I doing here? Enjoying myself, I deserve it. Ah, Masel, be honest for once: What are you doing? You meet a pretty girl and right away you want to charge off in pursuit of love.

She studied him with a cool, level gaze, her eyes now shockingly green. "George MacGregor?" she said. "Oh, you'll meet him in just a minute. I just thought I'd rescue you in the crowd. You were looking a bit lost. I knew your face from the picture you sent. I took the liberty of having several copies made for the Press."

Masel laughed brokenly.

"If you don't mind me saying, we're very excited about what you're planning for this year's Culture Festival." She turned to him squarely, and smiled, her eyes upon him like green laser light. "I hear it's quite a show you put on in America. And to be quite honest," - she leaned forward and whispered this - "we're all a bit fed up with opera and ballet."

Under normal circumstances this would have interested Masel, if only because her manner seemed to allude interest in him. But he was wobbly on his feet from his various anxiety attacks, the weight of his luggage and the possibility of love. He listened for elements of ridicule in the tone of her voice, but heard none.

"Follow me," Katy said, mildly. "I'll introduce you to George MacGregor."

Masel followed her through the dense but orderly crowd.

"So, what's with the getup?" he asked, gruffly, walking beside her and pointing to her glittering bow tie. The folk music expert wished he hadn't said that either, and was especially sorry about his indifferent tone. God take my testicles and let them be pecked by crows. May they name a disease after me. He wanted to make conversation, but it was coming out like insults.

"Getup?" she asked, tugging at her bow tie.

What kind of idiot am I? May cramps parade through my bowels.

She smiled, wrinkling her nose. "Oh this, Culture Katy 2080, that's me, the woman of the future."

There was a complexity in her tone he felt drawn to. He seriously advised self-restraint. He asked, "Why 2080, apart from the fact that it rhymes with Katy?"

Katy caught a short breath and beamed. "My real title is just Culture Katy, but I prefer to add the 2080. You see, I'm a woman of the future, so why not 2080? I work for the council to promote the Culture Festival." She paused for a moment to smile at him. "I'm the council's Culture Katy."

He guffawed, grateful for the gesture. "I like it," he said, aware of her blossoming perfume. "Makes sense, I guess." Grinning like an idiot, still considering it, he added, "Why not?"

Masel was on the verge of falling completely in love with her, when he tripped over a little boy chopping at his leg with a plastic cricket bat.

"Oy!" He went down with a cry.

His imitation leather travel bag and little valise went flying. Masel held his precious guitar in the air, although he banged his head on a stand-up ashtray while trying to get back on his feet. Masel saw himself floating in a white galaxy of stars and crescent moons. Star struck, he thought, when he came to. He lay for a moment on the airport floor in torment.

"Dr Masel, are you all right?" Katy raised her hand to her mouth to forestall laughter.

Masel admitted he would live, although he felt a blush ignite his cheeks. It was more a knock to his self-esteem, as she helped him up and then gathered his bags. This is all I need. He stood a moment, shaken, by the ashtray that had wounded him.

"Elliot," he said.

"What?"

He grinned foolishly. "You can call me Elliot."

Katy jabbed her finger into the distance, Masel's travel bag now over her shoulder. "Ah, there's George MacGregor over there," She seemed relieved. So was he, although his heart dropped. I warned you about this, he insulted himself.

Ahead, almost in front of them, Masel saw a man holding a slab of cardboard with the words DR MASEL on it, in large, thick, red-ink letters. This embarrassed him. A tingle of nervousness ascended to his chest. The lump on his head swelled.

"Mr MacGregor," shouted Katy, "yoo-hoo, over here."

MacGregor was a small, anaemic-looking man with off-white rotten teeth. Under an open green parka jacket he wore a plain brown suit that smelled of moth-balls, and fat grey shoes, like herrings. He had the face of Masel's old chemistry teacher, over-wrought and over-eager. Terrible dandruff too, yet in his eyes there was something sad, unfilled, but almost instantly likeable about the man. Masel, remembering with disappointment that he had failed his chemistry class, conjured up the image of a pig farmer come to the city for a day. Was this the culture king of Culture City? Him? Him with no chin?

MacGregor swiftly put his grey hand through his greasy hair and extended it.

Masel accepted with caution.

"Well," said the bureaucrat, wagging the expert's tired arm until it was limp. "Dr Masel, welcome to Culture City. All roads lead to Glasgow, eh? My name's MacGregor."

"Glad to know you," said Masel. Enough shaking already, please. MacGregor had an odd way of keeping still, like a fish trying to stand upright on its tail fin. His smile twitched absurdly.

Katy stared at Masel, as if reading the lines on his forehead. Out of the corner of his eye, he watched her watch him.

"Yeah, it's a pleasure," Masel added, after a moment. He rubbed the throbbing bump on his head.

MacGregor regarded him cunningly. He studied Masel's ponytail, his tentative, slender nostrils, his dark, sallow skin.

"We have quite a large Arabic community in Glasgow," he offered suddenly. "Mostly computer students if you'd like to speak to them. And there's quite a few Turkish restaurants springing up, and we have a Mosque in the Gorbals if you feel inclined to pray. Just make yourself at home in our..."

"Actually, I'm Jewish," Masel interrupted with a nervous smile. "Californian sunshine."

"Jewish, yes, well, we have a fine Jewish community here, too. Many synagogues."

Gevalt, thought Masel, he's an anti-semite. He doesn't like Jews. I might have known that. I'll bet some of his best Jews are friends. Masel reminded himself he came from a paranoid generation. In his youth, during the haze-filled days of Flower Power, he had developed a habit of flushing the toilet whenever the doorbell rang.

The bureaucrat manoeuvred a step sideways to stare. Standing on his tail fin, as if he were peeking around a corner, he added, "Did Katy mention we won't be able to reimburse you for your flight for another month or so? Wee cash crisis."

Katy coughed. Masel, rubbing his left ear, fixed a gloomy eye on the offending ashtray, then at George MacGregor. He gently groaned.

MacGregor proceeded sternly. "And of course you won't be paid for your shows until after you've done them. So I hope that you have enough funds to last a month or so. You can negotiate with the university yourself, although I'm sure your fee will be quite satisfactory." There was an uneasy silence. Grinning, MacGregor added, "I've set up a meeting in a couple of days. Katy has the details." He raised his voice, twisting slightly. "Don't you, Katy?"

"What? I'm sorry."

"You have the details of Elliot's meetings, don't you?"

Meetings? Masel thought, blushing.

"Of course."

MacGregor nodded. "I hope it's all not too much of an inconvenience."

"Actually, it is an inconvenience," said Masel, half-stuttering, sweating, blinking. "I had to borrow the fare from my ex-wife in New York. I only have five hundred dollars in travellers' cheques and maybe a hundred in cash."

Both MacGregor and Katy stared at Masel; he, almost in regret, she, more mildly.

Masel realised he had confessed his marital status, and God knows what else. Well, if so, what of it? They'll find out sooner or later, he said to himself. I've got nothing to be ashamed of. Marriages fail every day, don't they? Mine just happened to be one of them. God, help me. What have I got myself into? Out of the frying pan and into the dragon's claws.

"Well," said MacGregor, his mouth dropping open, as if he were having his leg pulled. After a moment, he chuckled, "Well, Doctor, you gave yourself away there, didn't you?"

Katy laughed merrily.

Masel smiled. Oy gevalt, he thought. On the way to the car, Culture Katy, her hood up, her perfume attacking Masel's nostrils, whispered in his ear, "Don't worry about the money. I'll sort it for you."

Masel worried about the money, yet couldn't shift his eyes from Katy, exquisite, lovely creature that she was.

■ Three

His new world seemed shiny from the rain. The wind died. A pale sun broke through, but then disappeared again. The downpour stopped then started, lessened then increased, and, in the midst of a thick shower, they sprinted through the parking lot to a black limousine. Katy, her head half hidden in the cave of her hood, winked, but Masel was too wet to blush, even if he was sure he had seen it. She dug in her bag for the keys and jumped into the driver's seat. Masel and MacGregor sat in the back together; MacGregor, sprawling himself over half the back seat, Masel, uncomfortably crouched in a corner, his long legs awkwardly cricked against the door. He had agreed to put his luggage in the trunk, but refused to part with his guitar. It sat between them like a polite passenger. Katy gunned the engine and took off, expertly slipping into the rushing traffic.

A jet roared and climbed above their heads.

"Wow," said Masel "This is my first time out of the States."

"And how do you like our weather?" Katy called from the front seat, her body turning slightly as she spoke, her breasts pointing toward western hills. "You must miss California already."

Masel shivered. "I thought it was coming up to summer time."

"In fact, it's still spring," said MacGregor, oddly chuckling. "Summer doesn't usually begin until after May. And that's what? Two days away."

Masel looked at the rain.

MacGregor's laugh was not unlike the bray of a goat. Katy smirked in the mirror, easing the long limo through the thick, wet traffic. Masel, reflecting the red, setting sun as it bobbed over darkish, green hills, wasn't sure what was funny. His flannel suit was already drenched, if not ruined, and he shivered with cold, not to mention the mental and physical exhaustion that was rapidly spreading through him.

"It feels like winter in Alaska."

"You'll get used to it eventually," MacGregor said, still smirking a little. "You'll be at home here in no time."

"AH-CHOO!" Masel sneezed suddenly, springing forward in the seat. "Excuse me."

"Bless you," said Katy.

"Masel tov," Masel replied. As far as he could remember, it was the first time in his life he had used the term. What possessed him? It was strange how foolish he felt, freakish, more than just an ocean apart from these people. Every word, every gesture, even sneezing, seemed a foreign act. MacGregor, rubbing his hands together, took it upon himself to describe the four seasons. Masel tried to relax and enjoy the ride. He nodded listlessly, almost dosing.

"That's quite something," he said absently.

"What?"

"The amount of rain you get here. Fearsome."

They drove along a busy rush-hour highway, other cars moving slowly around them in the dimness, their headlights and wipers on. Tyres hissed and splashed through the wet asphalt. The road was suspended, and on either side the land was muddy green, misty in texture, and seemed dredged, as though it were lower than it should be. Masel gazed at the scenery, keeping his distance. In his mind, he thought he heard the faint music of bagpipes, the sad, oozing lament of the Scots, the sadness of victory and defeat, of joy and loss. The occasional office block and grey housing area stuck out here and there from a distant quagmire.

"We're coming up to the Kingston Bridge," said MacGregor, "it runs over the River Clyde."

This interested Masel. He'd heard about the Clyde. Bonnie and Clyde? The bonnie banks of the Clyde?

"From here," MacGregor, twitching a smile, went on, "the river sweeps to the sea. This has been Glasgow's gateway to prosperity for centuries, from Roman times until now, really. Although, let's face it, times are not what they were a hundred years ago. Look at shipping, for example."

Masel looked and saw no shipping; he saw no prosperity either, only grey-white tower blocks beyond silent shipyards, with mangled, rusty scaffolding and old, bent cranes that looked like H.G. Wells Martians, a microcosm of industrial death beneath the low smog-like glow of a black cloud belly. It reminded him of south-central Los Angeles in late dusk, although he wasn't close enough to see any diamond-toothed pimps in white cadillacs. All the same, he was enjoying himself in a way, and he congratulated himself that he had, at least, gotten this far.

"If you follow the river westward," MacGregor coughed - for a moment he couldn't stop himself, his hand to his mouth, his eyes bulging, his chest heaving as though in convulsion. He took in a shallow breath and resumed, "Excuse me ... to the firth at Greenock, and then for another forty or fifty miles, you're in the Irish Sea."

The effect of the rain on the engine-warm metal caused steam to rise from the front of the car.

"The Irish Sea? Where's the Atlantic?"

"Beyond Ireland."

"Really?" Ireland interested Masel. He had planned to visit Dublin during his stay in Scotland. Maybe later in the summer I'll go. He imagined the rolling hills of so many folk songs. Among the rolling hills, he thought, I'll do no man no ill.

"What's that?" Masel asked, pointing across the city to a large black cloud of smoke, billowing upward and outward from somewhere in the centre of Glasgow.

"Ah," said MacGregor, his face suddenly emptying of expression, "I was just getting around to that." He coughed. "We heard about it just before you arrived. That, I'm afraid, is the GBH. The fire's out now, thankfully."

"Excuse me?" Masel inquired, a difficult smile on his face. "You're kidding?" He had a sense something was wrong. After a moment, he asked, "What's the GBH?"

MacGregor coughed again, more harshly this time, as though he were trying disguise the slight tone of solemnity in his words. "The Glasgow Baroque Hall." He spoke as if he were sad. "The GBH, as we like to call it." His grin twitched.

Masel was tired, but, abruptly, not that tired. Almost at once, the name clicked in place. There was suddenly an annoying ring in his ears. "Excuse me, isn't that - ?"

"I'm afraid so." MacGregor smiled a shabby, superior smile, displaying a black incisor on the top row of his teeth. He was trying to be cheerful. "But not to worry, we'll just transfer you to somewhere else."

Gevalt, he thought. Katy, cruising on, smiled in the mirror and, when she saw he was looking at her, burst into an almost nervous laugh. The rain lashed in sheets against the windshield.

"It's really not a problem," MacGregor said, after a moment, as if he were referring back to some long-forgotten topic they had once discussed. Masel smiled, embarrassed.

They pulled off the highway onto a broad boulevard of
shuttered shops and small, silver skyscrapers, sand-blasted
architecture and elegant buildings. The streets thronged with
cars and people huddling through the weather in a mass of
multi-coloured umbrellas. Katy indicated, but the road to the
left was all torn up and cordoned off. Some of its innards were
exposed: sewage pipes, telephone lines, electricity cables.
Police held back a milling crowd. Yellow-flashing traffic signs
and gigantic construction equipment blocked the opening to
the road, which went a long distance up a gradual hill. Almost
at the top of the hill, fire trucks with wheeling lights stood a
distance from a smoky building, its dense, black fumes rushing
skyward. This is Glasgow? That was the GBH? Masel experienced a moment of inspiration, then a chill.

"Ah, we'll go another way," said Katy.

MacGregor shot her a dirty look in the mirror.

She took a right turn, and followed the road down to a
railway station before swooping back through a series of small
lanes and alleyways. At last, they came up at a broad junction.
Masel lost all sense of direction. A moment later, he became
fearful when he observed cars driving toward him, the wrong
way around a round-about. The car slowed through a deep
puddle and a hotel abruptly stood up in front of him. He
couldn't believe what they had chosen for him; a Vacation Inn,
for God's sake, in the middle of Scotland. To step into a
Vacation Inn after seven thousand miles depressed him. Masel
secretly scorned American economic imperialism.

"Damn convenient for the city centre, I can tell you,"
MacGregor said, beaming, as Katy pulled into a too-narrow
parking bay in front of the hotel entrance. MacGregor grinned,
his head jerking back at the chin. "Our fair wee city's getting
bigger and bigger every day. I'm sure you'll be quite at home
here in no time."

"I'm sure it will be fine," Masel yawned, and faked a
laugh, a solitary hack. He was weary to the state of near-
exhaustion, yawned again and apologized. He saw that their
eyes were on him, and blushed deeply through a fatigued smile.

"I guess I'm just not used to flying across time zones."

"Well, sleep tight and we'll see you tomorrow," Katy said. She handed Masel her calling card and he studied it. "That's my office number. Phone when you wake up and we'll talk then." As an afterthought, she said, "Sweet dreams."

Masel, dazed, sighing, stole a last look at Katy and murmured to her his heartfelt thanks. He made various attempts to enter the revolving door. Fourth time lucky.

* * *

A tired porter of twentyish stepped into the space at his left, and the American, with some hesitation, let him carry his imitation leather travel bag and valise into the elevator. It has to be the top floor, he thought; my luck. The man offered to take the guitar, but Masel wouldn't allow it. In the room, the young porter, his bleary eyes barely open, held out an arrogant, ill-humoured hand. Now a schnorrer, thought Masel, handing him two gold coins from his pocket. Three-bucks-fifty to a porter; I guess I can live with that.

Masel quenched a hot thirst from the bathroom tap and flopped exhaustedly on the double bed; there was room enough for three - I should have such luck, he thought. The encased Gizmo lay beside him like a deeply-asleep lover. He kicked off his squeaky sneakers and stretched his cold toes. A few moments later, he laboured back to the bathroom, his scalp tingling unpleasantly. He was unable to get the toilet to flush; he didn't know whether to pull, push or pump at the thing. The shower was weak and his shivering continued. His nose dripped. He spent thirty seconds figuring out how the light switch worked because it was upside-down. Then, he cracked his ankle on a chair while trying to get past his valise. He was too frightened to touch the lamp because he guessed the plug had about twenty thousand volts in it.

"AH-CHOO." Masel sneezed again. "That's all I need," he muttered, hanging his wet suit over a frozen radiator. "Now I'm getting the flu." He felt his forehead. It was clammy and chilled. "I've probably got a temperature."

He beheld in the reflected window a vision of himself in

the grave, white and still, expressionless.

"Oh, Dad," he groaned in sorrow, wishing things had panned out better. His parents had been of the stunned generation, post-holocaust, never spoke of their past, and now when Masel had a longing to understand their pain and their fear, it was too late. I'm doing this for you, too, Dad. Masel made the same anguished gestures of terrible shame and panic that had irritated the hell out of his ex-wife. A hot tear welled up in his left eye; he wiped it away before it dripped.

Masel pulled the metal latch and opened the window; a cold, water-scented wind struck his face. The late, northern twilight seemed suspended in animation, never-ending, fiery, its red-orange light spreading in the faraway western sky with silky, glowing slowness. Glasgow fanned out before him from his eighth-floor window; a wonderland of twinkling lights and reflected car beams. The sound of traffic. Gazing into a thin, paling space between two distant, emblazoned clouds, he wondered how things happen to happen. I'm in Scotland, Glasgow, imagine, me, of all people, here, somewhere. The streets beyond the hotel seemed deserted.

Deep rivulets of rainwater flowed between parked cars and into the gushing gutter. A motorcyclist sped swiftly through the wet street just below him in a deep rumble of engine noise, black-clad, helmetted, like an alien patrol. Directly above him lay a low, grey-black cloud and the rain came down in thick lumps. He closed the window and went to bed.

Later, while Masel was asleep, moonlight slanted through the undraped window across his sloping shoulder and then moved into darkness. "God help me," he repeated in his sleep. He tried hard to dream of California sunshine, but the rain kept him this side of the sink.

 Four

His tee-shirt half over his head, Masel dreamed his ponytail was on fire. He awoke shortly before noon, fevered. His head ached and his classical nose dripped. That he would have to spend the rest of the day in bed troubled him; the room cost nearly £100 a night. "Jesus God," he sighed, "two nights, that's almost four hundred dollars." A fortune to a man who had to borrow an airfare from his ex-wife. For meals, he discovered, they charged like sin also; and the coffee, like his nose, was frozen. It was a good thing he was in no condition to hold down food, and it was pointless trying, because he also suffered badly from diarrhoea.

In his delirium, a thin gloom ambushed him. Am I a clever man or an idiot? If I am a clever man, what am I doing here? If I am stupid, why do I have a PhD? Do I have a stupid PhD? Masel concluded he had the makings of a clever man, but he wouldn't say he was clever now. If anything I am a masochist, and maybe I do have a stupid PhD.

On the telephone, he could get hold of neither Katy nor MacGregor. Nor did his stomach cease churning. Sniffling, uneasy, he left a message with a secretary who he wasn't sure understood anything he said. He certainly had no idea what she had said to him.

Sleep savaged him. In a dream, he saw himself, Gizmo in hand, fleeing from a mob of evil, blood-thirsty Jew-haters. His breathing impassioned, he used his guitar like a crossbow to return fire. Mostly, he was running for his life.

* * *

Late in the afternoon, he awoke groggy, a grown man deeply bent into a foetal position on soggy sheets, too late to check out of the hotel without first forking over another £100. His stomach felt better, though, his fever vanquished, and he crawled tentatively over the bed to switch on the television set. The remote control was broken. He figured there must be bad reception because he was getting only a few channels. The rest were snowy and made him feel cold again. Abruptly, out of the blizzard, he was astonished to find before him, there in glorious technicolour, Culture Katy 2080 giving an interview on the pros and cons of Culture Festival Year Five. Masel was helplessly struck by her plushing fountain of youth.

She was discussing cash for culture against a backdrop of unemployment. My God, she's beautiful. Control yourself. "Culture is hope," she was saying. "Culture is about freedom, equality, individual talent, expression. Freedom of expression is knowledge, and knowledge is the basis of a free society. Best of all, Culture is what we Scots have always had. Who cares if it's not the same as French culture or Italian culture or, for that matter, dare I say it, English culture?" Masel nodded as if hypnotised. Democracy? The American Dream?

He had, however, less than a minute to contemplate the issue; he was startled by a soft knock and the opening of his door. Love is the basis of everything, he concluded quickly, harping back to his hippy youth. He whiffed a sweet fragrance, and in a moment focused on Culture Katy standing at his bed. A fevered hallucination now? He put his hand to his forehead. He attempted to rise but realised that, except for a tee-shirt, he was naked beneath the sheets. He tried to seem casual, but was depressed that he had only his dishevelled self to offer.

"Feeling better?" Her breasts stood out and hallooed him. "I got your message. I phoned back, but there was no answer."

"I must have slept through it," he croaked. He gazed dreamily at her for a moment, then looked away. Masel felt a small, embarrassing silence. She smiled affectionately. His heart raced.

"You look different," he said. "You've changed your hair."

Katy let out an uncomfortable laugh. "Tireder maybe, I've been on my feet since six o'clock this morning."

He cautioned himself to behave. "I meant prettier," he said, shyly.

Masel, noticing her redden, couldn't believe he had said this. Sex was easier in the old days, when it was a religion.

"Prettier?" This seemed to amuse her. Her laughter tormented him.

In a moment of loneliness and daring, he asked, "Pretty enough to buy you dinner tonight? If you want to, that is."

Katy, her neck arched, blinked both eyes moistly. "I can't," she said, dutifully.

He clucked in sympathy with himself. "Why?"

"I have two babies." She smiled dimly.

"Babies?" He trembled in despair.

"Yes, two of them."

"A husband?" Masel apologized. He didn't see a ring.

"No husband."

He hesitated a moment, holding his breath. "Can we be friends or did I blow it already?"

Masel insulted himself for blowing it.

"I almost forgot," she went on, quickly. Out of her bag she thrust forward a small bouquet of flowers and a bag of grapes. Masel, moved by the gift, didn't have the heart, or the stomach, to tell her of his awful diarrhoea. Instead he thanked her profusely, only mentioned that he thought he might have a small bug, one of those twenty-four-hour things.

"Better not come near me," he warned. "It might be contagious."

She cautiously placed the grapes on his bedside table and retreated, with the flowers, into the bathroom. Masel heard the tap running. A moment later she re-appeared with a glass of water. She sipped it and then put it on a chest of drawers by the door.

"I left the flowers in your sink." She pointed to the television. "Well, how was I?"

"Huh?"

"On the television, how was I? You were watching me when I came in."

"Wonderful," he said, his mouth dry. "Truly."

"Aye," she said lowering her brow in mock seriousness.

"Excuse me." Masel blew his nose. "What about tomorrow?"

"I've rescheduled all your meetings. Tomorrow morning you're with the EPI Centre. On Saturday, you've got a two o'clock appointment with the council's culture committee and a four o'clock with the university."

"What's the EPI Centre?" he asked, cautiously.

She looked at him coyly. "Euro Pictish Institute. That's where your first concert will be now, since, as you know, the GBH burned to the ground. Anyway, the EPI Centre is all booked up. It's really just as good, so there's no problem,"

Masel, gulping, looked into her eyes. He thought he saw them twinkle.

"Very efficient. Don't you ever stop?" he asked.

"This is for your benefit."

"I only meant ..."

"Occasionally," she interrupted. "When I have to." There was that smile again. "I've a full-time career and two babies. My free time is limited."

He coughed embarrassedly and fiddled with a grape. "What am I doing after the university on Saturday?"

Katy hesitated, serious, but for a hint of enjoyment at the corners of her mouth. Then an almost serpentine smile emerged on her lips. She blinked twice in succession. "Having dinner with me, if you like," she said.

Her eyes flashed on him, and she smiled. Her hair seemed redder and lit up the pale-blue wall. Masel was taken aback, felt himself blush beneath the sheets.

"Yeah. I like. It's a date."

She chuckled, enjoying the word. "All right, a date."

How could he possibly refuse her anything? And a date, no less. He liked that word, too. When Masel was in high school, his idea of a date was to go over to Zelda's house and eat everything in her parents' refrigerator. Katy took hold of her bag with both arms and cradled it.

"I hope you don't get the wrong idea about me." she said.

"I don't think I have."

"Or about Glasgow. Everything's really in a transformation stage."

Masel grinned widely. "Me too," he said. "I've had my fill of San Francisco. Now I want to see the northern skies over my head. You know this is the first time I've been out of California, except for a disastrous two-day trip to New York."

"A parochial American? I don't believe it." She paused, her focus easing.

"What happened? Or shouldn't I ask?"

"It's the truth, we Americans are very parochial," Masel confessed, slightly irked at himself for dredging up his old failures. "Let's just say I swindled myself for a long time."

She turned sideways and, putting her white hand to her mouth, yawned.

Then Masel yawned.

"Sorry...the flu."

"Well," Katy said, her sharp breasts pointing at him, smiling. "I suppose it's time I got back to work. They have to pay me for something." She laughed, "I'll be in touch."

Masel smiled at her - he couldn't help himself - and watched her narrow behind as she half-turned, cheerily repeated a goodbye, and left.

He abruptly felt the pulse of his heart. Am I in love or am I in love? An energy filled his chest as he leaped out of bed, showered, and dressed. Love is warmth, he thought. Love is the cure.

* * *

He unpacked the Gizmo from its case, as though he were very gently lifting a child from a cradle. He was slightly self-conscious of the action, despite being alone in the room, and blushed mildly to himself. Masel's pleasure piece, a symbol of his own fragility, among other things. The instrument had, against his ex-wife's advice, cost him a small fortune at a time when he could ill-afford it. Now, lost in himself, he picked a gutsy ragtime on it. He enspirited the Gizmo and it enspirited him. The instrument rang out magically, creating a harmony with air. He thought of Katy's pronging breasts and, skilfully negotiating a slow melancholic change, croaked in a perfect bluesy-black-man imitation, 'You take Sally and I'll take Sue, there ain't no difference 'tween the two."

The failed performer was at peace, passionate. Playing the guitar was as natural to Masel as breathing. And he was reasonably accomplished, he knew, possibly good, perhaps on occasion exceptional; yet he lacked some uncertain quality he himself was uncertain of, couldn't quite nail down. If only he had genius. All nature uses what it needs to thrive; he had learned that from his study of Zen in '70. The thought made him hungry.

What he needed was a Big Mac - possibly two of them - but where, and how? Masel, in truth, was a junk food junkie an addiction that came into his own after Zelda had moved out. For what reason? Sympathy? Suicide by cholesterol? He had once - not long ago, in fact - eaten four quarter-pound cheeseburgers in a row. He pondered before him an imaginary soggy bun, two square slabs of meat wedged snugly inside, smothered in ketchup, mustard, mayonnaise and gooey salad.

He went for it.

* * *

The Vacation Inn receptionist, a big-boned, lanky Irish girl, gave Masel directions to the nearest MacDonald's. Masel, for a moment, considered giving her the eye, but on closer inspection, he found her frame lacking in flesh and decided against it. She seemed to croon at him in a foreign language.

"How far is that?" He asked, "Which way?"

"Five minutes," she said, her head tilted to the left, trying to glimpse his ponytail. Her tone was severely apologetic. "Straight down there to Argyle Street and it's on the corner at Jamaica Street. But we have hamburgers here, if you'd like me to order one for you, sir. You can have it in the bar or in your room. I'm afraid the restaurant closes up at ten o'clock. But it's not a problem."

"No thanks," he said, finally eyeing her as he walked away. The Irish girl lowered her brow at him, her mouth drooped. Why do I bother? he asked himself.

Masel stood motionless before the revolving door and studied the thick, dark rain. He also studied the revolving door, cunningly, slowly blinking. He dipped into a pocket, but came up empty handed. In the other, Masel found a solitary American nickel. He remembered he had no British currency. A beer and a sandwich at the bar, though he could hardly afford it whatever it cost, couldn't be that much. He would charge it.

The American chose a small table near a pretty, pale-cheeked waitress, her hair jet-black and curled into long ringlets, her face lean. Masel signed a bar bill for a pint of gassy German beer and two fatty roast beef sandwiches. He shrugged to himself; okay, it wasn't exactly a Big Mac , but what could he do under the circumstances? Flower boxes with plastic tropical shrubs separated his table from the bar. He took a couple of bites from his sandwich and found the roast beef gristled. The waitress looked at him but did not see him, her closed features staring out, expressionless, a thin, silver-coloured tray loosely held at her side. Masel lost his appetite.

He sipped his beer and furtively, through the plastic shrubs, studied two darkly-suited businessmen diagonally across from him, hovering around two big-bosomed blonde girls on barstools. Their method of attack was apparently to stare hopefully at the girls' healthy cleavages and buy them as many umbrellaed cocktails as they could drink in an alotted time. Masel was waiting to see how they fared, when he had to make a sudden dash for it. His swishing, liquid belly was acting up again. The fatty roast beef gurgled dangerously through him.

He sprinted up the carpeted steps to his room in distress. Why me? he thought. My God, one ordeal after the other. After relieving himself - in truth, it was partially too late - his stomach painfully cramped, he showered slowly and collapsed on the bed, letting out his ponytail. He thanked God for throw-away underwear. When he gathered what little energy he had left, he telephoned the reception desk, vaguely explained his predicament, and ordered a bowl of hot rice pudding. To hell with the cost; an emergency is an emergency.

Masel was throwing up into a metal waste paper basket when the Irish receptionist appeared with the rice pudding. "Come on in," he moaned. "Thank God."

"I'm already in, sir."

Masel, sighing with discomfort, heaved again. "So you are." He felt faint. "Just put it by the bed."

As she bent down to place the bowl on his bedside table,

their eyes met. She giggled. "You've let out your ponytail."

Masel vomited into the bucket. "God help me. Excuse me."

"Would you like me to call a doctor, sir?" the girl said, nonplussed.

"No thank you, " he said, trying to smile.

"Aren't you Elliot Masel, the famous one? I've seen your picture." She gazed at him.

"In the flesh," he said, weakly. "If you'll excuse me, I'm not in the best shape right now."

She was still staring at him, now a little coyly.

Masel suffered a gurgling pain in his stomach. "If that's all, I'm not really..."

She interrupted him, flapping a blue piece of paper in front of his dripping nose.

"Would you mind giving me your autograph, sir?"

"What?" He blushed in spite of himself. Although moved by the request, he was forced to decline.

"No, sir, I meant could you sign this so we can put your rice pudding on the bill."

Letting his rice pudding go cold, he signed his autograph and passed out almost at once. He dreamed of being engulfed by a great glittering bow tie.

■ Five

A wind, wailing, came up and blew bouts of rain at the window, like volleys of spears, then suddenly stopped. Pale sunlight filtered through low, mist-like clouds and into his hotel room window. The morning air was grey and cold. The telephone rang. Masel sprung open glued eyelids, the thin light assailing him like a blow on the head. His internal clock remained stuck somewhere in the foggy, San Francisco night.

"Huh?" he said, tightly pressing the receiver to his ear.

"Good morning."

"Huh?" Masel, his nose whistling, imagined Katy's piercing breasts. "What time is it?"

"Are you fit?"

"I guess so. I used to jog three or four miles a day, but that was last year."

Katy laughed, enthusiastically, momentarily surprising Masel. "You've got the EPI Centre at ten o'clock. Rise and shine. Have you forgotten?"

"What time is it now? I'm sorry. I over-slept."

The tone of her voice was calm. "Half-eight. You have an hour, so don't panic. I'll pick you up at half-nine in the reception area. Is that all right?"

Masel moaned.

"Righto," he said, flopping back on the pillow. Was half-nine nine-thirty or four? he wondered. He noticed, with embarrassment, the smell of the waste bucket half-full with vomit beside the bed. His face in the pillow, he screwed his eyes shut to keep out the light and forgot what he told himself not to.

Some time later his alarm clock went off.

He awoke with a yell from a dream of jousting with George MacGregor. He waved a long lance at the bureaucrat. Annoyed, Masel shook his alarm clock, clobbered it with a pillow. It was nine-fifteen.

He glimpsed himself in the bathroom mirror. One side of his doubtful face was creased. He pulled on a tee-shirt, and his replacement brown tweed suit and struggled hamhandedly with the laces on his squeaky sneakers. He tied back his ponytail with shaky fingers.

He glanced quickly out the window. The rain was off. A thick film of water remained on the streets.

"All right," he called, getting himself in a mood, "let's get this show on the road."

★ ★ ★

"I'm checking out at noon," Masel breezily informed a man in a blue jacket with his back to him at the reception desk on his way by. "I'll be back in a couple of hours." He could see a summerish sun glisten warmly against the revolving door at the end of the long lobby. He was also happy to find that the

Irish girl who had seen him vomit was no longer around.

The man, a patchy, reddish beard on his face, turned quickly. His close-cropped hair had an aggressive, military manner. He nodded sharply.

Masel walked the long lobby. Doubts began to assail him. Who am I fooling? he asked himself, burdened by the memory of so many past failures. Everyone. Me. Why was I asked to come half way around the world? Me and my bizarre little repertoire. Life is strange, but why me?

Katy, at that moment, spun through the revolving door in a torch of sunlight, her young and lovely face striking him, open mouthed, her hair combed back into a French twist, her neck arched regally, her head slightly raised, her breasts pointing enthusiastically at him, beckoning.

Masel felt his stomach gurgle and he passed wind. Thank God, he thought, only a false alarm.

* * *

After the rain, Masel was famished for colours, his eye searching for it in every light. Metal in car doors gleamed and reflected in office-block windows that seemed to jut out from towering shadows and angles. Cars and buses jammed the streets before him. For the change of season, Katy wore a Western-style embroidered blouse and a sky-blue cape that seemed to reflect Masel's increasing affections for her and his growing ease in her presence. Her hair was redder and her smile brighter. He enjoyed the hustle-bustle of the street. Masel liked cities, although probably through force of adaption; he had spent all his life in them, shlepping between Los Angeles and San Francisco. But he was a self-aware Jew, and Jews had spent millenia adapting and surviving, just as he was now, in his own way.

"Hope you don't mind," she said, "I thought we'd walk. It's lovely out and the EPI Centre is only ten minutes away."

"Fine with me," Masel said.

He raised his face to the warmth. A summer breeze blew across his eyes. To be on the safe side, however, he purchased an umbrella in a dark haberdashery shop under a railway

THE ARRIVAL / 31

bridge about fifty yards from the hotel. He hung it on the crook of his left arm as he walked. The road was encumbered with traffic, its sidewalks tight with pedestrians. A thin fog of diesel fumes from the exhaust pipes of buses dispersed through the sheen of sunlight.

"A sunny Saturday afternoon in Glasgow," she said, smiling.

The sun sucked Masel's flu from him. They crossed onto a broad walkway of shops and stopped at a golden sculpture of a whale's tail, its bronze reflection gleaming into the pink blossoms of a cherry tree. It's branches softly stirred.

"What does it mean?" he asked. He slipped on his Californian sunglasses.

"Nobody knows," Katy said, dismissing it with a wave, "but it was the council's first attempt at modern culture. That's the important thing. They paid some local sculptor to do it back in the nineteen-seventies. I forget his name."

Masel chuckled. The scent of her perfume exploded in his nose. He felt his desire stir, but checked himself. "I think I'm going to like it here."

Katy smiled. "We always look good in the sunshine, even if we are a bit ashen. But to be fair, you'd better get used to the rain, this may only last for a couple of hours. Long summers are rare. I think the last one was 1976."

"My God," he said, removing his jacket, revealing a black tee-shirt and dark arms. But his skin grew cold and goosefleshed in the weak, northern light and he put it back on again. He took off his sunglasses and hooked them at the front of his tee-shirt. Strutting along Sauchiehall Street, the failed musician saw that Glasgow, too, was in a state of confusion. Thirsting for evidence, his eyes wide, he began to identify himself with the city. Glasgow is a Jew, he thought, shocked by the idea. This was a modern city of skyscrapers and cars, but it was also one of dark, stone tenement halls, ancient peoples, the black dirt of the ages, cobbled alley ways. It was modern and fragile on the surface, yet old and hard below, sturdy.

"Me, too," he whispered to himself.

It abruptly occurred to him that beneath his very feet, Picts had once walked. And still their descendants walked, trodden to dust by history, yes, but still refusing to submit their identity; proud, stubborn, persistent, and deeply cultural, beaten but not dead. No wonder he could identify; I'm a Jew, am I not? This is my ball game, my territory. And now, what was this? A rebirth?

"Me, too," he repeated to himself, deeply moved. Me, Elliot Masel, a Californian Jew, wandering around all this reborn history. So taken by the thought was Masel that, for a moment, he wondered if perhaps he had stumbled upon a lost tribe of Israel.

Katy smiled, eyeing him. "Tell me about your shows."

"I like to think of them as histories," Masel said, at last relaxing, closing his eyes then opening them again. He laughed at his easy success, and turned to look at her. She was beautiful in the sunlight. "Musical histories. Just me and my guitar. I don't know if you could really call them shows, but -."

"What about your synthesizer? And your laser show? Are they coming later?"

"Synthesizer? Laser?" Momentarily panicked. He had never played a synthesizer.

"Yes, I thought you had one of those mini-synthesizers for all those strange noises."

"Noises?" Masel echoed.

He groaned. His throat gulped. He felt suddenly stifled. Can this really be happening to me? No. Yes. No. Yes. No. Yes. Can't be. Is. God help me. He put a hand to his face and pinched his cheek. He wasn't dreaming. He was back in the world again, his old world. He imagined his brain, swollen. He kept walking, balancing himself like an old work horse, sleep walking. He let a minute pass, possibly more. He breathed out thinly, but spoke solemnly. "Listen, Katy, I think there's been..."

"Ah, here we are," she interrupted him. "The EPI Centre. We made it at last."

Masel, his heart suddenly like thickly-vibrating bass

strings in his chest, suspected a terrible mistake. Gevalt, what now? Am I not who they think I am? He made a small attempt to escape, wandered past the EPI Centre as Katy walked in.

She ducked her head back out, "Yoo-hoo, in here."

* * *

Very rapidly now, he began to add together two and two. The invitation, he now knew, hadn't been for him at all. It was for a Eugene Madel, a musical and electronics genius, who since last year had been doing laser and synthesizer shows all over the United States and Canada. He once had an office next door to Madel, in Berkeley's Performing Arts building. The council's letter was addressed to an E. Masel. Holy shit, he thought, I'm the victim of a typing error. With the best of intentions, in fact flattered, Masel had written back explaining his modest act on 1960s' youth culture. The council had enthused. The Press were involved. It was Dr E. Masel they were expecting, but Dr E. Madel's laser show they thought they were getting. Holy shit, he thought, wanting to flee with the wind. His palms perspired thickly and his weak stomach gurgled. What the hell am I doing here? Now it became clear to him.

 Six

"This is Leo Plotnikov," said Katy, quickly leading Masel into an office at the back of a small art gallery.

A man puffing a cigar stood pensively facing a wide, open window, his back to Katy and Masel. Between them and Plotnikov, there was a small, pale laquered wooden desk and a spindly, antique-looking chair. There were papers all over the desk and a pair of bent, gold pince-nez. Plotnikov turned after a moment and smiled. He was a short, thin man, with a balding head of wiry, grey hair, a big, gold hooped earing and a Paisley-patterned kipper tie. A fly buzzed around his nose, and he swiped at it, missing. He looked up at Masel for a moment, his eyes still, deeply blue.

"Hi," said Masel, mumbling. "Glad to meet you."

Katy broke in, "Leo's in charge of bookings, among other things."

Plotnikov stood motionless, puffing his cigar. He had terrific posture for a man of his slight stature, Masel thought, almost frightening. Masel wiped his right palm on the thigh of his trousers and nervously offered his damp hand. Plotnikov shook it stiffly, holding on to it for a moment, squeezing slightly, after he had stopped shaking it. Masel's heart thudded. He bit deeply into his lip. The manager, though he seemed to disguise it, had the sharp look of having been through everything, if not more. It gave Masel momentary shivers.

"Beautiful day," said Plotnikov. Cigar smoke surrounded his head like a softly swirling dust cloud in the light.

Masel warned himself not to let a foolish word come out of his mouth.

Plotnikov, looking straight at the American, smiled casually and continued, "But first let me congratulate you on your talent and originality. Everyone is extremely excited about what you've got in store for us. Something a wee bit different. And variety, as we all know, is the spice of life."

"Thanks." Masel blushed radiantly, gulped. Should I confess now or later? Confusion and fear assailed him at once. He slammed his open palm against his forehead in an attempt to control himself, then scratched, pretending it was an itch.

Katy gazed strangely at him and, with a swoop of her cape, a piece of sky flashing before him, she excused herself and went to the ladies' room. Masel wondered if he had given her his bad stomach. He worried about his life.

"Follow me," said Plotnikov. "I'll show you the concert hall."

* * *

"What's your impression?" he asked, pushing open a wide, black door. The two men entered a smallish auditorium with a white stage and a black curtain. It held maybe five hundred people.

"I do a good Jewish Jimi Hendrix."

Plotnikov smirked. "I mean the auditorium."

"Er - it's fine, I guess," said Masel, his throat hot and scratchy. He regretted the humour. "I was joking," he affirmed. "I don't really do a Jewish Jimi Hendrix." I must be completely out of my mind, he was thinking.

"It's compact," said Plotnikov, as if he had built the place himself. "Although I know you're used to big arenas."

"Er - no really, really big ones lately. But I have done a lot of college lecture halls, and I've also done a bit of television. It's my nature," he confessed, "I was born a late bloomer."

Plotnikov smirked again. No doubt an anti-semite, too, thought Masel, his forehead perspiring. A drip of sweat ran down the tip of his nose. Probably a Pole with a name like that.

"Now, to get to business," Plotnikov said, grimly. "I have you booked provisionally for next Friday night."

"Friday?" Masel squeaked in fright.

Katy returned, seemingly distracted, from the lady's room. Masel grew pale.

"You can manage by then, can't you?" Plotnikov asked, plainly. "I'm not sure exactly what you need, but you can let me know by Monday and I'll see what we can come up with." He coughed. "Now to the subject of money, we get a small grant from the Scottish Arts Council and a modest sum from the district council, so how does a third of door taking sound to you? It's all we can afford. But with a full house, at seven-fifty a ticket, that's about twelve-hundred pounds. We're small, I know, but prestigious."

"A third? Er - that sounds fine." God, help me. He glanced at Katy. She smiled at him, beamed.

"Right, then it's settled," said Plotnikov, staring, as if through Masel's eyes into his cranium. He shot forward an eager open hand. The American took it in terrible fear. Masel's heart fluttered, jumped like a canary in his chest. He wiped his brow and rubbed another bead of sweat from his nose.

* * *

Masel confessed in the sun-lit street. "I think we're in deep shit." A sadness came over him, the old kind, the sadness of failure, reduction.

"How do you mean?" Katy said, her eyes fixing him.

"Maybe we should have a drink before I tell you this."

"Just tell me now," she demanded. "What is it?"

Masel spat it out flatly. "You've got the wrong person."

Katy laughed nervously. "Wrong person? What is that supposed to mean?"

In despair, he admitted, "The person you want is Eugene Madel. There must have been a spelling mistake and the invitation came to me. Madel doesn't even work at Berkeley anymore. He used to, but not anymore."

Katy shook her head in disbelief. "Are you telling me..?"

"I told you, I play folk music on my guitar. To be blunt, what I have is a singing lecture. That's all. I knew this was too good to be true. I've never been a very lucky person." He apologized. This was a terrible situation.

Katy stared intensely at him, her bottom lip trembling slightly.

"Pig. How could you perpetuate this? What about the sixties? Or is that this Eugene Madel person too. What about your act? What about the lasers?"

He admitted, "I'm afraid I have nothing to do with lasers. That's Eugene Madel. I'm Elliot Masel, a lecturer in American Folk Science, Phd. My act, if you're sure you want to call it that, is a modern musical history. I'm an educator. The 1960s, yes. I imitate the guys I'm talking about, that's all. It was a thing that started at Berkeley a couple of years ago to make the class more entertaining for the students. I used to get paid by class attendance. It was just an idea for a little fun and more money. Last year, I was a guest on a couple of television shows because of it. I assumed that was how you'd heard about me."

She looked miserable, then, desperate, as if she were about to scream. Masel wanted to crawl into the earth and fade away.

"Maybe I should go home," he offered, gently. "You know, just skedaddle."

She ignored this and, with flaring nostrils, angrily said,

"You could've told me before." She seemed to groan. "You have really got me in trouble. I could lose my job over this. And what about my babies? What am I supposed to feed them on? Air?"

Masel put his knuckles to his mouth in guilt. "What can I do? I'm a folk music expert. I play the guitar. It's not all my fault."

Masel wondered if he was to be forever bound by this spelling error. Is it my fault? Gevalt, why should I pay for someone else's mistake? Yet I did act upon it, didn't I? Am I responsible? Masel concluded he was the chosen one. How odd of God to choose the Jews, he remembered from childhood. And how odd of God to choose Glasgow for his diabolical fate.

"Think," Katy told him, the light of desperation in her eye. Her hair was wild; her skin, unearthly pale, beautiful. "If you've been on television, you must be able to do something."

Masel kept his tongue firmly between his teeth. She went on, her fists clenched and red at her hips, "Put it this way, if you don't do this show, we're both finished. I mean it, Elliot. I'll be out on my ear. And you'll be stuck here without a penny." She hissed at him, "You could die here."

He considered the option and shivered. "I can't do it," he said, depressed. "I don't know how."

"Friday, that's nine days," she plotted, her eyes darting around the street. "How long is your act, or whatever it is?"

"I hadn't really thought about it. Forty-five minutes, give or take." He twisted his lip between his thumb and forefinger. "I only expected to be doing a few songs. I thought there were others. I thought this was a culture festival."

"Alright, if you can do another half-hour, and you're semi-decent, I think we can give them a show."

"But they're expecting a laser show," he said. "What do I know about synthesizers?"

Masel feared a terrible fate descending on his head, saw himself a dead man in a foreign gutter, bleeding, penniless.

Panic went through him like a lightening flash. He could feel his jaw trembling. He sweated profusely. His heart raced, neck flushed. A dimness now came at him, his balance shaky. Abruptly, Zelda stood before him, her emaciated body swathed in voluminous skirts, her mouth violet.

She smiled wanly. "Elliot, do something for God's sake."

Masel, for the first time in his life, fainted away in the street, collapsing in a flurry among clucking pigeons.

The Plan
One

ON the floor of a cluttered, high-ceilinged Victorian tenement flat, on a West End suburban hill behind Byres Road, Masel woke to the sound of laughter and running water. He had been dreaming, as he had been for two nights running now, of dawn on the sea, rose light on the waves somewhere in the mid Atlantic, half way home. He smelled the womanly ocean as birds wheeled into the luscent sky. When he thrust his head from his perspiring sleeping bag, he discovered through semi-conscious vision a little boy happily making pee-pee over him.

"Oy gevalt," he cried. "What a feshstinkeh in here."

"Sam! No!" he heard Katy shout. "You dirty little man."

He felt entrapped. The room was streaked in the belated spring sunlight. Masel leaped from the bag and revealed a pair of awkward, blue boxer shorts, peppered with small yellow guitars. He was reminded of the frailty of his fate. My life is fog, a blob.

Sam, howling with laughter, continued piddling.

Setting down a baby girl from her arms, Katy rushed over, pulled the little boy up by his arm pits, his pee-pee making a zigzagging curve in the air before it pitter-pattered on the worn red carpet, and ran with him to the toilet. The boy's laughter echoed through the small apartment, turned to tears when he was sent to his room, then a moment later was pacified by Katy's gentle voice. Masel, his heart aching, hypothetically envisaged himself in her arms. He snapped out of it.

He furtively wiped his brow with a sock and, turning to the wall to slip on his trousers, wished he could flee. "Deliver unto us another flood," he breathed to himself, with a perfect country pastor's impression. He looked at his dripping sleeping bag and took the wish back. In truth, he didn't know what to do.

He was buttoning his fly, blushing, as Katy pushed past

him with a towel and a sponge. She accidently nudged him and Masel, panicking, dropped his trousers to his ankles. He grabbed for a belt buckle where there wasn't one.

From the floor, the baby girl giggled and made a face at him. Masel made a face back; it was the face of desperation.

"Don't touch anything," Katy warned, scrubbing his bag. She was nursing the beginnings of a cold.

Masel clumsily retrieved his trousers. "You were nice with Sam, considering. Does he often pee on sleeping bags?"

"I want them to remember a loving childhood."

"Was your's so miserable?" Masel felt at that moment she was a soul mate.

Katy stared harshly. "That's none of your business."

He apologized. I have to get out of here before she despises me, assuming she doesn't already. Sheepishly, he suggested, "Maybe skeddadling isn't such a bad idea after all."

"Not so fast." Katy clamped her teeth, glaring sharply, annoyed, her breasts pointing angrily at him. She put her hands on her hips. "What am I supposed to think? You've been moping around here for two days. I didn't leave you unconscious in the street, did I? Are you going to help me or not? Or are you just going to use me for whatever you have in mind?"

Masel, buckling his belt, turned away in shame. He honestly didn't know how to help her without making a fool of himself. He doubted his hopes were anything more than pipe dreams, demented yearnings that would obviously lead nowhere. He tried to smile, but his mouth twisted unconvincingly across his face. "I was kind of hoping you wouldn't have left me in the street anyway."

Katy charged into the kitchen and slammed the door behind her. Masel stood depressed in the middle of the living room, the baby girl salivating at him. He considered making a break for it. If ever there were a time to run, it was now. He saw himself fleeing with heavy bags, his guitar on his back. No one would miss him for at least twenty-four hours; a taxi, he could be at the airport in half an hour, and on the first plane west. He'd even settle for New York at this stage. Even the indignity of

Zelda's futon would be better than this. But his heart sank like a brick in the ocean; he had spent his airfare home getting out of the Vacation Inn.

* * *

Katy stood in the corner by the kitchen window gnawing a turkey drumstick, the light rising in her hair. He had fiddled with the door handle before entering, so as not to startle her and make matters worse. He could see she had been crying.

Masel grinned nervously. "Life's a cold bowl of chicken soup," he said. "Then you die." He laughed immoderately and stopped abruptly.

"I'm sorry about the sleeping bag," she said. She seemed unable to look at him, threw the fatty bone in the garbage and went to the refrigerator for another. Masel omitted to tell her the bag was new. He nodded. She was seriously beautiful in sorrow; he tried not to watch her chew. It seemed grotesque in the mood he was in, saw himself being eaten alive, devoured by her gnashing teeth.

"Hungry, eh," he remarked, attempting to crack the ice, his eyes fixed on her smooth jaw.

"My appetite grows when I'm pissed off."

He spoke gently to her. "It's nothing serious."

"It is if you get fat." She looked at the turkey leg and threw it, too, half eaten, into the garbage.

"I meant the sleeping bag."

Katy rinsed her hands under the tap and then blew her nose with a paper kitchen towel that half-hid a groan. Me or life? She twisted sharply to face him.

"Why am I always crying?"

He praised her independence. "You're under pressure."

"You don't understand. I've got myself into a terrible mess." She slowly seated herself at the kitchen table.

Masel scratched his nose. He leaned an elbow on the refrigerator and fondled a flowery napkin, which he crumpled and put in his pocket. He wondered why, then put it back. Then he seated himself across from her at the table. Katy, touching a tired, red-rimmed eye, picked up a cup from the counter and moved it around in her palms. Masel wanted to do the same, but there was only a carton of orange juice on the table. Uneasily, he said nothing.

"It was me who made the spelling mistake," she admitted abruptly after a silence. "It was me who typed E. Masel instead of E. Madel. When you answered MacGregor's letter as Masel, I thought the spelling mistake was in the directory. I didn't know until yesterday. I swear it."

Masel, rising hastily from his seat, upset the carton of orange juice. Momentarily, he watched the stain spread on the table before running to the sink for a cloth. Should he keep on running? Katy put down the cup with the sharp crack of cheap china.

He began to lightly dab the table, but Katy grabbed the cloth from him. She wanted to do it.

As she rubbed, her voice immediately rose and gained strength. "I'll be sacked. This is my first job, and I even bluffed my way into it. They wanted a glam girl with a degree to do PR for Culture Festival. I needed the job, so I lied on the application form. I'm not fit for anything."

Out of habit Masel shrugged, although he was not insensitive to the situation. "I wouldn't say that."

Katy sniffed. "I left university after a year, when I became pregnant. I never got a degree. There was really no point carrying on. Once the baby was born I wouldn't have been able to finish anyway. I could hardly support myself never mind a baby. Then Jenny came along."

"Where were your parents? Couldn't they help out?"

"My mother's a nice middle-class ex-hippy with no money. She lives in a commune now, somewhere in the south of France. My father left her when I was born. They were married too young, I think. I thought he was dead until I was fifteen, but I've never met him."

"I'm sorry. It must have been rough for you." Masel touched her sleeve, as if in apology.

"My stepfather was worse. They divorced when I was nine. They never really liked each other or probably she just saw through him." Katy flicked a look at him then down, her lips stretched. "They used to batter each other all over the place. Even when they had parties, they'd get out their heads and the guests had to call the police. And when we used to go over to other people's houses, and I played with their children, they were always fighting, and we'd have to leave after a few minutes. Once, when I was ill, and I went into my mother's bedroom, I found a strange man in her bed...when I ran into the living room there was another girl, a teenager, I suppose, on the couch with my stepfather. I grew up with..." She stopped herself. "So much for sixties' love and peace."

"How did you get by, I mean without money?" Masel felt himself shudder. "Were you on welfare?"

"I was getting cheques from the father of Sam and Jenny, but after three years they stopped. You understand, he was married, so there was trouble from the start. I had to get a job. Then, when MacGregor found out I lied, he was going to get rid of me. The only thing that saved me was this stupid sixties show. It was my idea."

"If you don't mind me asking, how could you fool them like that, the council I mean. They must realize I'm not Eugene Madel."

She grinned, glancing at him sideways. "I didn't know myself until two days ago when you told me. It's the Culture Festival. Anything goes. George MacGregor is the head of the culture committee, and he thinks you're famous.

Him? thought Masel. Him with no chin?

Katy straightened her shoulders, her breasts pointing. She let out a long, tired sigh. I doubt anyone will have heard of Madel anyway. You know the way it is, you're an American. Success is ninty-nine per cent hype, one per cent manipulation. It's like advertising, all publicity and lies."

Masel, glancing at Katy's sharp breasts, was surprised to find he was becoming sexually aroused. Looking away, he blushed more darkly than before. "That's very cynical."

She stared straight at him. "You think so? Look, it's you they're expecting now, even though you don't do what they think you do."

"That's ridiculous. If no one's heard of Madel, why am I here, as Madel or Masel?"

"I told you, it's the Culture Festival," she said. "What does it matter?"

He hesitated, gulped, decided to say nothing.

Katy went on, as if compulsively, "I heard about Madel through an old school friend, who emigrated to Canada. She wrote to me about a fantastic show she saw, and that gave me the idea. I thought I'd found a way to save my job, especially when this American guy wrote back. But unfortunately, Elliot, you showed up instead of Madel."

"Thanks a lot."

"Nothing personal." She half-smiled.

"Didn't you think it was a little strange that your friend got the name wrong too, or right, I should say? Once is..."

"I know, I know, I just never thought." She lowered her eyes, bowed her head.

Masel squirmed where he sat. He was the last resort once again, a second choice. Sweating, a nightmarish thought struck him. "What if somebody finds out?"

"It doesn't matter. Other people have lasers."

"But I don't."

Katy bit her bottom lip, her eyes tender, but shrewd. "I have a friend who's a professor at Glasgow University. He teaches electro-optics. I'm sure he could do something for me. He can do anything like that. And he owes me a favour."

He wondered what kind of favour, but dropped it. Did Masel dare? After so many failures and frustrations? Me, the son of Polish immigrants, a failed performer, a failed husband, a second-rate lecturer with a third-rate PhD? Could he refuse Katy anything? He was melting. Masel went to the sink and drank tap water from a child's plastic cup. First, he rinsed the thing thoroughly in case Sam had lately urinated in it.

"What do I have to do?" he asked, his voice resigned, doubtful. "I've never played in front of more than a hundred people before, except once, and I was booed off stage. I was a total failure."

Why did he say that? Nervously, he rose from the seat and sat back down. Fulfilment hovered somewhere near the outskirts of his consciousness, just out of his grasp. From the livingroom, he could hear the baby splutter out a wet rattle that seemed to vibrate her entire being.

"Jenny, darling, are you all right?" Katy shouted. Her concentration remained unbroken.

Jenny's sad, pouting reply came as, "Uh-huh." Katy nodded blankly.

She turned back to Masel. "Look, forget about that. You said you did impersonations of sixties music stars. What if we could make you look like the people you sound like? I'm sure that can be done with lasers or something. What do you think? This is your big chance."

Masel, a reluctant star, felt his armpits sizzle. Nervously, he winked an eye at Jenny, who was now crawling around the kitchen floor, waving a plastic brick at him. Then at once Katy burst into tears. Jenny followed suit. Masel didn't know what to do, wanted to take them both in his arms, dared not, wanted to escape. He held his ears.

Katy looked up, gazing at him. He was wide open; wide as a building. Always a sucker for tears, he darted an uneasy glance at the orange juice stain, and guiltily assented.

As he let his hands down, Katy kissed his earlobe in elation. Masel blushed deeply.

 Two

The folk expert, seriously doubting his sanity, practised impersonations night and day. Yet the more he doubted, the more his affections for Katy increased. He began with Bob Dylan, and spent dreadful hours wondering where his talent had gone. In despair, he wailed, "There are no truths outside the gates of Eden," and shrieked, "I ain't gonna work on Maggie's farm no more." He worked through the Rolling Stones and Country Joe

MacDonald ,"One, Two, Three, What are we fightin' for."
That one was good for his rhythm; cruised into Truckin' and
For What It's Worth, and cursed his ability, or lack of it when
he came to Hendrix's Purple Haze.

Masel slept late to make up for periods of wakefulness in
the pit of the night. He often dreamed of being strangled by the
suspected terrorist and spymaster he had encountered at the
airport. On other occasions he saw the man surreptitiously
dropping a bomb into the sound hole of his Gizmo, a wide,
toothy smile on his face. Yet Masel settled cautiously into the
spell of general contentment; he enjoyed the run of the house
after Katy had gone to work, taking Sam and Jenny to the
nursery. Alone, he crunched breakfast cereal and perfected his
vocal exactitude. His university and Culture Committee en-
gagements were cancelled. There was no time. Yet what little
freedom he had gave him pleasure.

Lunch times, he took long walks through the West End.
He wandered up the busy hill at University Avenue, Gothic
spires towering about his ears. Splashes of joyous youth swept
passed him, brushed his body. He pushed from his stomach a
deep sigh, his heart ransacked. Although the sun shone, Masel
hung his umbrella over the crook of his left arm, munched hot
steak pie and beans among the students in the university
refectory and was, if only momentarily, at peace. Afternoons
he returned via the botanical gardens and out through black
cast-iron gates, his heart eager to work on the talking parts and
the connections between songs. What a pleasure it is to walk
without fear of attack, he thought. Once, however, while
helping a youth dislodge his football from the branches of a
lone pine tree, he hit a camouflaged squirrel with a pebble, and
the animal rained on his head, scampered, stunned, into a stiff
meadow of daffodils.

Evenings, he ate dinner with Katy, which she usually
cooked after Sam and Jenny were asleep. Being so close, able
to smell her aroma, invigorated Masel. He occasionally walked
around the flat with his shirt off, flexing his muscles in an effort
to excite her; otherwise he plucked songs for her on his Gizmo.

Although for the most part he stuck to sensual love ballads, once he sang her a song about a raggle-taggle Gipsy who stole a squire's wife. Perhaps unimpressed, perhaps tired, Katy dosed on the small couch with paperwork propped on her breasts.

She often had bad dreams as she slept and woke with a start, bolting upright, the look of sadness creeping over her face.

* * *

Masel's affections increased, but he found himself as ever miserable in love. At night, he slept on the floor in his sleeping bag. In spite of summery days, the small hours were chilly and Katy gave him two blankets to sleep under. Sometimes it was so cold Masel's teeth chattered. I'm running out of voices I can do, he complained to himself. Why me? Inside, he was the old Masel. When he woke in the darkness, shivering, thinking of her, he knew from the depth of his heart he was in love with her.

Early one afternoon, after an unusually satisfying morning of practise, wearing a red apron with penguins on it, Masel took the rest of the day off to prepare a candle-lit, Jewish dinner for Katy and the children. Although he could ill afford it, he cooked chicken soup with soft cinnamon dumplings and noodles (as his mother had taught him after his divorce), sweet black bread, pot roast, cooked with carrots, potatoes and natural gravy, with cabbage and pickled cucumbers on the side. In a nearby deli, he found strudel with apricots and peaches for dessert. He included a cheap bottle of Italian red wine for atmosphere. At exactly two minutes to seven o'clock, Masel switched the lights out and put a flame to the candles. A kitsch time piece ticked loudly on the wall.

He paced restlessly as eight o'clock approached.

At nine o'clock, he drove a wooden spoon deep into the chicken soup, obliterating a cinnamon dumpling into a thousand soggy fragments.

An hour later, Katy rolled home drunk and childrenless. Arm in arm, she brought with her a friend, an older gent, a pipe in his mouth, also drunk. Masel stood helplessly by the kitchen door. The candles, dripping, gave a final flicker and expired in a cool, single stream of smoke.

"This is my old friend, Prof Longman," Katy said, breathlessly. She was slurring her words. "He's a scientist. Dr Longman, this is Dr Masel. Dr Masel, this is Dr Longman."

Longman removed the pipe from his mouth and grinned. Masel looked uneasily between him and Katy.

"Glad to know you," he said dryly.

Katy's cheeks beamed. She rubbed her body against Masel before collapsing in his arms. She chortled a little, and then flopped her face in his shoulder, her sharp breasts prodding his rib cage. Masel, cautioning himself, leaned on her for support; he got none.

"Where's Jenny and Sam?" he asked. What business was it of his anyway? he scolded himself.

"At George MacGregor's," she said, slobbering on his shoulder. "And what business is that of yours anyway?"

He apologized.

Eyes wide, she smiled and planted a quick, wet kiss on his mouth, which he could neither refuse nor avoid. He blushed in the company of the other. Why now, after so long? he wondered.

"Forgive me," she said.

Masel, groaning, told her he already had.

"Aldous Longman," said the professor, shooting forth his palm. He was a bushy, beer-barrelled man of fifty or more, with hairy ears, a meaty double jawline and plump hands.

Masel shrugged. He put his arms around Katy and guided her to the couch. She kissed him again, the sour, acid odour of alcohol on her breath assailing his nostrils. He interpreted the scent as fruity. Then, as though in acute pain, she jerked her head straight and, raising a frightened hand to her bosom, hurried to the toilet. Masel noticed a slight softness in her belly as she ran, but he loved the creaminess of her skin where her sweater lifted an inch or two at the waist. Turning his head to the side, he tried not to listen to her throwing up, but was unable. He began to sense deep beatitude in her presence.

"Terribly sorry about this," Longman said, breathing deeply, his chest heaving a little, his eyes bloodshot, his brow wrinkled like a rag. The smell of whisky permeated everything, and Longman, as if sensing it, lit his pipe and pulled his head back. "I'm afraid I'm responsible for this."

Masel warned himself to keep his trap shut. Did she not have a right to her own friends? "It's all right," he said, testily, "if she wants to drink she can drink."

Longman puffed smoke into Masel's eyes. "So you're the American, eh?"

"That's correct. San Francisco."

"Old hippy, eh?"

"Kind of, I guess. Not really." His affection for Katy calmed him. "It's my work now," he explained.

Longman hiccoughed. "Aren't we all? Halcyon times," he recalled. Masel looked warily at him.

The professor headed for the kitchen, but Masel embarrassedly directed him away from the Jewish food - and the wine - and back into the livingroom. Together, they sat on the small couch. Love, he thought, like life, is a cold bowl of chicken soup, too.

"You don't happen to have a wee smidge on the premises, do you?" Longman asked

"Excuse me?"

"A drink."

"I don't think so. Sorry."

"Cleaning products?"

"What?"

"A joke. No matter."

Katy, returning from the toilet, stumbled clumsily into the livingroom wall. Unperturbed, she ran her fingers through wild red curls as she wheeled herself around, her complexion ashen. "I have to go to bed," she announced thickly and then turned back on her heels.

With an aching heart, Masel watched her hurry from the room. He felt for her footing, her very existence, although in his heart of hearts for himself.

"Let her sleep," said Longman. He hiccoughed again. "Excuse me...Too much whisky."

Masel looked contrite, nodded slowly. "Are you the laser man?"

Longman puffed thoughtfully on his pipe. "My boy, I've something far better than lasers in mind." He rubbed his hands together. Masel wanted to unburden his soul, but checked himself.

"To tell you the truth," he admitted, "I'm not really sure about any of this."

"One must overcome one's fear of the unknown," Longman guffawed, leaned into Masel, face to face, his eyes wide. "See me, I'm as bold as brass. Now what about this?" He paused and took a deep breath. "...Dr Masel's Light Extravaganza...Take One...What do you think?"

Masel began to snicker, but stopped abruptly. He couldn't get rid of the ironic smile on his face. "God help me," he said. "Gevalt."

"Gevalt? You speak Yiddish?"

"Maybe twenty or thirty words. It's a habit from my father. It's my way of remembering. He was Polish."

"Holographs," said Longman. "That's the key to the whole thing." His eyes sparkled like quartz. "Exact, almost live replications of the musicians you impersonate and a few others for a band. What do you think?"

He's a lunatic, Masel thought. "A band?"

"Why not?" Longman's belly rumbled as he emptied his pipe in the ashtray. "They won't make any sound, you understand, but it will look wonderful." With "wonderful", Longman threw his arms in the air, as if it were a final gesture to mankind, and then collapsed back in the settee, coughing.

To haunt the past like this was worrying, to bring the dead back to life. Was it healthy? Was Longman healthy?

"Don't overdo it," Masel said. "We've only got a few days, five to be exact. It's next Friday."

"Don't use that tone with me, Mr Jewish American. I'm well aware of the limitations."

Masel asked lamely if Longman was absolutely sure such an idea could be put into practice.

"Of course it can. Leave the technical business to me."

"It's just that I've never heard of anything like it before."

"That's the point," Longman said, jumping forward. He looked cunningly at Masel. "It just so happens I've been working on a project similar to this for years. This is a perfect opportunity to see it on a large scale."

Masel gulped, his eyes unhappy. "You mean you've never done this before?" He had an unfortunate vision of himself, shamed, ridiculed, embarrassed. "What if something goes wrong. What if I get hurt?"

Longman tittered, "Don't be stupid. Calm down. Now listen, first we have to record the images. We'll use a..." Thinking, Longman rubbed his chin. "Imagine a big piece of holographic film, like the thirty-five millimetre film you get for a camera." Masel tried to imagine it. "It's going to be a big piece of that, and we're going to wrap it round to form a cylinder. It'll be about six feet high and I don't know how wide. We'll have to work out how wide."

"You mean like a person's size."

Longman nodded gravely, hiccoughed, coughed. "Excuse me."

"Righto." Masel shivered, a lump in his throat.

"As for the images, we'll have a statue or a model of the person playing the guitar and then just photograph it onto the holographic film. We'll paint the model with some highly reflective colouring and then blast it with white light. On the big night, the tube will be the same colour as the stage background, so you'll only see the image."

Stone into life, thought Masel. "How will it move?"

"Move the statue, my boy. It'll be made of plasticine. The end product will be a series of, say, four or five images, like a cartoon. Except we'll just repeat the images back and forth. Simple but highly effective, I can assure you."

"Very interesting," said Masel.

"Exactly."

"Will it look real?"

"Better than real."

"What are you going to do with me? Put me in a tube too?"

"Listen before you talk. For you, we'll photograph heads." Longman touched Masel on the arm. "This is the clever part. You'll wear special helmets, holographic helmets, one for each impression. Then we'll blast you with white light."

"But we need lasers."

Exasperated, Longman glared. "I've told you, you'll learn more by listening. Why use lasers when you can have holograms? Lasers are irrelevent to the entire idea. You're obsessed, my boy, completely obsessed."

"Because the audience will be expecting lasers."

"If you want lasers, you can have lasers." Longman's expression was restless. "We'll just blast them around, but the hologram idea is quite different, far superior really."

Masel hesitated, rubbed a moist hand on his lap. "If you don't mind me asking, what's in all this for you?"

He looked at Masel with a wide, intense gaze, and coughed. "If you mean materially or financially, the answer is nothing. Suffice to say I have a personal interest in the project, and particularly a personal interest in Katy. I have known her since she was a child and now she needs my help. That's all there is to it."

Masel dared not ask him for more. Instead, he began to have moody delusions of possible stardom, of doing a show the people of Glasgow wouldn't forget for a long while, a show even the whole world might hear about.

The professor, groaning breath, rose uneasily from the couch, struggled momentarily with his aplomb, and let out a belch and hiccough at the same time. It seemed to stun him. It stunned Masel. The combined affect was like a bull frog emerging from a pond.

"I'm terribly sorry," he said heartily, striding for the door. "Solar wind."

Masel followed. Longman hiccoughed again, then turned and put out his hand. They shook on it.

"I'll be in touch with you," he added.

Another of Longman's hiccoughs echoed in the stairway. Masel perspired.

* * *

After an hour of misery clanging back through years of his life, thinking useless thoughts, Masel, unable to sleep, wandered the Glasgow streets in an unhappy mood, adrift. He was burdened by fear and solitude, saw himself trapped within a flaming circle of camera film. Yet, perhaps Longman's crazy idea would in the end be his salvation and perhaps through it, he would win Katy. He loitered momentarily beneath a humming orange street lamp, then trundled across University Avenue on to the deserted campus, his shadow shrinking and stretching as he walked.

With slow, sure steps he climbed a back stairway, his spirit heavy in an airy opening of mazed cloisters. The architecture inspired him, reminded him somehow of an ancient Chinese chess board in the court of Kublai Khan, stealthily majestic. He was about to ascend the Gothic tower, when suddenly, a stupendous thought struck him: Why don't I write a love song? A wild rush of feeling stirred up like soup in him. What more intimate way of expression was there? A love poem put to music. Romantic in all its intonations. Truly, a labour of love.

Light of heart, Masel jogged home. It took him only half an hour, in the full flight of inspiration. He strummed light major chords with mellow minor ninths and, in a perfect Mick Jagger voice, composed: "Woke up this mornin' with love in mind." With increasing sadness, he moaned: "And I've seen love make a fool of a man. It tried to make a loser win. But I've got nothing to lose I can't get back again."

Then he bellowed a chorus, as if frantic: "Churches long preach sex is wrong. Jesus, where has nature gone?"

He stopped short in desolation, realised, Jesus, I haven't composed this song at all. It was somebody else's from somewhere in the distant past. How could I be such a fool? Where has my talent gone? I'm a failure and a plagiarist.

Embarrassed by the racket he was causing, Masel lowered his voice and chanted slowly to a solitary suspended minor seventh, "What am I doin' here. What am I doin' here?"

And then, "Daddy, you're a fool to cry, you're a fool to cry", until he did.

Depressed by his depression, he gave up the idea. I can't even write a love song for the woman I'm in love with, he berated himself. Each note weighed on him with anguish, became dirtied by the thrust of his fear of the past and future. I have no talent. Maybe I don't really love her. Maybe this is all some kind of weird psycho-simulation. This kind of thinking could go too far, he warned himself. Then it occurred to him in momentary panic: What if she heard me? That chorus! Sex is wrong? Give it up now, he told himself, abandon ship before you go under.

He wept for the sinking ship, his loss. Yet, unwilling to be enticed by his old habits of cowardice, Masel crept into Katy's room. She lay face down, half-undressed, and half on and half off the bed, conked out. Her clothing was strewn everywhere. Masel breathed a heavy sigh that caused a quick, sharp pain in the middle of his back. Unable to control his instincts, however, he began picking her clothes off the floor and placing them neatly on an easy chair.

Stirring in sleep, Katy groaned at him, "Is that you, Willie?"

Willie? What's with Willie? Who was Willie? Masel's heart plummetted. It was a hideous blow.

Berating himself for his stupidity, he remained in silence, almost too petrified to move his hands through the air, which he was doing to keep his balance. It was the same old story. Now there was Willie to consider. Then she turned over and, revealing sharp, naked breasts, fell back asleep. Masel giddily admired her pale flesh, motionless, not knowing what to do. What would she think if she wakened? Me, walking around her room in the middle of the night, picking up her clothes like a meshugenna, ravishing her flesh with my eyes, my wanting?

Now creaking atop guilty floorboards, Masel approached

THE PLAN / 55

her bedside. Without untying her laces, he pulled off her flat, black shoes, and her legs flopped heavily on the mattress. Then he unbuttoned the waist of her cute, little leather mini-skirt and lifted her under the covers. She was light in his arms, like a child. He was wondering if he should have removed the skirt altogether, when she put her arms around him and began to softly kiss his neck and face. Masel held his breath and felt his desire crackle. He smelled her skin, a concoction of perfume and sweat. Masel felt himself stir. What about Willie? His heart thudded. He wanted to act, but couldn't bring himself to it.

"Love me," she said, dreamily.

"Try to sleep," Masel advised.

He tucked in the covers sharply around her and, as her breathing became even, she sank back willingly. Do I enjoy this suffering? Have I no courage? Only as a masochist, that alone is where my courage lies; as a Goddamn masochist. Later, in his bag, Masel concluded he was not fit to be a man, never mind a lover and performer.

■ Three

Preparations grew frantic if not riotous, and Katy, who never once mentioned Willie or her drunken night, worked feverishly. With her brow furrowed, her eyes lit, her nostrils flared, she pacified councillors back and forth and made deals with Plotnikov, and relayed information between him, Masel and Longman regarding stage requirements.

There was constant rain, day and night, never ceasing. The roof leaked and slaters had to be called in, disrupting his routine for two afternoons running.

Longman telephoned half a dozen times a day. First, to check the colour of the curtain backdrop at the EPI Centre, and then fifteen minutes later to insist it be a smooth, velvet black. He had a fastidious, haughty, irritated voice on the telephone, and said the holograms would show up better against black. Masel said he would see what he could do, although he really didn't have much to do with any of it. Then, as more rain heavily pummelled the kitchen and living room window, George MacGregor telephoned. Although Masel panicked, MacGregor only wanted to know if he could wait another week before being reimbursed for the Vacation Inn.

"Figures," he said. "Do I have a choice?"

"Ha! You're such a comedian."

Before hanging up, MacGregor told Masel to break a leg. Masel was absolutely paranoid, and he knew it. A curse on himself. A curse on electro-optics, too, while he was at it.

He left the phone off the hook.

His tension expanded as the deadline loomed like an approaching thunder cloud. Despite his efforts and all his passion, Masel felt things were going badly. He returned to Bob Dylan again, experimented with Sergeant Pepper, Hendrix, the Velvet Underground, the Grateful Dead, Jefferson Airplane and Janis Joplin. Where was the summer? Was this it? Where was the light? He was sick of this grey, wet climate. He needed blue sky, detested the low, black clouds.

He looked longingly from Katy's livingroom window and seemed to remember every song he had ever sung. He heard them as if hearing time-worn classics for the first time, but then got them mixed up with each other. Although tormented with his endless variations, he gradually began to love the tones of his voice, the skill and perfection of his impersonations. Masel's confidence in himself grew. Alone at night, with what was left of his heart, he worked with hefty inspiration, as though he were composing the originals.

* * *

Loathed to be taken from his practice, Masel eventually assented to a photo session and Press conference, although he tried to limit himself to answering only the most basic of questions. Five reporters and eleven cameramen were present for the occasion in a small conference room at Glasgow District Council headquarters. But it was more Katy's interview than Masel's. Masel was backed into a corner, flashlights blinding him, pinning him to the wall. Katy, looking ravishing in red hot pants, her hair flowing, told them to expect a show so spectacular it would make Guy Fawkes night look like a council housing sub-committee meeting. The reporters grinned.

To one question, however, Masel, his hands held up in front of him, obscuring his eyes from the incessant flashing, retorted, profusely sweating, "If you piss in the wind, it'll come back at you twice as hard."

"Don't quote Lou Reed at me in that tone of voice," said a reporter.

Furtively, Masel attempted to leave by a side door while Katy told them about the laser show, but the newsmen railroaded him back into the corner.

Q. Is it true you were searched for drugs at Glasgow Airport? another young newspaper man asked.

A. No comment.

Q. Why sixties' culture? asked another, an older man with red-veined cheeks, thrusting a tape recorder in Masel's face.

A. I don't know for sure. It draws me. Because the music is excellent, has feeling, soul, enormous social and personal significance. I find the nineteen-sixties a moral time, in retrospect, despite the violence.

Q. If you don't mind me asking, how can war, drugs, sex and psychedelic music be moral?

A. It was a highly constipated time, no analagy intended. (A camera man tittered.) The response was moral. We wanted to change the world, improve it. I still do in many ways. In other ways, the Vietnam war ruined that for us.

Q. Excuse me, we're talking about the '60s, not your personal psychology of the time. Do you think you could confine yourself to the questions at hand?

Several reporters scribbled furiously to his left. More cameras clicked, flashed on the right.

A. I answered it honestly. It was an explosion of values, a chaotic reaction against the block-headed anti-intellectualism of the white Anglo-Saxon puritanism of the previous three decades. I guess the truth is you have to liberate yourself.

Masel, moved by the past, coughed to clear the lump in his

throat. He grimaced.

"Some of us saw the changes, but few will see the ends."

"That's an extremely strange thing to say, Dr Masel, but carry on anyway."

"That's it."

Q. What about the effect on the youth of today?

A. What about it?

Q. This is a great worry to many people, especially parents. In the sixties, if I recall correctly, liberation was achieved by way of drugs and sex. Is that the kind of example you want to set? What about AIDS? Have you ever used drugs, Dr Masel? Do you sleep around?

A. To both questions, the answer is yes, but not for many years. I think it's fair to say that drugs, among other things, like the Vietnam War also, for instance, destroyed the credibility of the time. Worse than that, my generation are now at the root of evil. We were the ones who were going to change the world, but stopped short. Now we have become like the generation before us; we grew up, became selfish, paranoid, conservative and greedy. I am as guilty as any, I don't deny it. The world is still a hell of a place. If I'm asking for anything now, it's a return to hope. I'm an idealist, I admit.

Q. So you would advocate another nineteen-sixties-type revolution, drugs and all? That's really what your show's about, isn't that it, Dr Masel? Why don't you come clean and be done with it? That's what our taxes and public money is going toward in this year's Culture Festival, isn't it?

A. I wouldn't know about that.

Q. Admit it, it's all about the promotion of drugs, sex and violence, isn't it?

A. You should know, that's your business. And frankly, I don't think I care for some of your comments. We're talking about a concert, a musical anthology of an era, not some drug-crazed orgy. I suggest that you come clean, not me. I have nothing to hide.

Q. We have a saying in Scotland: Your balls are mutton. Come, come, Dr Masel. You're clearly a man with a past.

A. Fuck off.

Q. What about your relationship with Culture Katy? Does your Jewishness have anything to do with your caginess?

Masel punched the tape recorder.

* * *

In a newspaper the next day, a headline - 'HIPPY HIPPY SHAKE UP'; sub-deck: 'American psycho-delic star in drug punch-up shocker' - appeared above a photograph of Masel and Katy. Masel wore his blue flannel suit and a black Grateful Dead tee-shirt, his hands on his hips, his head proudly in the air, turned slightly to the side, the length of his little black ponytail exposed in full. Katy, truly stunning in her scanty red hot pants, a low-cut white, frilly blouse, her piercing breasts pointing toward the camera, a silver Culture Vulture badge at her collar, lay sexily at Masel's feet, her head propped up by her palm and terse forearm, resting on her elbow.

She berated Masel severely for his outburst. MacGregor wasn't happy about it either, complained over the telephone that he'd lowered the tone of Glasgow Culture.

Masel, sporting a small, bulging black eye after the fracas, disturbed by the slander, apologized to Katy, said he didn't know what came over him.

"Idiot," she said.

"I couldn't help myself."

Katy strode across the kitchen floor. "On second thoughts, it's good publicity,"

Masel blushed in fear.

* * *

On Thursday evening, the night before the big one, Masel's black eye yellowed. He paced Katy's livingroom in a desperate mood, a bowl of crunchy-nut cornflakes in his hand as he walked. Longman telephoned again. The professor's voice boomed, then hiccoughed drunkenly, deep into Masel's ear. Masel, taken by surprise, crunched into the receiver. He feared the worst, swallowing.

"My dear, dear boy," Longman bellowed down the line.

"Was that you?"

Masel admitted it with a groan. "I'm sorry. I was chewing. How about you?" He would get no inspiration from the laser man, that much was obvious to him. He put down the cereal.

"Just telephoned to give you the good news.

"And what's that?"

"Everything is in order. It's final countdown, my boy. In other words, we're ready when you are."

Masel bit his thumb in fear. Touching a high, throbbing cheek bone that depressed his spirits further, a dreadful thought assailed him. "Are you sure you haven't forgotten anything? I mean, considering the condition you've been in."

"What condition might that be?" Longman snapped. "What are you insinuating?"

"Nothing," Masel said, lamely. "I didn't mean anything bad. It's just that you sound a little strange."

"You're a bit strange yourself, stranger than you think, in fact. Just make certain you get your part right. Katy and I will take care of the rest."

There was a long silence, then a thud. Longman had dropped the telephone. He hiccoughed as he picked it up. There was another silence, this one more disturbing than the last. Masel, breaking into a profuse sweat, panicked. My God, I'm trusting a dipsomaniac with my fate. He kept his mouth shut, leaned his clammy forehead on the livingroom window, the spring evening before him, and felt the glass vibrate as a truck rolled by on the main road.

After several seconds of fear and doubt, he asked, "Can I at least look at the holograms?" Masel was especially nervous about the helmets he would have to wear.

"I still need to optimise the lighting. Tomorrow's soon enough for you. Stay relaxed."

Longman hiccoughed and hung up. Masel's mind jumped ahead. All he could see was disaster. He was on stage tomorrow night. Alone, he pelted his nervous system with doubt and fear..

* * *

For dinner Katy, Masel and the kids ate garlic sausage and

tomato pizza from a home delivery place around the corner. Although Masel offered to pay, his heart wasn't in it. He told Katy about his call from MacGregor and she wrote a cheque.

Afterwards, he unpacked his Gizmo and performed a perfect Purple Haze, with exact Jimi Hendrix-like passion and nuttiness. Masel the professional; he played with anguish, and received rapturous applause from all in attendance, a standing ovation from Sam and Jenny. *I'm as ready as I'll ever be,* he knew, resigned to his fate. *Gevalt, my life will end in disaster.*

█ Four

Long after Sam and Jenny were asleep, and the American had practised all his heart would allow, Masel, frustrated, famished, overwrought, asked Katy, "If I were to promise to be a gentleman, do you think you might let me share your bed?"

Katy looked up from her paperwork. "How do you mean?"

He coughed, his heart lurching. He fumbled with his Gizmo, trying to get it into its case. "It'd just be for tonight." He smiled fearfully, bending again over the instrument. "And I promise to stay in the corner. You won't even know I'm there. I'm sick of the livingroom floor. I need a break."

Katy, momentarily expressionless, said nothing. She raised her fingers to her mouth and leaned far to one side, trying to get him to look at her directly.

"Please, Katy?" he asked, eventually, looking up.

She seemed stunned by the suggestion."You've got a real sense of timing."

"You've got a big bed." Masel sensed he had blown it. For several heartbeats he was silent. "It's just that tomorrow is the big night, and I've been lying on the floor for almost two weeks. The couch is too small, and my back is killing me. I've hardly slept a wink. I'm exhausted. What kind of performance can I give in a state like this? I was just hoping you might trust me, just so I can have a little rest."

Katy considered it, spoke as if she were addressing a child.

"Do you promise he keep your hands to yourself?"

Masel, overwhelmed by the possibility, crossed his heart and hoped to die.

There was a long silence. Masel felt his breathing race.

Katy twisted a strand of golden hair around her finger. "OK, then," she said, half-smiling. "But watch yourself."

"I promise." Masel all but cheered.

* * *

Katy undressed quickly and got into bed. Masel, after a long time of doing nothing in the bathroom, brushed his teeth twice - once before taking a shower and once after. He surveyed his build in the mirror, his flat form - or at least what was left of his flat form. He wasn't that happy about it; still, he had strong deltoids. His pectorals, however, and biceps looked let down. And that little pot belly. Let's face it, you're approaching middle age. Masel concluded he was a ball of muscle.

Despite his softening middle, he slowly became aware of a youthful, hardening erection. It lifted his boxer shorts like a tent pole. "Gevalt," he said out loud, ordered the thing to go down. It disobeyed. He even tried slapping it, but that didn't work either, against his will excited him further. A culmination of everything, no doubt, Katy, the concert, desperation, sex, impending doom. He had thought of making his appearance in his underwear; naked was out the question. I can't go anywhere like this. There he stood, helpless before the mirror. Then he thought about going in fully dressed, but that was ridiculous, too. Eventually, he discovered if he bent over, it wasn't really that noticeable. Yet, he couldn't walk into the bedroom like this, like a sexually-aroused hunchback.

He emerged suspiciously, crept into Katy's bedroom, his trousers folded neatly over his left arm, in front of him. The light was out but, after his eyes adjusted, Masel glimpsed Katy's huddled form in the far corner of the bed, her face to the wall. In the semi-darkness of the room, only her wild curls were visible. Masel put his trousers over a chair and climbed into bed. His erection, stubborn although now half-hard, continued to embarrass him. Katy didn't turn. Was she holding her breath? He was sweating again, blushed in the darkness.

Masel lay still, dared not utter a sound. He turned lightly on his side and, mocking a parallel position to her, brought his knees up and faced her back. He had never been this close to her before. Would he be again? That depended, he supposed, on several factors. Her odour entered his palpitating nostrils and drove him nuts. He was tense with desire, yet at the same time shivered with cold. She was inert, as if suspended in animation.

Abruptly, a gentle tone to her voice, she said, "I forgive you, Elliot. I want you to succeed."

"What did I do?"

She seemed slightly sheepish. "Everything, really, I forgive you for complicating my already-complicated life." She coughed, her hand moved behind her and touched Masel's leg. "What I really mean to say is, thank you for helping me when you didn't have to. I regret we didn't get off to a better start. I know that was my fault."

Masel told her to forget it. "Save it until tomorrow night," he said. "It's bad luck otherwise."

She told him to break a leg.

"MacGregor told me the same thing."

"In that case, break your nose."

Cautiously, he placed a hand on her shoulder, turning over possibilities in his head. Masel felt the smooth linen through the calloused tips of his left-hand, guitar-worn fingers. His emotion stirred, and she flattened her hand on his hand; the tiniest touch of skin on skin caused his heartbeat to race.

"Elliot," she asked, "can I ask you a question?"

"Be my guest." He was trying to seem casual, but his erection seemed still to be growing.

"How long were you married?"

Masel shuddered, his member abruptly deflated. "Seven long years."

"You make it sound like a jail sentence. Did you leave her for someone else?"

"I hung on to the bitter end. It's my nature. I loved her very much. That's also my nature."

"Did she cheat on you?"

He hesitated and breathed out deeply. The question caused tears to well up in his eyes. Guilt? Self-hatred? The ache of a desire he was afraid to act on? What kind of person am I? What am I for? If only he knew. He did know that he would do anything in his power now to be able to seduce this beautiful creature beside him. Furtively, he wiped his cheek.

At last, he said, "We both developed our own little crises, became isolated, she in her life and me in mine. We became irrelevant to one another. At least I felt I was irrelevant to her. I was playing in a rock band at the time; she was studying business at the University of California. We never met in the middle."

"So what happened?"

Masel's feet rustled the sheets. "Nothing, the closest I ever came to success was a song I wrote called No Rest For The Wicked. A band called the Mindwarpers recorded it, and it got to number a hundred and seventeen in the Hit Parade. It made me three-hundred dollars, and that was that."

"No, I mean your wife, you never saw each other?"

"I suppose occasionally at nights, when we were both home. Rarely really. It sounds emotionless now, but it really wasn't like that. Maybe I drove her a little crazy. Maybe she just got tired of my obsessions. Like I said, it's just the way the thing panned out."

"That's sad. I'm sorry," she said. "I think I like your obsessions." He felt warmed. She dreamily closed her eyes and paused motionless in the darkness, biting her lip. "I haven't been much help to you, have I?"

He said she was, whether she knew it or not.

"And before that? What was it like, I mean the sixties?"

Masel, groaning slightly, was smacked by a vivid memory. He saw himself burning dollar bills and American flags in between songs before a rowdy bar-room crowd in Tehachapi, California, a seventeen-year-old radical, eyes foggy blue, shooting his mouth off about the six million fried in Nazi ovens, and how many had Nixon sent to their deaths in the jungle infernos of south-east Asia, etc.

"Before that?" he said, "I only caught the tail end of the era, but it was the Haight Ashbury hippy family. You must have heard of it, Hashbury. Sociologists call it the 'Haight Ashbury Experience'. You know, love, drugs, music, liberation, revolution, the Utopian vision. Those were the days when most women laid down for me. I came from a long line of missionaries. Nowadays, it's different."

Katy laughed. "Do you have children?"

He hesitated, startled for a moment by the directness of her question. "It would have been a mess." His voice weakened and dropped. "Besides, Zelda didn't really want any. She had a miscarriage about six months after we got married and went on the pill after that. She became very career minded, not that that's a bad thing in its own right. She works in the stock market in New York now, on Wall Street. She got what she wanted."

She stared at him with interest. "And you?"

"I didn't get a thing. I had to pay alimony for four years."

"I'm sorry," she said.

"Don't be." Masel felt his heart thud. He tenderly stroked her hair, as if she were a child. "I want to be here right now."

It was the truth, although, all things considered, he no longer remembered why he was here. Katy touched his nipple with her fingers. On second thoughts, he did remember. She turned and they embraced passionately. "Don't worry about tomorrow," she said. "We'll do fine."

"What about Longman?"

"What about Longman?"

Masel felt his forehead perspire. "What if he's drunk tomorrow night? What if everything ends in disaster?"

"Calm down. It won't. He drinks all the time, it's a fact of life. He knows what he's doing."

Masel continued to worry. His heart raced faster as he moved his hand down her arm. Now she touched his hand. Then, gazing into his eyes, she affectionately touched his ear. Masel's heart skipped five beats, the sixth rattled his rib cage and made him hold his breath.

"Katy, I ... you're ..." he stuttered. He hesitated, nervous, aroused by passion. "You really are beautiful."

Jenny started to cry in the other room. Masel hiccoughed uncontrollably. Then he did it again.

"For Christ's sake," he mumbled, irritably. "Why me, already? Why does nothing ever go right?"

"Don't get excited, Elliot," she said, "It's only the baby. She's probably hungry or thirsty. I'll be back in a minute."

When she returned, Masel had drifted asleep against his will, although, vaguely, he heard her remove her dressing gown in a swift swooping motion. He had been on the threshold of a dream - a nightmare of riding a unicycle over Leo Plotnikov's forehead - when she clasped him where it counted. His heart thumped and he smelled her sweetly scented flesh.

"My poor, poor, crazy Elliot," she said. "Warm me up."

Masel hiccoughed.

The Concert
One

AROUND noon, on a warmish, pleasant summer's day, a Glasgow University coloured van - red, blue and yellow - edged along a shadowy cobble stone alleyway and stopped outside the back entrance to the Euro Pictish Institute Centre. The steamily-clouded morning had made a run for it, and the sun had burst brightly in its wake. Masel, his guitar case gripped in his right palm, dark glasses on, stood in a patch of sunlight at the other end of the alley, waiting. He was jostled briefly by a gang of rowdy football supporters; they surrounded him in good humour, singing team songs. They chanted primitively for maybe thirty seconds and headed on their way. Peering through a rare rippling heat haze, Masel saw Katy perched in the driver's seat. She was intense at the wheel, her hair wilder and redder than ever. Longman sat firmly in the passenger seat, gripping steadfastly to the safety belt around him, as if for his life.

Masel, his arm half rising in greeting, felt his knees tremble; he secretly wished the van would drive by him.

Katy honked the horn. It was a deep, quacking sound. To Masel, it was a beautiful honk, a honk of love.

His heart paused thoughtfully, but momentary panic accelerated the beat. He was deeply affected after making love to her. Thus, whatever might lay in store for him, Masel began to interpret certain events of the recent past and present as being of good fortune. My fate is fame, he told himself, trying to psyche himself free of fear. The day was warming. Karma-wise, he figured, he was being groomed for success. In evidence, Masel noted the council's confirmed invitation had arrived on the same day he had lost his job at Berkeley; it had hardly been his fault, he remembered, that a pretty student had tried to seduce him in his office after one of his 'Summer of

Love' lectures; it had hardly been his fault that, as he was fighting her off, the dean had walked in; nor was he to know the student was the dean's daughter. Had fate instructed it all? Had fate instructed Katy to make that absurd spelling mistake and perpetuate the consequences? Also: two weeks before his flight, Zelda had remarried and at the wedding had, out of pity or perhaps a desire to get rid of him, loaned him $1000 for his airfare. Masel became convinced these were signs that destiny had winked at him. Even the fact that this concert was now a reality, after so little time to prepare and organise, seemed to Masel not too much short of the miraculous. And, last night, making love to Katy; was that not the ultimate signal? Imagine a man like me doing something like this. Things in this world do not just happen, he remembered as a thirteen-year-old boy in a distant, near-forgotten Hebrew class. Not even a blade of grass exists without having its roots in something higher.

He stared smilingly at Katy for a moment, recalling the touch of her electric flesh. Is it love? he wondered. And if so, what possibilities? If I love her, how do I know she loves me? What if she doesn't? He had warned himself to get tough, but was assailed by a battery of ancient logic. Jewish logic? He considered: What if I'm being set up for the biggest fall of my life? Gevalt, what a mishamagas. Ancient questions; cause or consequence? good or evil? Be on your guard, a voice from a dusty Talmud advised him, there are no truths, only interpretations.

Masel, munching a chocolate bar, watched in fear as Longman, coughing bronchially, stumbled from the vehicle. He wore a green hunting jacket and a tweed deer-stalker that sat slightly askew on his head. Masel, crinkling the chocolate bar wrapper and stuffing it in his pocket, swallowed, gulped.

"How are you, Masel?" Longman called, rubbing his fat hands anxiously together. He was wearing a pair of steel-rimmed spectacles that seemed to bend around into the shape of his head. He looked as though he'd spent the night lying on his face with his glasses on. There was a roughish smile on his lips, mischievous, almost chimpanzee-like.

"Nervous." Masel laughed nervously. A wavering flush came over him, but he steadied himself.

"Nobody will notice. Just keep your mind on your work and don't forget the order of the songs. Remember, the computer is programmed on the information that you specifically gave me. So, whatever you do on that stage tonight, don't sing the wrong songs; or, for that matter, the right songs in the wrong order. If we get that right, we're more than half way there; otherwise, chaos will ensue very rapidly."

Masel gulped. "No fear."

Masel, sneakily staring at Longman, couldn't tell if he was bazookaed or not. The folk expert abruptly felt deflated, an old emotion, flattened like a tyre; Masel's own father, Joseph, had been a lush - the word was painful to Masel - and had died after a lost weekend, as he staggered blindly into a milk truck at 6 a.m. on a bright, dewy Monday morning. He had let Masel down for most of all he could remember. A little Masel, barely eight years old, had looked on in anguish from his bedroom window, milk-white rivulets running into blood, catching the glint of sunlight as it surely flowed to the gutter's edge, tears streaming down his face in horror and disbelief.

Masel snapped out of it.

Katy opened the back of the van and smiled furtively. She looked delicate today in her short, black fringed skirt and leather jacket, narrowed her eyes, her lips apart; her breasts, as ever, protruded forward. If he had expected to find uneasiness in her, he detected none. When he searched her eyes for guilt, he was distracted by their warmth.

Masel had to concentrate to force his stare away from her to focus on to the three massive, black film cylinders before him in the open van. His heart bumped. As he drew a breath, Katy went to find Plotnikov.

"Well?" said Longman.

"My God," Masel said, rubbing a drop of moisture from his hairline. "What are they?"

"Magnificent creations," Longman said, his hands on his hips, his voice deep and intense with satisfaction, almost in awe, proud, the veins on his cheeks purple. "Take my word for it, they're all magnificent." He paused for a moment to consider something, smiled. "Every one is magnificent, if I don't say so myself." He took a deep breath and announced loudly, "Meet the band."

Masel stared in fright, couldn't exactly see a band.

Longman laughed to himself, cocked his thumb up. "Magnificent."

Masel laughed politely, so heartily that probably not even Longman could see his true fear. He looked around for Katy, but was unable to find her.

* * *

The two men, loudly huffing and puffing, carried the equipment into the auditorium. After the first trip, Masel, a bulky black speaker box on his back, broke into a profuse sweat and was unable to breathe for several seconds. Longman's eyes bulged like eggs beneath the weight of his computer and various boxes and attachments, which shot forth an intertwined plexus of multi-coloured wires, like psychedelic snake-hair. The equipment, which was at times so heavy that it had to be tackled by the two them, grew heavier with each load. Longman wheezed, holding his big chest, his face like a tomato. Masel's muscles ached.

On the final trip, staggering in sneakers along the back of the dark stage, his heart erratic, the chocolate bar wrapper fell out of Masel's pocket and he slipped on it. The spotlight in their hands turned, seemed to totter in mid air for a moment, before it thudded to the ground.

"Oy!" Masel fell on his ass, and twisted his foot as he went to the floor.

Longman, in an effort to keep his balance, caught his leg in the metal bracket at the side of the light. As he hit the ground, a bottle scooted out of his pocket and slid across the floor to Masel. Masel groaned, dread engulfing him: How was this ever going to work with a dipsomaniac at the controls? He was now face to face with a half-drunk bottle of vodka. As if by a miracle, neither the vodka nor the spotlight were damaged.

Masel touched his lips with his furry tongue, said nothing. The truth was he didn't know what to say.

Longman stared at the bottle, incensed yet restrained, asked, "Can I have it back, pleas?"

"You promised."

"Did I?"

"You promised Katy. She told me."

Longman rose from the floor. He eyed Masel powerfully. He took a deep breath, as if to bolster himself. The professor and the American glared at each other in hate, eye to eye.

"Just give me it back, and that will be the end of it."

After a moment of contemplation, fear, daring, Masel asked, "What if I don't?"

"Then you'll do this show on your own, without lasers, holograms and without a band. And be it on your own head, whatever that might look like after the crowd get hold of it. I dare say they'll be somewhat tetchy after paying good money for their tickets and getting you, and only you. They're expecting a laser show, remember?"

"You would do that to Katy?" It was his paranoia, he knew, that linked Katy and Longman as conspirators.

Longman, thinking, his eyebrows forcibly lowered, said solemnly, "She's with me."

Masel felt more alone than he had ever felt in his life.

Katy and Plotnikov ran in from a door at the back of the hall and stopped. "Everything all right?" Katy yelled, tipping her head forward as if trying to hear some faint sound in the distance. "There was a bang."

Masel darted a quick glance at Longman and nervously considered his options. He furtively slid the bottle back and gulped.

"Dropped a light," Longman called. He slipped the bottle in his pocket. "It's alright. Nothing to worry about."

"My goodness," said Plotnikov, approaching the stage. "No roadies?" Longman smiled faintly. Plotnikov smiled, too, or rather winced, and broke away, shaking his head.

Katy, catching Masel's furtive glance, waved quietly and

turned in trepidation.

Why is everything against me?

* * *

An hour went by.

In near darkness, backstage, on a pile of wooden crates, Masel hammered out Bob Dylan's Most Likely You'll Go Your Way And I'll Go Mine. He was trying to calm himself by strumming the fear out of his system, attempted to beat it back with a vibrating Gizmo. What will become of me? What if they laugh? What if Longman...; he tried not think about Longman. Didn't a failed musician have enough to worry about? Gevalt.

Masel battered his Gizmo, and out came, "Lay lady lay, lay across my big brass bed."

 TWO

Sometime during late afternoon, an alien purple ray peered onto the brooding folk music expert. He was paralysed for a moment. Within a solid purple ring, the light pinned him where he sat. It projected weirdly and created a bumped arc on the outskirts of the ring, where it passed over the edge of his guitar. Masel, stunned, his heart racing, tried to look up at the source.

"Click it off, for God's sake."

"What do you think?" Katy called.

"I can't see. Click it off. Quick."

Masel couldn't see a thing. He guessed Katy was in the gantry and had swivelled the light round to the back of the stage. The light abruptly clicked off.

"Good, eh? It's our centre spotlight with a purple filter on it. What do you think?"

"Thank God. I think you've blinded me." He saw spots before his watery eyes. He blinked rapidly.

"You're always exaggerating. You better get used to it."

Masel continued to blink.

Longman, swaying in mid air, sat on a stool behind a computer on a suspended platform above the back of the auditorium.

Masel, clonking nervous heels, stalked the stage. He studied the holographic cylinders (three were life-size; the other was huge), the circular platforms, the eight stack speakers, and the lonely microphone. His stomach burned when he looked at the sea of empty seats.

"What about my helmets?" he asked cautiously.

"Behind you." Longman jabbed his finger in the direction.

Masel gazed in fright. On a longish off-white table in the dimness, there were the dozen or so hollow tubes that were supposed to go over his head, strange helmets with cutouts around the eyes and the mouth. Masel took one up cautiously in the tips of his fingers and felt ridiculous when he put it on his head. What happens if I get an itch on my nose? he wondered. His ears perspired. He heard Katy laugh from somewhere high above him, and he pulled it off quickly.

"Get up on the stage," shouted Longman. "I want to see what you look like."

He waved. "Katy, flick on the switch."

Masel put the tube back over his head, staggered, lost his aplomb and tripped over a wooden stool.

"Have I got this on straight?" he cried. "I can't see anything." His voice was nasal. This will never work in a million years, he thought, trying to get back on his feet. He tried turning it around.

Longman guffawed noisily. "Take the tape off the eye and mouth holes," he yelled.

Masel, severely berating himself for his stupidity, fumbled with the black masking tape. Use your brain, he advised, you have a PhD.

Katy shot on the over-head spotlight. It blasted down a thick, powerful column of white light, perfect, circular and solid, as though it were some potent energy from outer space, a bold ray from heaven.

Masel, stumbling forward, his head encased in a roll of holographic film, thought he would frazzle if he walked into it.

Sweating profusely through his blue flannel suit and black tee-shirt, he moved forward a little, so the beam would be directly above him. He tried to look up at it, but it was blinding and he snatched his eyes away abruptly.

There was stunned silence. Masel, only conscious of loud breathing - mine? he wondered- feared the worst. What was this? a circus, a freak show?

Longman, fingering his scalp, his mouth opening, took ten seconds before he could bring himself to say anything. "Oh, my," he finally said. "I don't believe it."

"What? What's wrong with it?"

"It's magnificent. I've done it. I'm a genius." Longman's voice echoed through the hall in exaltation, boyish and excited. "It's perfect. A magnificent creation. I've brought Jim Morrison back from the dead. It's truly a miracle."

"Turn around," Katy yelled, excited. "I want to see."

Masel turned. He felt like Frankenstein, but in fact he looked like Jim Morrison; long, flowing, black hair, deep, youthful features, dark, sullen stare. Masel was a sixties sex symbol, albeit a dead one.

"Oh my God," she exclaimed. "It's real. It's him." Katy began jumping up and down.

Masel's heart thudded.

"Hee-haaa! Yeahhh!" Longman bellowed, his deer stalker flying off his head. "I told you I could do it. Stupendous." Unashamedly, he took a slug of vodka in celebration. He was gung-ho.

Masel whipped the mask from his head and clasped it between his hands. Stunned in the flood of light, he beheld the magnificent image of Longman's counterfeit creation - the neck and head of Jim Morrison. The American held it fearfully in his hands, as if it were the head of John the Baptist himself.

"Now you're talking." Longman flapped his arms three or four times in the air. His voice was loud "Get off the stage. Stand back and you can see the band."

"You work everything from back there?"

"I work the band," explained Longman. "And Katy will

track you with the spotlight. The reference beams for the other holograms, the band, are stationary."

"Righto," confirmed a confused Masel.

He gulped and nodded unconvincingly. My God, he thought, what have I done?

"The band is all wired up to this Macintosh Plus computer, which controls the speed of the holograms. I spent an entire week writing separate programmes for each song. Clever, eh? What do you think?

Stunned, Masel said nothing.

Longman chuckled. "Well, I can assure you it's a work of genius. I can even slow it down or speed it up, depending on how you do the song. Remember the list you made for me? To put it simply, I rotate the platforms at the right speed and then bingo. Katy hits the holograms with the reference beam and we have two individuals playing the guitar, one on keyboards, and one banging drums. Ah, the wonders of modern technology."

"Drums?" asked Masel. No one had mentioned drums to him.

"Wee surprise." Longman laughed. "You can run through a few songs in a minute. Plotnikov, I understand, is working the PA."

Masel's heart pummelled his chest.

"First get off the stage and watch this." Longman gave Katy the thumbs-up. "Are you ready?"

Warily, Masel asked, "Have you got the lasers?"

"Of course I do. I told you not to worry about that. I'll just blast them around the auditorium. They're wired to the computer, too. It'll be a masterpiece, a visual extravaganza, believe me. In fact, how about Dr Elliot Masel's Super Light Extravaganza And His Journey Through The Past!"

Masel apologized, fearful. I must be out of my mind, he thought. Katy giggled, and gave him a stiff salute from high in the gantry. Masel, blushing beneath his clothes, stepped off the stage and stood sweating in the front row.

Then: Ping!

"Awesome," Masel said.

It was a wonder to behold.

■ Three

Most of the crowd arrived on time, but lingered first at the bar before taking their seats. Masel sat somewhere back stage, and fingerpicked fast rag-time in a panic.

The quietness in the small auditorium thickened and rose up like noisy mist.

Masel, always a sucker for tradition, was determined to be at least a half an hour late. Backstage, peeking through a crack in the velvet curtain, he watched the hall slowly fill, his throat parched, his heart whamming, his nerves biting like a drill on his teeth. Longman and Katy were already in position. Masel looked up and saw Longman take another swig from his bottle. The American gulped.

Plotnikov moved quietly about backstage. "Are you there?" he asked, peering into the shadows. In the dim light, motionless, Masel clung fast to his Gizmo D25 with both his hands. He nervously whispered his whereabouts.

"Where are you?"

"I'm here," he said, groaning.

"Ok, we're ready to rock."

Masel, psyching himself into a trance, gripped the sweating curtain. In truth, he wanted to fly, flee across the Atlantic and hide in someone's cellar; but yes, he was ready to rock, as ready as he would ever be.

Without expression, Plotnikov casually stepped out from the side of the stage, and went to the microphone. He took care to avoid the table, only just visible in the darkness, on which sat Masel's dozen or so holographic helmets in a neat row.

The crowd, momentarily restless, cheered thinly and waited for Plotnikov to speak. Katy switched on the spotlight. No drum roll? Masel had forgotten his band wasn't real.

"Ladies and gentlemen," he announced, an electric grin on his face. "I have the great pleasure of bringing to you tonight, all the way from San Francisco, California, another winner for Glasgow's own Euro Pictish Institute, please give a warm, warm welcome to ... (he shouted this) ... Dr Elliot Masel's Super Light Extravaganza And His Journey Through The Past!"

* * *

Masel was stunned by the name of his own show, but tried not to let it get him too excited. The stage was clicked back into darkness. There was violent clapping, but it died hastily. Can't run now. Masel waited thirty seconds, and like a somnambulist, emerged from behind the curtain. Can they see me yet? he wondered. Enough. I am a man. I am a professional. Shame on you for wanting to run; but he still wanted to run. Guided by the red light of his fuzzbox footswitch, Masel made his way to the table and picked out the first mask. The thick silence crushed him inwardly. Seeing only his outline, the crowd exploded in a burst of polite applause.

Deeply, he forced out, "Good evening, Glasgow."

Another round of mild applause burst forth, followed by rapt attention. Masel's cheeks stuck to the inside of his helmet.

His ears burned.

Pulling away from the microphone, he tilted his head back and yelled skyward, "Ok, Katy, let me have it."

Whoosh ...

The spotlight was on, and at once Masel was imprisoned in a thick column of white light, solitary and alone. His head bowed over his guitar, the hologram distorted, out of position, he stood a moment in silence, his eyes closed and perspiring in meditation. Tension built up within and without. He waited for the crowd to quieten and then, as if someone had gripped him by the back of his collar, he snapped himself upwards and revealed his counterfeit identity. It was Janis Joplin in a blue flannel suit.

It was as if the entire audience, as if one solid entity, breathed in sharply.

His eyes wide and bloodshot and sweating under the mask, Masel strummed a chunky succession of E Majors and then went into an A with a passionate blues change and then back to E Major. Slowly, but with energy and feeling, he screamed at the top of his lungs, "Cryyy Cryyy-y Ba-bee. Cryyy-y-y Ba-bee."

Who would ever have suspected Masel of having talent like this? Not me, Masel breathed to himself. Where the song paused for a second in mid-climax, as if in mid-air, and starts again, Longman flicked on the band: deceased soul singer Otis Redding on rhythm guitar, the Grateful Dead's dead Pig Pen on keyboards, over-dosed Rolling Stone Brian Jones on lead guitar and crazy-but-dead Who drummer Keith Moon on drums.

Masel, never daring to peek behind him, battered breathlessly through his repertoire. His heart, though, somehow relaxed now, had gone north to the bottom of his throat.

Longman blasted out the lasers, and they fired everywhere like fine beams of crimson metal that reflected and twisted and turned into magic, unrecognizable shapes around the hall.

"Drivin' that train, high on cocaine, Casey Jones you better watch your speed."

Drenched in sweat, Masel tasted salt water on the tip of his tongue. He shook his head to remove a drip on his eyelid.

"Purple haze is in my brain," he bellowed deeply, through the dank and sticky Jimi Hendrix helmet, scrunching and grundging and thrashing out powerful assaults from his fuzzbox.

"...Lately things don't seem the same."

As Roger Daltrey, with a wild look of either madness or terror, he cried out, "Why don't y'all just f-f-f-fade away...Talkin' bout my generation..."

For the sentimentalists, he whipped on his Gary Puckett head, cleared a lump in his throat and sang, "Young girl, you're breakin' my heart."

Soulful Otis Redding, defying all true gravity, did a double somersault and began to play Masel's chunky chord rhythms with his teeth on his phantom instrument.

Masel clinked a series of high peak notes, that seemed to

suggest one of those dread-filled moments in a horror movie or an awesome star-fighting scene, white sparks flying and plummeting toward the camera.

If the audience were aghast, it was not noticeable over the thick chord manoeuvres. Although so life-like were the holograms and so perfect were the impersonations, Masel thought he heard one woman cry out, "Jimi Hendrix is dead. It's the work of the devil."

Then, as if by heavenly insight, he burst into Voodoo Chil', and jumped in the air.

Katy, high above him, tracked his every move within the fiery beam, like a bright moon.

Lost somewhere in a trance, Masel's guitar playing chugged. It became hypnotic and spellbinding as he ran his fluttering fingers in wizard-like incantation along the length of the fretboard. He astonished himself. His ability and speed seemed to surpass even his own imagination, surprised the surprise.

"Behold!" cried Longman, although not many people heard him. He shot a green laser blast at the microphone stand, which transformed into an upward-wriggling, wiggling serpent. The crowd gasped, a spasm of air going through them. Masel fled three steps backwards.

Catching his heavy breath, his Gizmo D25 still humming and distorting, he slipped quickly into his Grace Slick helmet and solemnly cried out, with feeling, "One pill makes you larger, and one makes you small...feed your head. Feed your head."

And with all his heart, "When logic and proportion have fallen sloppy dead..."

Silently, the band grooved on. Pig Pen - perhaps he was grateful to be dead at that moment - coolly ran ghost-like riffs up and down the electric organ, and Keith Moon went into a spasmodic frenzy, as did Longman. The laser show became frenzied too, and zapped at everything in sight, streaked in wide, crazy sweeps around the auditorium.

Squinting in a blinding haze, the lurid spotlight on his

head, Masel saw only darkness before him. But he concentrated away from it, as though it were a terrible void, a black hole. He also tried not to think about the helmets, which were now sticking to his cheek with hot perspiration. During Imagine, one of his quieter numbers, Masel thought he heard the low rumblings of laughter in the audience.

Suddenly, there was a succession of muffled hoots and cries.

Then he heard, "Fegghgghhhhghgghhhhhhhhh!"

God help me, he thought, it's a heckler. He tried to make out the offender, but saw only red laser light streaming through darkness.

"Fegghgghhhhghgghhhhhhhhh!" From somewhere deep down in the rumbling gut of the audience, there it was again...and again and again...like the persistent roar of a waking sea dragon, "Fegghgghhhhghgghhhhhhhhh!" And then more laughter, too. What?

"You may say I'm a dreamer..." Masel, doing a good impersonation of a professional musician, wound his way to the end of the song, hardly faltering.

Then something hit him on the shoulder and clattered as it banged off the neck of his Gizmo. He stopped playing. A deafening roar of feedback surged and screeched out of the PA system. Masel cringed, was stunned. The audience erupted like surf. Oh God, help me, anybody. Ouch! That hurt! There seemed to be a commotion from somewhere about half-way back in the hall. What the hell was that? He couldn't see anything out there. Christ, there it's there, at his feet, a can of beer, unopened! What kind of Scotsman throws an unopened can of Tartan Special at anybody? he wondered.

The commotion grew louder. A nervous murmur rose up at the front, then more yelling and more screaming towards the back, but Masel couldn't make out any of it. Everyone was pushing and shoving. He gripped his guitar for dear life. I can't believe this is happening to me.

Why me? Panicked, he pulled off his holographic head and someone shrieked. Cameras flashed in his eyes as he peered, wide-eyed, at the mask in his hand.

Gevalt, he said to himself, pleaded with the earth to open and swallow him. It was the wrong face, he was wearing Janis Joplin instead of John Lennon. And worse, he had it on upside down. With a groan, he felt himself sinking into a quagmire; heart first, then head.

What do I do now?

"Not again," he sighed.

Masel felt the old twinge of failure and berated himself once again for his stupidity. He insulted himself for not taking more care. He should have known something like this would happen. He had come into this show with an oy and now he was leaving it with a gevalt.

Momentarily, he considered putting on another mask, but it was too late for that. Only when his hand refused to move did he become aware of how frightened he was. Longman stopped the band and then the lasers. The ghostly group stood silent, motionless behind him, the reference beam still blasting white energy, feckless, as if waiting for Masel's execution. Longman tried to climb down from his platform, but an angry mob snapped at his feet. Katy gave Masel's spotlight a jolt and shot the beam into the audience. In the confusion, however, she overlooked the band and left on the reference beams; the band stood stationary, silently engrossed in the impending chaos. At the back of the hall, on one side of the large room, maybe two dozen youths in blue and white football jerseys threw cans of beer, waved fists and chanted, "If you hate the fucking Celtic clap your hands." Then, "RA-A-N-GERS-RA-A-N-GERS." Who the hell were the Rangers anyway? Texans? Why me? And what in the name of God were they doing at a '60s culture concert? My concert. Gang warfare? On the other side of the room, just below Longman's suspended platform, a similar number of youths, this group in green and white shirts, chanted "CE-E-ELTIC, CE-E-ELTIC. Up the 'RA", throwing fists and beer in the air and occasionally at Longman, but missing. Mashed together, the two opposing chants sounded like, "Fegghgghhhhghgghhhhhhhhh!"

"Fegghgghhhhghgghhhhhhhhh!"

"Can we keep it calm, please," Masel announced passively into the microphone. "Please, come on, let's try and keep
this peaceful."

A fight broke out near the door, and within seconds a full-
scale melee had blown up. A bouncer ran in but was knocked
to the ground, kicked savagely. Trapped, the crowd gasped and
rushed the stage. Longman climbed down from his platform
and escaped through the bar. Plotnikov was lost somewhere in
the middle.

With batons drawn, hats flying, a hoard of police rushed
in and attempted to wedge the gangs apart, threw themselves at
the crowd. Now fists were flying all over the place and more
violence erupted towards the front. Masel was petrified where
he stood, breathing heavily. Now he didn't know which direction to run. I could get killed here. Gevalt, what a terrible
situation, and it's getting worse.

"Hurry up," screamed Katy, backstage, somewhere in the
shadows. Her voice was shrill and panicked. She had climbed
down from the gantry and was about to make her getaway, but
Masel couldn't see her. "Let's go! Hurry! The stage door!
Quickly!" she called to him. Masel, backing up, knocked into
one of the holograms, and sent Pig Pen and his organ rolling
into a black flurry of confusion. Everyone seemed to be
shouting or screaming. Then he got hit on the chest by another
beer can. Some of the crowd, eyes like stone, climbed up on the
stage and blocked his exit. Masel suddenly found himself
surrounded. The crowd closed in front of him. Some of those
in blue and white began to laugh. Masel knew enough to laugh
with them and, momentarily seemed to have their sympathy. A
large, stout man in green slapped Masel on the back. Then
someone threw a punch and the stout man went down. Masel
grew conscious of trembling knees. A woman with snaky, grey
hair grabbed his arm.

"Jim Morrison. Mr Mojo, we will never forget."

Masel twisted his arm free.

He looked again, but it was too late; Katy was gone. He

was now trapped. It's out of control. It wasn't easy for him to remain calm. Men and women fled in every direction. Then someone unbolted the fire door and the crowd, grunting, screaming and thrashing about, spilled out like oil into the street. His precious Gizmo pressed tightly against his chest, Masel elbowed the woman with snaky, grey hair in the rib cage and followed suit.

Four

A bulging moon skated over the first real summer's night sky Masel had come across in this northern city. It was a warmish night, almost Californian in its windlessness, and he removed his jacket. With only the jingle of Katy's spare front door key in his trouser pocket, he wandered the streets in a miserable mood. He sighed at the moon. Where do I go now? Momentarily, he was dizzy with confusion, lost his bearings. Where's home? Time and again, he returned to the dark alley at the back of the EPI Centre - he was running in circles. and he knew it - in the hope of glimpsing Katy or Longman. Maybe they would come back for him, but he knew in his heart of hearts they were gone. After a while, even the police cars left and so did Masel, his heart heavy.

He slung his Gizmo minstrel-fashion over his shoulder, and headed into the west, his palate thickening with thirst. What's happened to everything? He hurried past anonymous red-clay tenements on grey back streets amid stone buildings, over Charing Cross and up Woodlands Road. To Masel, this strange Glasgow world was suddenly a very threatening place, full with extremists, anti-semites, drunks and hoodlums. Despair and terror tracked his every step. I am a failure. I can't do anything right. It is my nature and my fate. Masel cursed himself. To hell with this new life. Nauseated amid urine-smelling hallways, sick, grieving, he thought, I want to go home.

He continued westward, climbing University Avenue, his

eyes fixed on the sad, oppressive Gothic spires (his own pathetic image) and the hoards of students that bumped passed him, many drunk. It was Friday night; for most, it was the end of the work-a-day week. Crossing Byres Road, he felt the rage of helplessness. The pubs were beginning to empty and the street thronged. He cut through them like sharp glass, his eyes down, and made his way along Highburgh Road and then up Bowmont Gardens. Abruptly, he found himself before Katy's tenement.

For two hours, Masel haunted her street. He stood beneath a deeply hued weeping cherry blossom tree that stood in the gardens across from Katy's building and looked up at the flat. The darkness behind the window seeped into his heart. He was waiting. Asleep or no one home? God help me. What was he waiting for? Christmas? He was desperately in love with her and he knew it, but how could she love a man like him? With his past? And how could he face her after tonight? She would despise him. From the beginning, he knew, he had bitten into unearned bread, and the natural consequence of such an action could only be embarrassment and shame; Masel consuming the Bread of Shame, in his mind. His courage was a mess and his love was a slaughter. He had failed again. He berated himself, thinking it out, but his logic was his own worst enemy.

Masel was abruptly startled by a cough and a tap on his shoulder. He turned to find two policeman standing at his elbow, studying his ponytail. One of them informed him that there had been a number of break-ins in the area recently, and that these were private gardens, admissible only to residents of the street.

"But I am a resident." he protested politely.

The two of them looked at Masel suspiciously. "Do you have proof, some identification?" one of them asked.

Masel searched his inside pockets and pulled out his passport.

"American?" asked the other.

"Yes."

They returned the passport and caught site of the guitar

leaning against the cherry tree.

"About to serenade someone, are you?"

"No, no, nothing like that."

By force of habit, Masel crossed his heart. He felt stupid. The policemen, shaking their head in unison, gave him an intense stare.

"Can you tell me why you're standing under this tree?"

Masel felt himself blush. He looked up at a sleeping blossom.

"Er - I love this tree."

One of the policemen, still shaking his head slightly, said, "We've driven round here four times in the last hour and you've been standing here every time."

"Really? An hour?...I was just getting some air, but I think I'll go up now."

His heart whamming, he ascended the stairway.

He knocked on the door several times before he was willing to believe that no one was home, ready to bolt at any moment. He turned the key and entered silently, like a cat burglar. In a way, he was relieved, but he was also saddened. He packed his leather travel bag, his sleeping bag, slung his guitar back over his shoulder, and for his own good, as well as hers, decided, if he ever had her, to give her up. He was going home as soon as he could think of someone who would wire him the money.

Against his better judgement, ridden through with guilt at the thought of thieving, Masel searched the flat for cash. He found none. Then he wrote her a note saying he would be back in a few days for the rest of his things, and signed off, Yours in deepest regret, love, Elliot. He wondered about the word "love", but left it there. What did he have to lose. Maybe tomorrow would be better. Things could always get worse. Maybe tomorrow I can face her. Emotion blinded him. He couldn't get her out of his mind; nor could he scorch the terrible guilt he felt nor the image of the chaos he had caused. Where could he go without money in his pocket?

Sweet home California was out of the question. He

headed for a little cinema he knew on Ashton Lane, behind Byres Road. The late show would be starting soon. Maybe he could play some tunes and make enough there for a cheap hotel for the night and a small breakfast. After that he would decide what the best course of action was. Get tonight over with first, he advised himself. If he could play to an audience at the Euro Pictish Institute, Goddamn it, he could play to a movie line.

The sky, yellowish-black, seemed to open above him. Masel walked up a cobble-stoned lane and took a right onto another, similar, alley, where the cinema was situated. On a night like this, anything is possible, he said to himself. The warm air gave him the will to survive. The line of late-night movie-goers lengthened. He stood athwart the queue, against an old white-washed stone stable building that was now a restaurant and, admiring the architecture, tuned into it. Even before he began, the crowd were already dipping in their pockets for change. Strumming loudly, his fingers afire, he ran through his Bob Dylan repertoir: Blowin' In The Wind, Mr Tambourine Man, Hard Rain's Gonna Fall and Just Like a Woman. His ears still burned from the holographic helmets, his mind dark with love for Katy, his voice resonating and echoing sharply against the old white-brick alley way.

When the cinema line had disappeared, Masel, coming out of his dreams and memories, moved back against the stone wall, sat on a step, and counted his earnings. He was more than surprised, and snickered at himself inwardly, ironically. Who needs fame anyway? He could make a living at this. It was the little successes in life that counted, the essential ones. Fifteen pounds wasn't enough to get to California, but it was enough for a cheap hotel and a small breakfast.

He stood for a moment, his head bowed, the rush of reality abruptly coming back at him. In the luminous dark, another busker, holding a violin in one hand and a bottle of wine in the other, detached himself from a small group and approached Masel. Other than Masel and the group, the alley was empty.

The violinist was heavily built, with a pale, hard, intense face, unruly greying red hair and thick, bent legs. He walked forward slowly, almost cautiously, save the exaggerated heave of his shoulders, his eyes roving around.

Masel gathered up his money in his hands, deposited it in his pocket and stood up to meet him.

"How much did you make?" the violinist asked, sneering.

"Enough," Masel answered. "What's it to you?"

"What?"

"Why do you ask?"

"Because this is my fucking patch, pal, and you're fucking on it."

"Patch? What do you mean?"

Masel, trembling, staring hard at the violinist, felt his heart putter at a terrific rate.

"You Canadian?"

"American."

"What?"

"American."

The violinist thrust forward at Masel his sickly face and his darkly-rimmed, bloodshot eyes. "Well you're on my fucking patch. This is my spot, right. I play here."

"It's a free country, isn't it." Masel took a small step to the side.

"Look, you're not in fucking Yankyland now."

"What do you want from me?"

"Fuck off back to Yankyland."

Edging back against the wall, he noticed two other men, perhaps buskers too, at his side. As he turned to look at them, the violinist struck Masel a hard blow on the head with the butt of his wine bottle.

"Oy gevalt," Masel cried out in a rage, then in deep panic. "Somebody help me."

He flailed his arms, tried to lash out with his fists, but the violinist backed off and savagely kicked him to the ground. The accomplices put the boot in, kicking him with their dirty boots and punching him with their meaty, fat fists. Masel, holding his blood-streaming head, his thoughts black, passed out.

With their clammy hands, the violinist and his accomplices raked the pockets of his blue flannel suit and took the fifteen pounds. With clamped teeth, grunting, they crushed the Gizmo beneath their heels.

* * *

Masel woke some time later, his hands clasping his bloody, pain-wracked skull. They hadn't taken his sleeping bag. At least that's something, he said to himself, gathering it under his arm.

He picked up, too, the splintered, broken remains of his Gizmo and, with tears in his eyes, wandered off into the Glasgow night, adrift, without a guitar to play.

■ The Wilderness
■ One

MASEL smelled the living earth around him and, doing the best he could with crude implements, whistling, took a leak in the icy water of the muddy River Kelvin. He pushed a perfect hyperbolic arc high into the air and watched it drop. A bushy-tailed squirrel scuttled behind him without bothering, and bounded up the trunk of a leafy silver birch. Being at one with nature, Masel, a reluctant cave man, didn't bother either. Elliot Masel, disgraced performer, unemployed musician, now inner-city survivalist, dropped from the world into a mossy, Paleolithic-like cave dwelling in a thickly-wooded park below Glasgow's Royal Botanical Gardens. *My worst enemies should live like this.* He had hit rock bottom, was imprisoned within and without by poverty, guilt, angst, though he could think of worse places. He had planned to stay here only a day or two to get his bearings, so to speak, but his sense of direction addled, not that he had much of one in the first place. The world beyond the park was humiliating, frightening. *How can I go back now?* In short, Masel lapsed into faint insanity, flipped out, in.

Loneliness lived on his back. Masel the mountain man, the Jewish Pict. His troubled skull throbbed with the sound of his own voice. He spoke to the black walls; they answered. *Oy vey.* For a long time he had distrusted this cave, because of the strange, on-occasion rosy, dim glow within that made him feel slightly uneasy in the evenings. *How can there be light where there is none?* He discovered, too, that sweat sticks and, as a matter of survival, warned himself to be attentive of things that happened in nature. In his frayed flannel suit (now of no distinct colour, buttonless), Masel, amid voluminous rose-lit dust, wrestled a blossoming cloud of midges and cursed his weak soul, this God-forsaken cave. He saw cloud within cloud, red within black, black within red. With bony hands, he fought the approach of panic. Even if he could bring himself to escape, he was bereft of sufficient funds to go anywhere, if there was anywhere to go. So he stayed put, and waited for something to happen.

His ponytail abandoned, he blew his dirty nose on a fern and noticed a tic had attached itself to the side of his penis. He lit a match and burned it, screamed in agony; it did the trick. Then his zipper jammed a quarter of the way up, and tore a hole in the material. A gentle wind blew as the morning rain drizzled on his miserable, bedraggled head, pockmarking the warm, clayish soil, his tattered sleeping bag wrapped around his neck, a stolen duffel coat huddled over his shoulders.

Once in a while he ate; it was good for morale. At night, he dreamed of gefilte fish. During the day, Katy beat his brains. His deepest desire was to be with her, but he punished himself severely whenever he thought of it: idiot, numbskull, fathead, onanist. Yet, in a nervous reverie, he recalled the touch of her creamy flesh, her shoulders, the touch of her fingers on his skin; he imagined her beautiful body with the clothes stripped away; her breasts hanging above him, the collarbone like wings, her perfect, wet mouth, her eyes, like the sea. On several occasions, he considered returning to her, but each time stood helplessly at the wrought-iron threshold of the park, fingering his greying, freying whiskers, as immobile as a rock . If she ever wanted me in the first place, would she still? Did she ever? He found terror and embarrassment affected him worst of all, horrible emotions that flashed back again and again from his childhood.

He continued to wait; nothing happened. He grieved heftily. I have got to get her out of my fucking mind.

Days passed.

Masel dreamed he fell from the dizzy heights of a lofty tree. Why he had been up there in the first place, he had no idea, but he knew he was dropping fast. Death was a rapidly-approaching certainty. The uprush of air assailed his face, a hurricane in his hair, open mouth, nostrils. He was gaining momentum, velocity; Masel, a dead duck in a vacuum. Panic went through him; only one way down. He prayed that he be smitten by a cardiac arrest before squishing against a rock. But the tree was inordinately tall and, to his amazement, his heart pounding wildly, he continued to plummet. Whoosh! Masel flapped his arms uselessly. A darkness rose to meet him, the world dimming into windy timelessness, his feet, legs, elbows flying in every direction, apart. Then, by a miracle of determination and self-transcendency, he grabbed hold of a protruding, gnarled branch.

"Help!" he cried, dangling precariously on one arm.

The American nervously glimpsed the rocky earth a long way below him. Above, sunlight poked through an entangled thicket of wooden limbs.

Abruptly, a great yet gentle voice from somewhere high up intoned, "My son, do you have absolute faith in Me?"

Masel replied, "Yes, yes, help me. Please."

"Do you trust Me without reservation?"

"Of course I do, Lord. Quick."

"Then let go of the branch."

"Let go of the branch?"

"I said, 'Let go of the branch'."

"Excuse me," Masel asked, "is there someone else up there?"

The branch snapped and Masel awoke with an ache in his solar plexus, winded, miserable. It was a warming, early-summer morning.

* * *

Later, out of control amid reddish dust, Masel feverishly removed his shoes and socks and flung them angrily at the wall of the cave. He couldn't seem to shake off the depressing effects of the dream. With a cry, he leaped at the rocky portal, and ran bare-footed and howling through the warm trees until he came to the steep, stony embankment of a cliff, his heart thudding. His nose filled with pine, out of breath, he wondered, If I am a man like me, what should I do? Masel sneezed and searched his mind in desperation. Have I come here to jump? How far down is death? Too far; that crazy, I'm not. Out of mercy to himself, he decided deportation was as good a way out as any; his only ticket, he figured, if you discounted further charity from his ex-wife, the shame of which was too much for him even to think about. There was only one thing left for him to do: he had to get himself arrested.

Self-disgust enraged him to fury, replaced the vast and meaningless grief that had plagued him for weeks now. He clawed his face and climbed warily in haste to a thin, brown crevice above him, stripping away his ragged clothes with stride and stretch until he reached the place where he wanted to be, a rock jutting into the air. His behaviour both astonished and elated him. Then, naked as the day he was born, bar the stolen duffel coat which he removed then replaced, sweat gleaming in beads on his dirty forehead, he booted a rusty tin can a hundred feet down on to a children's play area. Masel, you old devil, you. He heard it clunk and rattle and scrape to a halt.

He could hold back no longer. At the top of his lungs, Masel, screamed, "Fegghhgghghgghhh!"

A young mother, pushing a little girl on a red plastic swing, looked up, stunned.

Frozen, he peered into her eyes; he gazed as though they had once been lovers but the affair had ended. Masel, too long alone, thought for a moment it was Katy. How can you end something that never really started? he wondered. He saw himself strapping on a parachute, white, fluttering in the warm breeze like a bird, about to leap a thousand feet from the door of a plane. Or a tree? God help us all. He laughed wickedly and, with red, jerking muscles, pulled open the duffel coat.

He stood flexed, statuesque but for his eyes, wondering what to do next now that he had done this. His breathing was heavy. The woman continued to stare at him in alarm, her mouth seemingly unhinged, her eyes wide, head tilted.

Masel yelled, "If God made all men equal, where's mine?" His face beamed beneath dirt. "I'm a man, too, huh?" he went on with increasing volume, the coat flapping frantically, as if he were glued to it, and was trying desperately to free himself. "Where's mine? Where's my equality? Every man has a right to a little equality."

Masel the public nuisance. Gevalt, Masel the lunatic flasher, the weeny wagger.

The mother picked up the child and, covering its eyes, fled hurriedly, her head turning every so often to glimpse the nude survivalist. Masel picked up his clothing and, descending abruptly from the crevice lip on the skin of his ass, escaped to his cave.

Alone, he wept bitterly, the duffel coat over his dirty face, his sadness enlarging fatigue. What will become of me? Masel had no answers, only black thoughts. He sank like a rock into a profound gloom, longed for a guitar, something musical to soothe his soul. With a blunt bone, he carved an awkward, squeaking flute from a stubby pine branch. Depressed by the inartful conclusion, he snapped it in two and pitched it at the wall, waited for the police to come, his mouth dry. His eyes stung sharply, as he chain smoked cast-away butts from a pocketful he had. The cave stank of emptiness. I'll never get out of here; why do I wrestle with the fact? A clod of mud fell on his head. To the dank, black walls, he complained, "See Glasgow, see culture."

* * *

Masel was lying on his back, sunlight streaking his face. The heat was penetrating him, when a car screeched to a halt somewhere near by, below him, a rosy dust cloud floating ethereally above him, like a miniature galaxy in a featureless, still cosmos. Doors banged fiercely, jarring him. This is it? At first, he couldn't distinguish the sounds around him from the incessant mumble in his head, the distant suggestion of voices, felt severe nausea. Every despicable detail of this hole in the wall seemed to him unnaturally sharp, sickening, black rose: black rock glistening like fading rubies, black earth, black sky within, his own few revolting possessions. He could feel the heat on his eyebrows and lashes as the murmuring continued.

A woman shrilly shrieked, "It was here. It was up there."

A chill startled him, went through him. Masel, ceasing to breath for several seconds, knew his moment had come. The police would take him away, and that would be that. He crawled dazed to the edge of the cave.

On his belly, he wriggled to a vantage point, and saw two policemen scrambling up the adjacent hill, where he had previously committed the dirty deed. The cops had him. Their tight jaws and determined, square mouths told him so. The young mother stood against the wheeling, blue-lighted squad car, the child in her folded arms, its face buried in her shoulder. Masel felt the throb of remorse in his stomach. On reflection, in a predictable moment of self-effacement, he flinched at the path he had put himself on, his madness.

The American feared deportation would go badly for him. What if they put me in jail first? His nerve dwindled into panic. He rose furtively, like a frightened combat soldier, gulped and swiftly shinned up the nearest tree. He fell off, shinned up again, like a bear cub in a fire, and hid, huffing and puffing, behind three leafy oak branches. Masel on top of old smoky, escaping from escape, his bony limbs knocking.

He squeaked at the approach of the enemy, bit his tongue, his breath. Whatever courage he had previously managed to muster was now gone, had sunk downward. The fierceness of his grip against the thick branch stung his palms. It was hard to hold on with bleeding fingers, skinned buttocks, an oak leaf in your eye.

The two policemen were below him now, their white faces pouring sweat. Masel, above a gentle, continuous, trembling groan, could hear what they were saying.

"Have a quick smoke, while I take a piss."

The more gangly, youngish of the two, drew the last of his smokes from a packet and threw the empty box on the ground. He lit up with a sigh. The other ducked behind Masel's tree and urinated against it. Masel looked away in embarrassment and terror. Gevalt, now who's flashing what at who down there?

The peeing cop whistled a shrilled, cacophonous tune.

"That's better," he breathed steamily.

"Hurry up," said the other. "That'll teach you not to drink so much tea at the station."

The cop, zipping his fly, swiftly came out from behind the

tree. A leaf was tickling Masel's nose. He wanted to sneeze, but bit into his lip to forestall disaster. His mind otherwise occupied, the survivalist drew blood, shivered. Don't look up, he begged them silently, shaking. He attempted to calm himself, but anxiety lashed out and pummelled him. He had no idea where it was coming from. He held on in silence, true fear cudgelling his brains bloody.

"What's your hurry?"

"You have one more look around the other side, just to keep that wee woman happy, and I'll look in that cave down there. Then we'll call it a day. This is too much like hard work."

"There's nobody up here. And if there was, they'd be long gone by now. This is a waste of time. To tell you the truth, I could do with another cup of tea."

The other policeman hesitated for a moment, then sighed. "You're right, let's get out of here. I'm sick of crawling around up here. Will you look at the state of my uniform. It's filthy, and it's not even lunchtime yet."

They nodded at each other, the older one in an exaggerated fashion. The younger one, his face acned, turned and, for a moment, stopped still. He seemed to be staring at Masel's tree. Then he looked at the dirt on the ground, like an animal tracker.

"Look," he said. "Foot prints. Bare feet."

The other one laughed. "Who do you think you are? Davy Cockeyed? John Wayne? Don't be daft." He chortled. "Come on, get a move on. The wee woman's waiting down there."

Masel, shuddering, thanked God. Blessed isolation, humiliation-free. He trembled violently. When the cops, their heads shaking at one another, disappeared around the other side of the hill, Masel swooped down from the tree, gathered his belongings from the cave and, with fear somewhere up in his throat, took off in haste. God help me. I'm doomed. He felt as though he were living in a house with a hundred rooms - in each room there was a bed, and that he was tossing from bed to bed for the rest of his life, never getting one good night's sleep.

He took with him a few old newspapers he used for

blankets, a creased snapshot of his ex-wife, a mouthful of cold
pizza, a curled half-eaten sandwich, and two dusty slabs of
rosewood, one with a hole in it, that used to be a Gizmo D25.
What he didn't wear he carried.

Masel on the run, a fugitive flasher.

Briskly, over stony nooks, through thorns, he skipped
across the Kelvin, considered jumping, but the river wasn't
deep enough for his purpose. A lone dove cooed overhead, and
he climbed up the lip of a terraced hill to a more secluded cave
he had found days ago, behind three tall spruce. He stuck the
snapshot of Zelda to the dirty wall with mud and sticky sweat.
His face drained of blood, he put his head on a smooth boulder
and, staring into the eyes of his ex-wife, wept in desolation
before taking a nap. I can't even get myself arrested. He
insulted himself. He had moved caves, but remained in the
same hole. If you're dead, how do you go on living? In his sleep,
curled and indistinguishable from a boulder, he wept again.

* * *

Amid an air of sex and death, Masel caught sight of Zelda
in the dim, rosy darkness of the new cave. A black magistrate
outfit open around her shoulders, a black cloak swooping in the
hollow void behind her, her voice was deeper than he recalled.

"Elliot," she said, with an air of authority, her eyes dark
like plumpits, her cleavage mountainous and freckled, "How
much longer can a person be expected to wait, eh?"

Masel sat against a porous boulder, fearful, trembling.
"How much longer I don't know. Soon. That's why I'm here.
I was hoping you'd reserve judgment until I had something to
show you. Then, maybe you'd change your mind."

Her lips and nose were hawk-like, her Tunisian eyebrows
flaming like a wandering Jew in the Saharan wind. "Don't
make me laugh, Elliot. What have you ever achieved, here or
anywhere else?"

"Well, nothing, but I'm honestly trying this time. It's just
that I've got nowhere else to go right now."

"Go where you like, it's a free country."

"I can't leave until I've accomplished something. It's

important to me to be better than I am, that all those years of talk and dreams weren't just talk and dreams, talk and dreams. I've learned that freedom isn't a natural phenomena. You have to create it for yourself, maybe even invent it."

"So why are you in such a state? Why don't you do it? What's all this cave business?"

"That's the way I am nowadays. It's for you. I'm trying to transcend myself. I admit that at the moment I'm not much to look at, but, like I said, I was hoping you would wait so I'd have something good to show you. It'll just be a little longer, I promise you."

"Transcend shmanscend. Why don't you come back now, Elliot? Just you and me, just as you are. Remember how I used to make you chicken soup after we made love?"

"I can't. I need to accomplish something first."

"Don't be so proud. It's a fault in your character. To be proud is to be in prison, less than a man, a statistic. Aren't you at least a man?"

"Not without achievement."

"You know, everybody says your dead. If you weren't you would telephone once in a while. You're also charged with not taking a shower for at least a year."

"I thought it was three weeks. I've been counting."

Despite his trembling, his answer evoked in her a hearty outburst of laughter. His mind whirled. He imagined he heard guffaws from a distant, invisible gallery.

"Be a mench, won't you?" she advised, suddenly indignant with annoyance.

"I'm trying."

"Don't think that you can come back to me after this. If you can't live with yourself, how do you ever expect to live with me? Or anyone else for that matter?"

Masel, irritated, blurted out, "But Zelda, I'm doing this for you and you know why."

"I'm no longer obliged to listen to what you say," she interrupted. "Your defence is pointless, because I will depart this life regardless of whatever you do or don't."

Masel sat with his mouth agape, his heart thudding wildly in something beyond trepidation. "Departing where? Zelda, you can't leave me twice. That's too much for anyone to bear."

She approached him with an angelic smile, rose waves of light emanating from beneath her swooping, voluminous, black cloak, her hands outstretched in swirling light. Very gently, she placed a white, rubber diaphragm on his crown.

"There, that's better, now at least you have a yarmulka. Now you can say Kaddish."

"But who's dead?"

Two men, it was Plotnikov and Longman, dressed in animal skins and bowler hats appeared at the mouth of the cave. With clubs in their hands, their eyes and feet like chiseled stone, they advanced and beat Masel hard on the head until he woke cringing in sorrow and fear.

■ Two

Long past midnight, when the park gates were locked and the survivalist couldn't escape, even if he could muster the will to do so, a waxish moon rose clear and pale in a wide, star-specked sky. He wandered around the Botanic Gardens like a phantom nomad.

In the dark wood, an owl hooted in a leafless hooped elm.

He thought of Katy as he fiercely embraced the cold, wrought-iron bars that looked out on an unfamiliar road, at civilization, and, with a shock, remembered his dream of Zelda; Zelda and Katy, Katy and Zelda. He loved them both and tried, not without bittersweet nostalgia, to butt them from his mind. But predictably they returned, assailed his concentration, languished him.

Masel, famished as he crept through a light tuft of sleeping buttercups on a food-scavanging excursion, managed to side-step that crisis with other, more immediate ones: I've got to eat; I'm going crazy; I've got to get out of here; fuck deportation; I've got to face me before I can rise above me; I've got to beat this rap of entrapment in the past, guilt, obsession. He side-stepped that, too, and turned to reverie. He imagined himself an accomplished artist sitting before a grand piano composing peaceful melodies in a spacious livingroom on a sweeping lake-front. Children played around him. Beautiful Zelda appeared through a door, her thick, black hair drawn behind her ears, a loving bowl of chicken soup in her hands. Then Katy appeared at the window, her smile gently warm, enticing, waving, therefore making the moment self-defeating, wounding. He hated these little aspirations, hopes, pointless dreams, like birds bred in cages. Love and hunger cannot live together, that much he knew for certain. When hunger came through the door, love fled through the window. With a start, a warm, serene breeze touched Masel's cheeks. He listened, heard nothing, only silence, wind in his ears, night, the rush of the cosmos. How come I'm still sweating? he wondered.

"So, that's why I'm here," he later sarcastically informed the wall of his new cave. "To find a way from the old me and return with me anew, enlarged. A little recognition wouldn't go wrong either, just so I have something to show people."

"What's to recognize?" the wall answered in reply. Masel showed no surprise. "You have to do something worth recognizing before I can recognize."

For reasons he couldn't fully fathom, this cave was rosy, too. Masel asked, "For instance, like what?"

"That's your problem."

"But I've already tried to leave the park and failed. So where do I go from here?"

"That's because you weren't ready to leave. Your body says one thing, while your soul says another. Those who find a difference have neither."

"Really? Maybe you have a point there. I suppose it's not every day you get advice from the wall of a cave."

"Yes, really. The freedom you seek is entirely relative and, I'm afraid, entirely individual."

"How do I know what's individually right for me?"

"That's the catch. When you must you will."

Masel cagily asked with a hiss, "What's the secret of

success?"

"You have to resist your ignorance and your past. But be warned, failure can lead to a life-time of misery."

Masel scratched at success, then his ear. He punched himself in the eye, and the wall fell silent.

* * *

It had been years since he had imagined things watching him in the dark. The survivalist hungrily made his way to a row of wire garbage cans near a row of green-painted benches, the night around him creaking, groaning without apparent cause. The immediacy of his whining belly helped him concentrate his slowly unhinging mind. To the rich God gives food, to the poor he gives appetite.

Then abruptly - shocking in the night's stillness - he heard fleeing footsteps in the rustling bushes. Or did he? Then a light flashed up behind him. Masel turned quickly. A small, stubby tree was on fire. The flames leaped upwards in a tremendous glow, wavering orange light amid the crackling, dry, summer branches and leaves. The fire, shimmering with heat, shaggy as a wolf, savagely rose in two, sometimes three, forks, like the golden horns of some magical, mythical ram, like phantom fingers. Masel breathed in the smoky air and choked. Street kids, he thought to himself, watching in alarm.

Then his attention shifted in fear, Masel froze stiff in dread-filled uncertainty. In that moment, his eyes transfixed on a grotesque face lit up weirdly in yellow-flamed reflection against the black window of the Victoriana greenhouse; a bedraggled, long-bearded figure before him, or rather behind him, in reality. He stared in astonishment, mute. Is that me? Either I'm crazy or this is another dream. I've had Zelda, Plotnikov, Longman, Katy and a talking wall, why not Jesus Christ?

A voice beckoned, moaning, from within the burning tree. "Masel, Masel."

Masel, trembling, shook his head with a jerk, ignored the call, reluctant to acknowledge what he was sure he didn't really hear. Oh no, not again.

The call was repeated, as if carried on wind, howling, entered his brain through a tunnel in his ears.

"Masel, Masel," the voice wailed.

Masel gulped thickly, chilled. Flicking away a perfectly smokeable butt, he turned quickly, every nerve suddenly alert. God help me. In the wilderness of the park, he examined his mind in fear and astonishment, concluded he had gone insane. Masel figured it was a game as long as he played it.

"I'm here," he offered meekly. "Who are you?"

The flames on the burning tree subsided as its branches began to glow fiercely, like violet neon in the warm breeze. From behind the luminescent entanglement, out stepped not Jesus Christ, but a near-skeleton of a figure, older but about the same height as Masel, same hair, longer, whiter beard, but the same dirty face, loitering near an expanse of tulips, red sparks like a swarm of fireflies circling his head in the frenzied rush of hot air. What the hell's going on? Masel eyed him warily, his heart whamming like a rubber ball in his chest.

The stranger grimly took a step forward, stopped short of the shadows. A burnt, orange glow hung on his face.

"I am Yahweh," the stranger called powerfully in scorn, his eyes heavily bloodshot and rheumy, either from emotion or disease. Delirium tremens perhaps?

"What do you want from me?"

"Your cries have stirred me to compassion," he answered. His voice, although at times strained, otherwise boomed. "I have come to deliver you from bondage."

"Excuse me," said Masel, conscious of quaking calves. "I didn't catch the name."

Yahweh stood oddly motionless, his expression irritated, his head thrown forward, only his mouth and eyes moving in the dim, waxy, light.

He spoke dully accented, but loudly; he had a tendency to shout. "Shalom. I am that I am that I am. I'm also out of work."

Masel mumbled nervously. "Wh-who?"

"I appeared before your forefather at the well at Midian and now I'm here before you."

Masel thought he would be struck dead, but nothing moved - not him, not Yahweh, not the burning, glowing tree. His face whiter than pale, whiter than white, Masel tentatively asked, "How do you know my name?"

"How do you think? I read newspapers. I hear things."

"I don't follow," Masel said, his throat gulping noisily, his palms gushing.

"I happen to know that in your absence, you achieved fame, well, to a degree. You're also a missing person. Do you follow now? Many think you're dead. But I knew you the moment I saw you. I've been watching you. And by the way, that was quite a stunt on top of the hill." Yahweh chuckled, his chest vibrating violently, until he began to cough. At last his body rested. He went on, "Pity it didn't come off. Better luck next time."

"How famous?" He was interested to know. Masel couldn't help blushing amid his fear.

"Well, famous is maybe an exaggeration."

Masel tried punching his eye; it didn't work. Yahweh stood passively in silence before him.

Masel backed off through the cowslips, panicked. By now frankly famished, he studied Yahweh's long spindly legs. his trousers grey and shiny and baggy at the knee and rear end. His coat was ripped and shapeless, his sleeves pulled up to grey, stringy biceps, his battered shoes, his rough leaden face, the bottle in his pocket. Sadly, though somewhat relieved, Masel saw that Yahweh was in fact a man. Not that he had doubted it for a moment.

The survivalist, his heart at last calming, wondered how this man had gotten into such a terrible state, but left the question unasked. If I'm not careful, I could be saddled with this guy all night. So what if he saw my picture on an old newspaper? He was probably using it for a blanket at the time, not that he could think of a better use for it. The less said about my old life the better, he figured. His relief incited testiness.

"Keep your distance," he warned, "These are my garbage cans, see?"

"I have no interest in your garbage cans," said Yahweh. "When the wind blows the garbage flies. What else can I tell you?" He paused a moment, rubbing his hands together, as though he were cold. "More importantly," he went on, "the Devil will smite you down if you're not careful. And then He'll piss on you from a great height. You'll know all about it then."

"Well, then," said Masel after a moment, coughing. "It's been nice knowing you. Shalom and be seeing you."

With a nervous grin, Masel fled hastily in the direction of the now-calm Kelvin, toward the hushed sound of running water on brown pebbles.

Yahweh called loudly after him, "There are three things in this life you can't hide: poverty, love and coughing. Unfortunately, you qualify in all three departments."

Masel raced across a bridge on to a trail that rose steeply between two lichenous rocks, like a twisting waterfall, only slackening his pace when he was sure he heard silence behind him. But Yahweh followed cautiously, furtively stalking the survivalist into a dark, moonless cavern of interlocking trees. A dog howled monotonously in the distance. It seemed lost and suffering. Masel shuddered.

"What now already?"

"I'll say this to you, the man who thinks he can live without others is mistaken. The man who thinks others can't live without him is even more mistaken."

Masel chose to ignore the remark; he hastened up the trail. "Go away."

But Yahweh pursued him, puffing heftily. In full stride, his arms shaking around him, the tramp coughed brutally trying to keep abreast. "The greatest pains, Mr Masel, are those you can't tell others."

Everyone wants to give Masel advice. "That's about as much help as throwing a bean at a wall," he said, turning with a sigh. He faced Yahweh squarely.

"Your not going to hit me, are you?" Yahweh was suddenly fearful.

Masel felt lousy, rotten to the core, a heel. "Of course I'm not going to hit you. What's the matter with you?"

"Promise?"

"I promise already." However, he proceeded unperturbed, his head tilted upward. "Look, I'll make this simple. If it's no skin off you, I don't feel like any company right now. So why don't you just leave me in peace?"

Yahweh, his eyes cast at his shabby shoes, reluctantly slunk back down the trail. Masel guiltily walked up the hill to his cave. The moon shone like a yellow hole in a black sheet.

The warm wind blew and circulated the stony chamber. Nothing new in the food department. Ravished, Masel kicked a boulder and bruised his toe. When the stomach is empty, so is the brain. Outside, the trees rustled and clicked, and absently, he chewed a final mouthful of hard, stale pizza. He washed it down with water from a corroded Coke can, and let out a deep belch. What will become of me? he questioned himself miserably, stretching out on his battered sleeping bag. Leaning his head against a rock, Masel closed his eyes and lay his hands over his shrunken paunch, trying to unwind himself and relax. At least I got rid of the shnorrer.

■ Three

Yahweh stepped out from behind a leafy tree at the mouth of the cave. He fixed Masel with a powerful stare. "Are you dead?"

Masel, vexed, rose in astonishment. Is there no escape from this man? "What this time? What do you want from me?" he asked, flushed at the man's nerve.

"I was thinking we'd share a dram? Do you take a bevvy?"

At last he comes to the point. Although annoyed, Masel, resuming his seat on his bag, controlled himself. "If that means a drink, forget it, I don't have any. If it's money, surely you can see I'm not exactly a rich man. Don't let this duffel coat fool you. I stole it. If it's food you want..."

"Whether you know it or not, you need me," Yahweh interrupted bluntly, his eyes hungry, kindled. "You're lonely.

Look at you, you're a wreck. You can't go any further down. But take me, for example; I just wander around like a bedouin. Believe me, there's a lot further down I can go. For instance, I could be deprived of the right to wander."

"Give me a break. I thought a man like you would at least have a little sympathy for a man like me."

"Just as I delivered the children of Israel from their bondage in the land of Egypt, so I will deliver you from your bondage in this park, if it's the last thing I do."

"Don't start that again."

"I shall produce proof," Yahweh insisted. Standing awkwardly, he thoroughly scratched his balls.

"That's it?"

"The proof is before you. You've seen how I bore you on eagles' wings and brought you from bondage and misery in a foreign land. The problem is, you changed your land but not your state of mind. You're still in bondage and misery."

"Excuse me," Masel said, impassioned. "For your information, it was a plane that I arrived on."

"Don't get so excited. It's not good for you. Planes, eagles; same difference."

"Who's excited?"

Yahweh's eyes shifted across the cave. "Now, then, you shall see further proof." He put his hand deep into his breast and pulled forth a bottle of deeply-hued purplish wine.

"So now you're a magician," said Masel, a smile on his face with good humour.

"Look before you scoff," said Yahweh, mirthlessly. He handed Masel the bottle. "After you."

Masel studied the label, slowly reddening with amazement. "Where in God's name did you get a bottle of Jewish passover wine?"

"I thought you'd be interested in that. Don't ask. Just drink. It's better to be dead drunk than dead hungry."

Masel jumped to his feet. "What did you do, rob a synagogue?"

Yahweh took a step backwards. "Don't get the wrong idea

about this," he said, jabbing his finger at the bottle in Masel's hand. "That bottle's mine. It's my lucky bottle. I've had it for years. It's rum and wine that's in it now. Taste it and see."

Masel looked at him in disbelief, his mouth, he knew, was twisted and open. He removed the screw cap, sniffed the bottle and, contemplatively rubbing the shag on his chin, not without guilt, apologized.

Yahweh let out a fruity cough, clearly knew an opportunity when he saw one. "Would you mind if I sit for a minute? My bones are tired."

After reflecting a moment, Masel, grieving at the grey in Yahweh's long, scraggly beard, assented. "So sit already."

Masel stuck out his hand, but Yahweh was busy with something in his pocket; Masel's hand hung heavily in mid-air. A little embarrassed, he withdrew it.

"Why don't you sit already?" said Masel, irritated.

Yahweh perched himself, finely balanced on the edge of a boulder. Masel, his caution blasted to the moon, gulped heartily at the bottle.

"L'chayim." said Yahweh, with a chesty guffaw. "Always be thankful to beggars, because they give you the chance to do good."

Masel tipsily thanked him. He asked, sarcastically, "Where did you learn Hebrew, eh?"

"I used to work in the Middle East, then for a time in the United States. I told you, I lost my job. It's a long story. I won't go into it. Lack of interest all round, you might say."

Masel continued to slug greedily at the bottle. "Where do you live now?"

Yahweh drank also, and passed the bottle back. "Here and there. Sometimes in trees. I like trees, always have. They're very safe and very peaceful."

"Why don't you live in civilization?"

"Because people would knock out all my windows. What about you?"

He gave no answer.

The moon fell, and the breeze in the cave grew cooler.

Yahweh, with a bronchial wheeze, blew breath into his fist. He held forth bluish arms, goosefleshed, as if in evidence.

"At least roll down your sleeves."

"It doesn't help."

Masel hiccoughed.

Although he was flushed from the rum and wine, he rose energetically with a stumble to gather stray limbs of birch into a pile in the centre of the cave. With his last match, he ignited the wood. Then, feeling an uncontrollable urge to sacrifice something he threw on the remains of his Gizmo D25. With wet eyes, he watched the dusty rosewood blacken and burst forth into fire. He fed the flame with stubby, leafless beechwood.

Yahweh, spitting on his meaty palms, rubbed them together and placed them before the fire. Masel, the heat on his face, had the feeling of being as far down as he could go. He threw over one of his butts and took another swig.

"Pass over the wine," said Yahweh.

But Masel continued to drink, intoxicated, was trying to quench an unquenchable thirst, his eyeballs reddening, his head fogging rapidly, drunkenly.

He began to hallucinate. As the flames rose, as if spewing from the centre of the earth, Yahweh, his face aglow, rose with them. His body levitated, floated, became engulfed within billowing wings of fire.

"Oh, my God."

"Now you begin to see, Mr Masel shmasel," said Yahweh.

In drunken fear, Masel said, "All You do, Lord, is certainly best, probably. But if You help total strangers, why not me? If You don't, I'll have to ask Zelda again."

Masel pointed vaguely in the direction of the cracked snapshot on the dirty wall.

Yahweh answered, "Because all you do, day after day, is nag me and nag me"

"I know that You will provide, but why can't You provide until You provide?"

"Don't ask me to change the laws of nature just for your benefit. Who do you think you are? Me?"

"Then advise me. What should I do?"

"Well, if you can't escape from your past, I'll need to think of something else. Don't be so proud. Pride isn't courage. You're also a bit shy, which doesn't help."

Horribly, Yahweh pulled off a fiery nose from his face and flung it at Masel. He screamed in terror. Dizzily, his mind shot through a swirling kaleidoscope tunnel to the wet, green lawn of a cemetery, nameless white headstones flatly stretching back and forth in the rain. There were six people at an open grave. He wasn't one of them.

Beneath a dripping tree, Katy, her face veiled behind a thin, black net, asked, "What was the cause of death?"

"Life," Zelda replied, tearful.

"What life?" Katy asked.

Yahweh, his nose abruptly and grotesquely bloody, descended with the slowly-shrinking flame. Yawning disgracefully, he fell asleep.

Masel spun dizzily back to the cave. In twenty seconds, maybe thirty, he too was asleep, his head propped up by a bumpy rock.

Yahweh woke an hour later. Staggering sideways, he heaved Masel into his sleeping bag, zipped him up to the neck, and pulled the draw-string tightly into a bow.

"Bless you," he said, and departed, after first picking up his bottle and swiping from the wall Masel's snapshot of Zelda.

Four

Spring got down on its hunkers and summer climbed on. All nature joined against Masel, but his spirit rebelled. Enough was enough. Whatever he had waited for, or sought, or hungered after in this deathly solitude, he could wait no longer. A body, he discovered, and a soul could take only so much punishment. Masel, his heart racing, his face now crimson and blotchy, found he was trapped inside a sweating polyester sleeping bag, and couldn't move. Gevalt. He was frying alive. Sweat drenched the back of his neck and flowed profusely from his armpits. His limbs and hands were pinned, wrapped.

"Yahweh," he called, repeatedly, "help me."

Yahweh was gone. No one heard him.

He rolled over, half-somersaulting, in a bid to free himself, but failed; he caused a friction-burn on his cheek. His head ached, and he wanted to throw up. Masel, flushed with a hangover as it was, rested a moment, his breathing thick and hard. From where he lay, he had a view of the morning: high pearl clouds against a wide fissure of blue sky, trees smothered in blossoms. A soggy clod of hair deposited a fat driblet of sweat on his forehead, and then dripped to his eye. He tried again to move, but found he could only roll on his shoulders. His mouth burned dry, his tongue fastened to his palate.

An unusually hot morning sun rose sharply and glared down, edging creeping light into the dimness of the cave. Inside the bag, the heat was unbearable. For some reason, he remembered his father's drunken death under an early-morning milk truck. He remembered how the sun had risen sharply then, too. In a rage, he tried to dislodge his hands to loosen the zip and draw-string, but he was locked into position, his body clinging like fly-paper. When he noticed that Zelda was gone, he wept, rolled in the dirt, struggled, wriggled, wiggled, shook, cried out in a fevered flurry. Gevalt! Which way out? His arms pressed tightly against his sides, he tried biting away the material around the zip lock, but that was useless; wild-animal proof, thermo-reflective. Masel was a prisoner in a fiery sleeping bag that was also a straight-jacket, incommunicado. Am I dreaming? He tried standing, thinking it might be easier to wiggle out of the bag, but fell on his ass twice. The pressure of the stretched bag on his thighs, his own body weight pulling the material tighter, was too great and he lost his balance.

Exhausted, Masel bent his neck, wiped his forehead on the bag and sat watching a spider on the damp, rock ceiling. He gazed in fascination. The spider failed twice in its effort to make a web, but succeeded on the third attempt. Likewise, Masel, drawing inspiration from the bug, momentarily afraid of falling a third time, seriously attempted to get on his feet.

He made it, but lost his balance and fell again. He was like a turtle rolling on its shell, groping for anything. On the fourth attempt, however, pushing his nose on to a tiny jagged cleft in the rock face, he pulled himself up in a rage, the tip of his nose bleeding profusely. Leaning heavily against the black wall, his bag embalming him in grease, Masel wept again and, for a moment, didn't know where he was.

I could die in this God-forsaken place. Adding insult to injury, his bladder filled and cut into him. Maybe, if I can make it to the greenhouses, someone will help me. With great effort, Masel found he could hop, two-footed, as it were. As long as he remained erect, he would be all right. He practiced springing from one end of the cave to the other. It only hurt when he landed badly, which was often.

In a moment of daring and desperation, he leaped savagely from the cave, his expression mad with concentration. A beam of sunlight bolted into his eyes and made dappled, hypnotic spots before him. He had visions of plunging into the muddy river, drowning, as he bounced over the thudding wooden bridge. Unable to hold back any longer, after all the bouncing, Masel emptied his bladder. Now, there was a puddle at his feet. Hopping was easier than shuffling, he discovered, as long as he was careful. Sometimes, he felt as though he were landing on a wet sponge, although he twice descended on hidden, sharp rocks beneath the tangled grass, and bruised the balls of his feet. Watch out for those damn nettles; he had already been stung on the ear after a minor fall.

He laboured, like a vaulting cocoon, up the narrow, rocky steps to the greenhouse, bouncing step by crooked step, his eyes tearing, his knees jarring, his calves aching with strain. He puffed and panted, his lungs stinging as he exhaustedly breathed. His scraped nose hurt like hell, seemed filled to the brim with blood, pulsated. Where the sleeping bag rubbed at his sides, a purple, stinging rash came up. At last at the top, breathless, he was tempted to collapse, but propped himself carefully against an oak tree in case he couldn't get up again.

Then, with a shock, through savage sweating, bleary eyes, he watched a crowd of people accelerating across the lawn towards him. What the hell was going on?

"Masel, Masel."

Their calls stirred the drowsy air like buzzing mosquitos, as they neared. Long, black lenses aimed at him. Gevalt. Which way out? Masel's heart raced. He groaned desperately. Cameras were clicking at him. A fluster of note books shook at him. Then more cameras clicked. A television news apparatus zoomed strategically in from an adjacent mound of bright, yellow buttercups. At the head of the multitude, just slightly in front of them, ran Yahweh, his long grey beard swaying in the wind, a leafy crown on his head, his arms thrown forward.

"Oh my God. Yahweh. Snitch."

"It's for your own good," Yahweh called, rocking back and forth as he ran; no easy trick, the survivalist thought. "You have pride, but your courage is lacking."

Masel, in severe alarm, hastily fled back down the stony steps. Bouncing as he had never bounced before, he leaped three or four levels in single bounds, with long, pained stretches. At the bottom, he ducked left on to a secret short-cut through thorns, past the children's play area, to the other side of the park. A group of students casually crossed the long expanse of lawn, and eyed a suffering Masel, puffing, sweating, first warily, then with amusement.

"Help me," Masel cried, his eyes watering, his voice strained. "I'm trapped. Help me."

He bounded toward them eagerly, his mouth wide and hot, breathing hard. Expressions of disbelief on their faces, the students retreated, laughing, exited the park. One of the boys yelled back, "Where's your hang-glider, pal?"

Dispossessed of all dignity, Masel hopped after them through the big, black gates that had imprisoned him, but the students' pace quickened and they vanished into the street.

Masel cursed them all. What he would give for a dirty, old, half-smoked butt now. Flustered, exhausted, sweat swimming with God knows what else inside his bag, not looking where he was hopping, he just missed knocking into a blue-haired woman walking a poodle.

Breathlessly, he pleaded, "Excuse me, ma'm, could you unzip me. It's an emergency."

The woman picked up the poodle and, cradling it, stood for a moment gazing at him in distaste, her bad-tempered mouth quivering, her eyes horrified.

"Please," Masel begged, squinting, over-excited, trying to focus on her. "It really is an emergency." His smell was putrid, he knew, like a sick animal. Sweat filled his eyes. His beard dripped. "I'm going to do something terrible if you don't unzip me. Have mercy, lady, it won't kill you."

Masel hopped at her, but she clouted him on the temple with her handbag, and he bounced back. The woman departed hurriedly, gasping, the poodle yelping in her arms.

"Up yours," Masel yelled, "and your poodle."

His scraped nose throbbed, and he began to have heart palpitations. There was a pain in his stomach, but he couldn't tell if it was hunger or something else. Gevalt. God help me. His whole body shook in terror. His nervous system was shot. Heat tortured him. Panic wracked his brain.He hopped onto Great Western Road, keeping close to the dull-green painted metal railing in case he collapsed. He felt as though he had emerged from a jungle. Masel down from the mountain. Traffic blazed by him. Pedestrians hurried around him, gave him a wide berth, some ducked, poking others on the shoulder, grabbing their collars, staring at him as though he were Death himself. Cars sounded their horns after him, some drivers waved their fists or raised two fingers. Others cheered him on. Masel hopped on. Abruptly, he experienced the strange sensation of seeing himself as he was; he saw himself as a pathetic madman, a lunatic bounding frantically along Great Western Road in a sleeping bag. Where did he think he was going anyway?

* * *

Consciously, he had no idea of direction. He hunted for a landmark, but it was as if some disaster had occurred and the streets had been altered in his absence. He shook his head, unaware he was doing it, his heart still thudding, his mouth dry, his body slippery and raw in the bag like a skinned eel. Subconsciously, he was bouncing towards Bowmont Terrace, the street of drooping cherry blossoms, Katy's street.

While bobbing obliviously across Byres Road, a white Mercedes Benz grazed Masel's ass, and he went rolling into the gutter. He cracked a tooth on the verge of the pavement outside the Presto supermarket as he went down.

A crowd of morning shoppers gathered, encircled Masel in silence. Then some of them laughed when they saw he was conscious and, for the most part, unhurt. Others looked on, as if witnessing some gruesome form of execution.

Dazed, he lay mute and helpless in the gutter, blushing in the sunshine at the pain, the heat, the attention. He lowered his head to the ground, spat blood and wiped his mouth on the shoulder of the bag. He felt severe nausea when he thought of what he had got himself into. What a terrible way to die. There was a sharp pain in his chest. He felt dread strike his gut. The driver screeched on his brakes just past him. A white door flew open and a large, bulky man jumped out, hurtled toward him. The man fought through the gathering mass with large, clawing hands. When he reached Masel, he stood above him, blotted out the sunlight, and gazed wide-eyeballed, as if deeply horrified.

Sharp-faced, high-voiced, the man called nervously, "You were walking, hopping, in front of the car. Hang on a minute..."

Bleary-eyed in the long shadow, Masel looked up and asked meekly, "Can you help me?" His words seemed jumbled to him, but he tried to go on anyway. The driver wore a long-sleeved blue shirt. Masel wanted to make out the red-stitched letters above the pocket, but was unable. He tried hard to focus on the face, but could not do that either. "I'm trapped in this sleeping bag," he cried softly. "I can't get up."

Masel was beginning to focus. At the same time, the man's stare grew intense.

"You're what?"

Masel breathlessly repeated the problem.

The man's eyes suddenly widened in anger, his brow red

and tightly-knotted.

Gevalt, why me? thought Masel.

The man waved his hands in front of him. "I don't believe this. You're a fucking loony. I have two children in that car."

Biting his bloody lip, Masel hadn't the strength to deny it. "I'm sorry, I can't get out of this bag," he said, his heart racing.

A murmur of sniggering rose up in the crowd. A number of them shook their heads, put their fingers to their mouths.

Masel heard someone say, "Isn't that Hamish Maurin, the rugby internationalist?"

The man abruptly calmed himself, although his breathing remained agitated. He looked around him, as if seeing the crowd for the first time. He gave a false smile.

Masel expected a fist in his bloody mouth, but instead, the man lunged at him.

"You're coming with me, sunshine."

The man clutched Masel brutishly around the waist, slung him over his shoulder and carried him to the white Mercedes.

"It's all right, folks, I don't think he's hurt, but I'm taking him to the hospital just in case."

The crowd applauded.

Masel was bundled head-first into the back seat. He began to struggle, but something in him gave; he felt his body go limp. With difficulty, he could see the crowd cheering. If there's a hell, thought Masel, I'm in it. Blood beat in his eardrum.

The rugby internationalist gunned the engine and took off, his tyres screeching, at break-neck speed. He instructed his two children - a girl and a boy of maybe seven and eight - to get in the front seat, which, reluctantly, they did, scrambling wildly over Masel's wrapped and bound body.

"Put the safety belt on right." The rugby internationalist warned them.

With a tremor, Masel asked, "Where are you taking me? To the hospital?"

"To the jail, where you belong."

"What about the hospital. I need to go to the hospital."

"Shut it or I'll shut it for you."

The little boy leaned over the front seat and prodded Masel in the ribs with both hands. The little girl peered around the side of the seat and giggled.

Masel groaned, his breath short.

"Daddy, he smells."

"Hold your nose, Fergus," Maurin told the child. "He's a dirty man."

Masel, lying crookedly against the back seat, did not attempt to speak. He tried to straighten his pained, twisted body, but was met with predictable frustration. He felt shame at his filthy state, and let out another groan. The clean plastic of the seat assailed his palpitating nostrils.

"Daddy, why is he wrapped in a sleeping bag?"

"Because he's a fucking idiot. Now leave him alone, and put the safety belt on."

"But his nose is red."

"That's because he's a bloody alcoholic tramp who almost got us all killed."

"Gevalt," said Masel, exploring his broken tooth with his tongue. Fear exacerbated his weakness.

"Daddy, is he foreign?"

"No, he's drunk."

The child pressed the survivalist's red nose. Masel, amid fiery heat, was getting weaker suddenly. What was happening to him? The car jolted to a halt. Masel fell onto the floor.

"Right." The rugby internationalist's door shot open angrily, and he leaped out. Masel knew he was in for it now.

"Can we come in, too?" the little boy asked.

"No, stay where you are," Maurin ordered.

Savagely, he pulled Masel from the back seat, and doubled him up over his shoulder. Masel dared not open his eyes, couldn't if he wanted to.

* * *

"Vay iz mir," Masel moaned, the words of his father coming back with a shock, trembling, half conscious now. If there was anything in his stomach, he would have vomited.

"Shut up." Masel was dumped like discarded wares, a

dead dog, on the counter at the police enquires desk. "This bloody drunkard nearly got us killed. I want him arrested."

The room was hot and close. Masel snapped open one eye in fear.

The officers, there were two of them there at first, then others came, were watching him with suspicion and disbelief. One, stout with large, white hands, was trying to unzip him, but couldn't. An oldish officer, with grey hair, fat cheeks, and thick pursed lips was eyeing the rugby internationalist.

"Aren't you Hamish Maurin," he asked, almost bashfully, "the rugby internationalist? Can I have your autograph?"

"Never mind. Just arrest the bastard." His face was purple.

"I'm sorry about this, Mr Maurin," he said, fairly patient, "but we'll have to get some details."

Eyeing Masel often, threateningly, and with disgust, Maurin excitedly told how a lunatic wrapped in a sleeping bag had hopped back and forth in front of his car on Byres Road, while he was taking the kids to school. He had had no choice but to ram the madman. The story deepened at every turn, had Masel leaping on to the roof of the car, the furrows on Maurin's forehead twisting and rippling. Then his excitement took on new blood. He seemed suddenly overcome by a convulsion of inner frustration, and began yelling. Masel closed his open eye.

"He was hopping...He's drunk," Maurin stuttered, unable to express his outrage. "Look at him."

"Fine, Mr Maurin, we'll take it from here. Thankfully, nobody seems to have been hurt."

"What?" he yelled. "This demented bastard hopped onto the road in a sleeping bag. He nearly got us killed."

"Right, that's it," said the grey-haired cop, now impatient. There was an air of natural insolence about him. "I want you out of here now. Thank you very much for bringing him in. Now please leave."

Cold sweat prickled Masel's back. He was convinced he was dying. Sour breath whistled in his nose. He could smell the dank, rotten odour of himself, and clamped his teeth to keep from shuddering. He did, however, let out a groan.

The rugby internationalist stomped angrily to the door. Three officers lifted Masel from the hard-board counter to a wooden bench in an adjoining room. He experienced an overwhelming sense of death. He wanted to say, "Help me," but was unable. He was being boiled alive in his own sweat. His kishkas were melting.

"We should call an ambulance," said one of the officers, studying him closely, prodding him. Masel heard their voices as if the words were being slowly spoken inside his head.

"Do you smell drink?"

The officer bent his head down. "Only sweat," he said, pinching his nostrils.

"Better call an ambulance. He doesn't look good. Pass me a knife from the drawer and I'll cut open this sleeping bag."

The officer carefully sliced the sleeping bag at the seam and, immediately, a putrid stench blasted out. Masel felt the fresh air massage his body. His own pungent air nauseated him.

"Gevalt," he called out faintly.

"Sarge, he said something."

Masel slowly opened his eyes and felt his scalp burn. He stared down at himself in horror, at his grey hands, his bleeding feet, his tattered body. He felt tears, but shook them away. He tried to fan himself with his free hands, but stopped when he began to shiver. The officer wiped Masel's brow with a cloth and put a blanket over him. The woollen hair irritated his skin and Masel threw it off.

"Oy-oy-oy. Too hot."

"Can you give us your name?" There was a frown on the cop's face. "Do you have a fixed abode?"

"Masel," he sighed softly. "Elliot Masel."

"Elliot Masel, the famous one?"

Masel admitted it. He feared the worst.

"All right, Elliot, the ambulance is on its way. I think you might have had a wee shock."

Masel spoke hoarsely. "I can always hang myself later. Can I make one phone call?" They said they'd do it for him.

He tried to remember Katy's phone number, but it had

gone from his mind. Instead, the officer, as instructed by Masel, called Plotnikov at the EPI Centre and asked him to pass the message on. Plotnikov, Masel was told, was busy with an 'I Belong to Glasgow' sculpture exhibition, but would contact Katy at his first opportunity.

The sergeant, holding his hand over his nose, fed Masel a cup of tea. A large-boned policewoman held his head up, and he gulped greedily. His teeth and back ached from when the car had knocked him onto the kerb. He was dizzy. His bleeding feet ached. He felt himself fainting away, but fought it. His heart pounded tensely, and Masel, deathly weary, became aware of a rapid pulse in his skull. Was this it? The end?

The ambulancemen came and two men put him on a stretcher. Masel numbly stretched out.

Just as they were lifting him, Katy breezed through the door of the police station; it was as if she were floating, her face, smile, like a rainbow, a flower, her hair, a halo.

"What you need is a good kick up the arse," she said.

Masel, holding forth a trembling, dirty hand, feeling the weight of his heart, moved by the sight of her, wept with joy.

■ The Marriage
■ One

THEY married casually in late October, in a red-bricked registry office, across the street from a naked, dripping elm tree. Masel gazed out for a moment, as if with purpose, through a long, latice-worked window in the hall, anticipating the pleasure he and Katy would feel when they were next between the sheets - as a married couple. As he observed, the swirling autumn wind threw soggy, brown leaves at huddled pedestrians and high into erratic loops in the frosty air. Icy cloud banks, black-throated, like waiting convoys, lay still athwart a wide, steep fracture of winter-blue sky. When Masel looked he sensed his own life breaking open, as if poised to spill forth in endless possibility at any moment. This makes it even, for the chains that fettered me for so long. Something was happening to him, even as he stood at this moment peering from the window of this near-empty hall. He was sensing an emotional change of weather, felt a plushing fountain in his being, glowed warmly. Katy had saved his life. When a man is in love his sins decrease. For months, Masel had been aware of an increasing desire to be near her at all times. His spirit descended the depths when he was bereft of her. Women, he thought; I suffer before I get them, while I have them, and after I've lost them. Then he remembered lying miserable in his cave, wondering where the hell Zelda was and what she was doing, and relieved that he didn't know. The same went for Katy. Yet, he felt his old fears waning. This new sensation was entirely different, enlarged.

That morning, while nibbling affectionately at Masel's ear, Katy had mentioned it was time to start thinking about another concert. Masel, swaying a little, agreed to think about it. Other matters occupied his mind. His cheeks ached from smiling. His thoughts wandered like a child in a dark wood, and then returned. Katy had drawn him home. She rose deliberately from the bed into the cold room, and stood naked for a brief moment before the long mirror. She raised her pointed breasts with cupped hands and sighed as she let go. Masel, bingeing on reverie, reflected on every curve of her beautiful body, the way her pale skin smoothed over womanly hips.

"Earth to Masel. Earth to Masel. Come in please." She waved her hand hypnotically in front of his face.

You move me, he told her. You touch me. I will do anything for you, and everything. I love you. You are beauty's rose, the fairest creature I have ever known. Katy kneeled on the bed, her breasts pointing at his face, choosing him. You make me affluent in feeling, he told her, tender as feathers. She gathered the covers around her shoulders and said she felt the same, was sick and tired of being so much by herself; although for most of the time she wasn't, Masel knew what she meant. So, later that day, in the crispy late-October afternoon, they married to be more together. Masel the romantic.

There were seven at the secular ceremony: the registrar, a catarrhal, frowning man of fiftyish, with dark, dyed hair, small blue eyes, and long, greying sideburns; Masel, his ponytail restored, fully bearded now in an ill-fitting rented dinner jacket, and Katy, lovely bride in a tight, purple mini-skirt; Aldous Longman, moody witness and serious in a plain, black suit; MacGregor, the other witness, eagerly smiling, otherwise expressionless in fat shoes; and Sam and Jenny, well-behaved but looking bored. The wind blew light rain, like arrows, against the voluminous many-windowed chamber. Katy and Masel looked at each other, a torch of white-grey light cutting across them. At last, he moved. She followed, and together they assented to the oaths, and, in turn, signed the large, black leather-bound book. It was over in minutes. They kissed open-mouthed, her wet lips stirring him.

Sam and Jenny clapped with delight. Masel felt deeply proud of them. He was also proud of himself. He felt free and energetic; even happy and aware, a rare harmony for the American.

Within minutes of being out in the open air, Masel,

enjoying the moment, in a rapturous mood on the porous, grey stone steps outside the registry office, was struck in the eye by a wildly-thrown grain of rice.

"My boy," Longman apologized profusely, his eyes narrowing, his expression dismal. He grabbed hold of Masel's arm. "What can I say? I'm deeply, deeply sorry."

"You could have at least waited until after the honeymoon," Masel said, his hand held to the side of his face.

"Come, come, you don't think it was intentional, do you? I think you're over-reacting somewhat?" Longman's voice was husky, offended.

He cleared a frog in his throat, and Masel did the same. "What do you mean? You just assaulted me in the eye with a rice grain." Masel's words seemed to make the situation ridiculous, embarrassing him. A rice grain? He bit into his pursed lips to distract his mind from the acute pain, forcing out a grimace. His heartbeat boomed to the base of his throat.

George MacGregor, an oblique smile on his face, stood next to Katy, silently watching. His body was unmoving, save his rapidly blinking eyelids.

Longman, in a slow, meaningful gesture, extended his arm and offered Masel his palm. "Let's settle this amicably," he said. "It's your wedding. Congratulations, my boy." He nodded furtively, like an assassin. "Take marvellous care of her."

Masel smiled unwillingly, one hand covering his eye, the other in Longman's palm. One half of his face hurt like hell and swelled unpleasantly in the chilly autumn afternoon. Longman, a man vulnerable to smiles and agreeable gestures, chuckled, his eyes skimming off, lighted with relief. Masel turned away, his gaze falling on the beautiful face of Katy. She drew her new husband into an emotional and familiar embrace, and then drove him to the hospital to have his wound treated.

* * *

They had hoped instead to drive north for the honeymoon, find a small, romantic hotel on the bonnie Isle of Skye and hole up for a week or two of amorous pleasure: they would walk hand in hand over sweeping, green hills, on golden beaches, the

salt wind on their cheeks, kissing tenderly, drink hot broth by
the fire in a cosy white-stone pub, and make love later, or
sooner if the inspiration moved them. If they felt like it, he
would take his guitar downstairs and play a song or two in the
bar over a rare, peaty single malt. It would be a nice thing to do
in between twice, thrice in bed, Katy clapping, buoyant,
affectionate.

He remembered he no longer had a guitar, but kept the loss
to himself. For the most part, his hand remained cupped around
the swollen rice-grain injury. His cornea had been scratched
and the doctor told him he would have to be back at the hospital
in two days for a check up and then again four days later.

· A nurse with iron-grey hair told Masel to drop his trousers, and then injected him twice in the left buttock; one to
thwart infection, the other to dull the pain.

"You may feel a bit foggy-minded later," the doctor said,
his long blond locks wrapped around his balding head like a
turban. "But it's nothing to worry about."

Masel said he felt fine, save a throbbing eye. "I just got
married."

"Tough luck," said the doctor. "About your eye, I mean.
Go home and relax, if you can." He furtively winked, grinning.

Katy had her own ideas, her hair now attractively long and
unfurled like a golden flag. In exchange for the honeymoon,
Masel was shlepped to the city centre to pick out his wedding
present - a replacement Gizmo D25. Katy parked her little car
in a multi-storey and led the rest of the way on foot. He didn't
exactly jump for joy, his eye bloodshot and emotional beneath
a dipping, heavy, white head bandage. Masel the pirate.

"Oh?" she said, her face, for a moment, frozen. She
seemed unnaturally awake. "Considering the circumstances, I
thought it would be a nice wee surprise."

In his heart of hearts, Masel desired the instrument, but
feared its ramifications, assented only because Katy had asked
him, and because Katy was Katy.

They walked along Sauchiehall Street, past the Euro
Pictish Institute Centre, closer to one another than Masel could

ever remember being to anyone, the icy wind cooling his hot face. He wore longjohns, thick dungarees, a red-checked lumberjack's shirt beneath Katy's big duffel coat, and his white sneakers. He watched her as they walked. They took detours and huddled together like ghosts against the rain and the wind. She took him down on to Cathedral Street, pointing out the tall medieval tower and stained glass, doubling back through a low, squat, semi-constructed amphitheatre.

Masel made no comment, although every nerve in him seemed to be alert. They lingered in bars and had lunch in a restaurant she knew. They talked about their childhoods, their parents, their plans for the future, and of the possibility of her having another child, their child. Masel said that was what he wanted. On occasion they embraced warmly and kissed across the table or in the breezy street. What more could a man like me ask for? he wondered.

Before asking Katy, Masel asked himself, for what do I need fame anymore? With nearly four months of it behind him, he had had enough. Since emerging from the park, his days and nights had been overloaded with newspaper interviews and appearances on television chat shows. Everyone was amazed that this apparently wacky American had hid out in a Glasgow park, depressed and unnoticed for four weeks. Masel's public, it seemed, were even further astounded to hear he had thought his acclaimed performance at the EPI Centre had been a failure. At Katy's instigation he went on the air to confirm it personally. Masel, the star by proxy, had cringed at the attention.

They crossed the street on to an open walkway, lined on two sides by the green-white skeletons of gnarled trees. Masel almost stumbled in a manhole, but furtively side-stepped it. For a moment, he was conscious of the fact that he hadn't fallen over and into it, the spooky sense of impending humiliation and pain lingering all the same. A hole may be nothing, but you can break your neck in it, he thought.

"Did you see that?"

"What?"

He pointed to the black hole. "What do you make of that?"

"It's a wee hole in the ground," she said.

He felt foolish at making a big deal out of it, because that was the old Masel, stuck, head first, in a lightless hollow. This was Masel in transformation, he berated himself, in metamorphosis. The simple truth was that he didn't give a shit anymore about manholes, orifices, puddles, archways, ditches, low fences, trip wires, wet leaves, the banana skins of life.

Outside an organic wine shop, he unlinked his arm from Katy's and nervously stooped to pick up a butt from the pavement. He scrunched up his nose as he lit the thing, smoke assailing his one visible eye.

"Hon - " he began. Katy looked at him, amazed. He halted his words, as though someone had switched him off.

"Elliot, when are you going to get out of that filthy habit?"

Masel's face frowned and flushed darkly. Feeling suddenly imperiled, he dragged furiously on the butt and, staring at it, threw it away. The sky was sunless, greyly clouded, chilled. Shaking his bandaged head, he lost his train of thought.

The late-autumn rain icily spritzed their heads. "You're right, it's a nasty habit."

She reached over and softly touched his cheek with her fingertips, then withdrew them. Her lips parted tenderly. "What's the matter with you now?" she asked.

"I know we've discussed this, hon," he protested, after a moment, his bad eye throbbing. "but I don't want to be a star anymore." He felt as though it was all an illusion, undeserved and unreal.

Katy let out a lungful of breath. It steamed through the cold air onto his face. Then, shyly, she confessed she had several days ago booked him in at the new Glasgow Baroque Hall - GBH, for short - to perform a Hogmanay concert.

"A Hogma - " Masel began, but stopped abruptly. He felt panic attack his throat. "I thought that burned down months ago. Wasn't that what was on fire the day I arrived?"

"They're building a new one. Actually, we walked through it about an hour ago. That amphitheatre thing. It's due to be

finished next month. What did you think?"
Masel gulped. "But New Year's Eve is only two months away. How can I possibly be ready by then?"
She shook her head stiffly, ignoring the question. Masel was to be the new GBH's first performer. It was quite a coup, Katy explained, and a chance in a million. He couldn't possibly fail as long as he was in a New Year party spirit.
Masel shivered, a little irritated. "Why didn't you discuss it with me first?"
"Because you would have objected. I'm looking after your interests. I'm still your manager, remember? Besides, it was mentioned in your initial invitation, if you recall."
They crossed back on to Sauchiehall Street. "If you're happy, you're happy." he said. "Why sneeze at happiness?"
Masel sneezed dramatically in the cold air.
"AH-CHOO!" It was a bad joke. Neither of them laughed.
"It has absolutely nothing to do with happiness," she said after a moment of gazing incredulously at him. Now she spoke rapidly. "You have to earn a living somehow. How long can you go on giving interviews about one concert and a crazy month in the Botanical Gardens? You're making a fool of yourself, Elliot, and me."
Her words hurt him. His eye throbbed. "You're the one who set up all the interviews."
"Consider yourself discovered," she advised seriously.
He gave her one of his twisted, half-ironic smiles that always irritated her - probably because she couldn't seem to fathom out what it meant, if anything.
Katy squinted her eyes at him, and quickly shook her head. "You've got the talent, Elliot, not me. You should capitalize on it, make use of it, take something worthwhile from it while it lasts. Look at all we achieved last time. We make a good team, you can't deny that, Elliot - your talent and my organizational skills." Then she looked at him coyly. "Didn't we move the earth?" She paused for a moment, sternly thoughtful. Now she was staring harshly at him. "If there's something else you can do besides sing and play the guitar better than

anybody I've ever seen or heard, now is the time to speak up."

He couldn't think of anything off hand. All of a sudden, she's an expert on playing the guitar, he thought.

Her powerful eyes fixed him and, vexed, she called to him, "Watch your step."

Masel abruptly had a vision of himself alone in the wilderness, womanless, garotted, miserable in a lousy, stinking rathole. He was a prisoner to love's logic and his own interpretation of it. He wiped his one wet eyelid, and decided he hadn't given up show business after all. He was heartened to have recovered her, even though it was he who had been lost.

Love, he surmised among other things, had disturbed his mental equilibrium. But he had misread her signs. As he pondered his fate, he found his foot on the verge of skidding through a soggy piece of dog excrement. At the last moment, he arrested himself and, in an effort to keep his balance, wildly leaped in the air. He manoeuvred, like an acrobat on a trampoline, a sneaky double shuffle and somehow, as if adroitly, landed back in step with Katy, amazingly still on his feet.

Katy gazed at him strangely. "Elliot, what in the name of God are you doing?"

"Nothing," he said, a little too quick, embarrassed. That was a close one, he thought.

"You're crazy but I love you."

Masel glowed like a beacon. She took his hand and kissed it, hugged his arm, near the shoulder, on tip-toes softly held his head between her fingers and lightly kissed his bandaged eye.

The wind grew more intense, now depositing sporadic hail. They ducked into the doorway of a small, sparkling shop called Gizmo Glasgow. Masel halted at the revolving-door entrance to the music store - to Masel, the ultimate obstacle before him. A memory came at him violently - the young Masel, a little, white-tassled prayer shawl around his narrow shoulders, his small head capped, standing next to his rocking, bearded father, dream-like, athwart the open Ark of the Covenant. Watching. Wondering. Why this? he wondered.

Katy, on her second trip around the revolving door, took

Masel's hand and softly pulled him in. Her green eyes twinkled at him, as if to say to him, "Together we can make it; together we'll be safe."

There was magic in the air, like when he was a child.

* * *

The bright walls of Gizmo Glasgow glittered thickly like Christmas trees with gaudy, reckless, up-to-the-minute designs - some of them with curved, horn-like headstocks, bent, convex backs, sunken shoulders, artful necks. Masel studied them all, a silvery-bearded salesman hovering irritatingly at his elbow. Masel nodded at him.

"Fine collection of Gizmos you got here."

"Cost you a fortune these days."

Frowning at the difficult decision before him, Masel was unable to resist the most expensive one in the range. The salesman seemed to draw away, but for a moment stayed where he was. When Katy approached, she whispered something in his ear, and the man backed off, over-politely.

"A pleasure to serve you, Dr Masel," the man said. "If I can be of any assistance just call me. We're quite used to having celebrities in here, you know, so just make yourself at home."

Masel grinned nervously. He lifted the instrument from the wall, pleasantly conscious of its smooth, wooden body. He crouched down on one knee and rang out a sweet progression of major seventh chords. Masel in seventh heaven. The ex-performer listened to himself with fascination, and relaxed cautiously. Is that me? He continued to listen. I know I'm good, but this good? Katy stood against a large, orange amplifier, her legs shapely, gorgeous, in black woollen stockings, womanly, at ease, always good to see her in those short mini-skirts. Only the spiritually bereft can live without passion. It was the first time Masel had touched a guitar in months. The thing felt odd in his hands, almost like a reverie. Katy smiled at him, attentive. Dreamily, his fingers swept across the brilliant, austere lines of the instrument.

Then, in clumsy excitement, he abruptly stopped, rubbed an open palm quickly over his face, as if his whiskers were on fire. "Well, hon, what do you think?"

"What do you think?"

Masel looked into her eyes. They seemed pale as the Arctic Circle. "I don't know, what do you think?"

"Oh, come on Elliot, don't start that again, please. What do you think? You're the one who's going to be playing it."

Masel watched her crispy, diamond wedding ring - it had cost him a small fortune, although now he could afford it and didn't mind - glisten coldly against the shiny, new varnish of the instrument, as if shamanistic. He feigned a cough, although he didn't know why, and, to a scrambled rhythm continued quickly to play another run of notes. They were jazzier this time, and he finished on three funky minor ninth chords. The salesman watched Masel's fluid hands in wonder.

In spite of himself, Masel groaned loudly, his fingers nervously in motion. He had forgotten how good he was at this. He played softly.

Katy flattened the palm of her hand and smoothed down her purple skirt. Her eyes were gentle. "I believe in you," she said with emotion in her voice. "Do you believe in me, Elliot?"

Masel stopped playing and said he did, felt his heart beating; and it was true, he believed. He drew in a shaky breath as Katy's scent rushed up his nose and into his chest.

"After the show" Katy said, "let's go away somewhere together for a few weeks. We'll be able to afford it properly then. Let's go away to a warm place, like Tahiti; some place exotic, where we can have a real honeymoon in luxury."

Masel said that was what he wanted. He was famished for the sun. He was also famished for Katy, his beautiful bride, felt trepidation at denying her what she obviously wanted, and deep down he felt the fear of being once again divorced, alone, abandoned, miserable. He racked his brain thinking how not to fail her, for her sake and his.

Katy's eyelids batted at him slowly, moistly, and she pulled him from his crouch into a slow embrace. They kissed passionately amid the flashing wah-wah pedals, her long, silver earrings clinking faintly in front of him.

The salesman furtively observed them from behind a grand piano, like a sneaking child glimpsing young lovers.

"I'll take it," Masel called over.

Katy unrolled a large wad of bank notes from her purse, her arms still loosely around her husband's ribcage, and flapped the bunch of notes behind him like a little flag. Her lips tenderly touched Masel's. The salesman, suddenly appearing before them, slightly bowed, his face smiling as he accepted the cash.

Gevalt, Masel thought. He wondered, what hath God wrought for me this time? It was a freezing afternoon. Their honeymoon was already into dusk.

 Two

They drove home on the expressway through sharp sleet, and cut off at Partick Cross, the new Gizmo laying lightly across the back seat, encased as though in some supernatural burial tomb. Katy double parked her little car - a leaping yellow frog - outside a small supermarket, and asked Masel to run in for a box of nappies for Jenny. A sense of irritation floated into his mind. On one hand, he was seeing himself armlocked, muted, being thrown onto a black stage before a massive, restless Hogmanay crowd; on the other, he was a man re-born, in love and, at last, in life. Marriage is a question of compromise, he thought, you lose this and get that, lose that and get this. He experienced a sense of loss, but checked himself. Without the hedge, Masel remembered his father saying to him, the vineyard is laid to waste; without a wife, a man is a homeless wanderer - and who trusts a band of armed vagabonds? The memory of his father trickily remained, like a vapour trail, in his head.

"What the hell are nappies?" he asked, snapping out of it.

Katy clucked like a hen. "Diapers," she translated, her eyes narrowing incredulously.

She gazed intently into his unbandaged eye, for a moment searching hungrily, then, with a good-humoured look on her face, told him to hurry up.

He ran through the icy drizzle, his mind elsewhere.

Masel, reflecting on the thought of his beautiful new Gizmo guitar, and all that it meant, wandered the narrow aisles of the supermarket in a foggy dream. A hefty Asian woman behind the counter, playing with a large gold hoop in her ear, eyed him suspiciously in a high, angled corner mirror. He noticed, but then forgot about her. Katy came into his mind, and Masel furtively fondled a pair of unripe melons, exotic and strangely pointed. As he meandered through the household appliances section, he began to worry about the little time he had to prepare for the GBH. He shook his head. At once, he felt spacey, almost weightless. His ears began to burn and crackle; it was as though someone were holding a red-hot strip of holographic film to his tender lobe. Masel sucked his lower lip, as if he were considering some complex puzzle. Now there were voices in his head that seemed to shoot all around him, muddled, unintelligible, clattering. Then rumbling and hissing came at him, as though from a furnace. He was also vaguely aware of the hum of refrigerators. The yellow-white fluorescence of the store cracked in his eyes like lightning.

A violent prickling went through his body, like some sudden chemical change in his being, that came rushing up his gullet and out through his ears and eyes, like light blasting through the face of a mountain. He hastened up and down the aisles, trying to shake it. His balance faltered and he hunkered down at a bread counter, holding on to it to steady himself. The store changed colour into a dullish blue. He put his arms out like useless wings to balance himself. Whether this was real, or the effect of the injection at the hospital or the after-effects of his wedding and the adrenalin that had pumped him into a new life, he couldn't tell. "Insane," he whispered. Was he conjuring all this up of his own free will, supplying whatever drug was in his system with his own crazy, black fantasies?

"Masel," a voice called from behind him, sharp with familiar annoyance.

At first, he was more startled by the stillness. But when Masel turned, slowly, as if he might set off a booby trap with the slightest movement, he gasped as he saw the bodyless head of his mother, floating in mid-air, as it were, tilted, as if she were listening to a very faint sound. Her face was the colour of ash. He stared in astonishment. His heart raced; he had a strong sense of being sickeningly drunk.

"Mom," he mouthed to a face he'd seen only in old photographs, but no sound came. He would have cried out, but his voice froze in his throat. He breathed in shakily, and held it. He was also having difficulty with his tongue.

Then he saw his father, robed in white, glassy eyed, his face dented like bread dough. He wore a cold, dreadful, drunken frown. A boy, maybe twelve or thirteen, was with him, weak-jawed, lazy-eyed, smirking. There were other children and others he didn't recognize, and birds and a dog. Masel felt a knot burgeon in his stomach. He stood immobile, observing, like a small, terrified child. Zelda, clinging to a broken bed, hovered above him, her lips pressed together in a look of concentration. (The ghost of his failed first marriage? As far as he knew, Zelda was alive and well, living somewhere in New York City) His heart leaped. Aunt Julia, who had raised him after his father's drunken accident, long-since dead, materialized across the aisle from him, poking her index finger into her cheek, her face repose in scornful glee. For a moment they all were still, fearfully watching him; was he the ghost? Sweat gathered on his forehead. He drew his hands to his face, as if he were remembering some shameful act in his past. What is happening to me? His mind shocking as lightning, awful as death, he leaped up from his crouch and doubled-back in a burst of speed past the frozen foods and into the vegetables.

The pack of ghosts flew after him, coming at him with the slow but sure advance of blood. When Masel ran, they hastened after him, some now swishing past him and back again. They seemed to be all around him, muttering.

He turned abruptly into the alcoholic beverages section. Why me? Why is it always me? He jogged around the aisles, the vision of his bodyless mother penetrating his conscience, until he had come full circle. He clung to a wine rack to catch his breath. Heat sprung into his throat. That this was actually happening to him, Masel knew, was unlikely in the extreme. When he closed his eyes and tried to concentrate away, he got an image of a little boy crouched on a front porch, crying because his aunt had wacked him hard across his bare buttocks with a big black comb; he had wet his pants. Masel hadn't remembered that in years, the terrible unfairness of her punishment still clinging to his subconscious. When he snapped open his eyes, the ghosts were advancing with speed straight at him, lightning in their eyes, their mouths black within.

He dodged through them frantically, faking left and right and right again, and the pack of phantoms swivelled around, as if one, in chase. They flew behind him and past him, as he darted furiously up and down the aisles. Then anger came at him. He manoeuvred sharply into the dairy produce section, and abruptly turned, facing them, their faces decaying and waxen, as they rushed toward him.

"What do you want from my life?" he said, shouting at them, waving his arms as if he were shooing chickens. "You've had years of my past, what more do you want? Enough is enough. Leave me alone. God-damned ghosts."

The phantoms, a look of abject fear now on their dark faces, attempted a screeching halt, tensing against his words. Masel insanely raised his clenched fist at them. It was as if they were trying to dig their heels into mid air, but instead flew straight ahead and over him, and crashed through a precariously-constructed stack of cottage cheese. They disappeared in a symphony of howls, and invisible crackling that slowly grew fainter and fainter. Almost at once, the dullish blue light turned into yellow-white fluorescence. It was over, the vision gone.

Masel stood helpless, catching his breath, amid the mess of spilled cottage cheese and broken containers that covered the floor like ectoplasm, his heart quaking.

An Asian man in grey overalls rushed out from the back of the store, waving Masel away, ignoring his apologies.

"It was an accident, I swear."

"Okay, okay," the man said, with the patience of someone

who had spent years of his life looking after an elderly relative.

Masel breathed deeply, his heartbeat steadying, and was surprised to discover in his arms three bottles of red wine and a long stick of bread. He forgot about the nappies. He shook his head. Had he seen ghosts? He wasn't sure. Or had he simply fallen asleep on his feet. Yet he had plainly seen them. Either way it seemed that all those who had made him insane had come back to haunt him. That was it, he thought, just a dream, nothing more than a hallucination induced by a drug. God-damned ghosts. Acid rose from his gorge to his mouth and he unpleasantly swallowed it.

As the big Asian woman rang up the cash register, a gentle, vaguely Celtic voice behind him called, "Is it a party you're having?"

What now? His heart hammered in his chest. He hesitated for a moment before jumping around. Gevalt, he thought when he saw her, another ghost? He looked down at the girl's white, limp hands resting on the trolley. She was real. He was rubbing his hand against his chest.

"Elliot Masel, you surely remember. The Vacation Inn. You were throwing up in a bucket when I saw you last. I brought you a bowl of rice pudding. I nearly didn't recognize you with your beard on. I called over to you a minute ago, but you didn't answer. "

His mind was snagged on the oddity of his hallucination. Then it clicked. It was the Irish girl. He had a sudden recollection of her watching him throw up, but said nothing. In the store's yellow light, the girl's hair and clothes looked washed out, and she had a pimple on the tip of her nose that drew attention to itself. All he could do was give her a crazy smile.

"And what happened to your eye?"

"Twelve pound thirty eight," the big, Asian woman said, flatly accented, expressionless. With a blush, Masel quickly drew his money from his pocket, and handed her a twenty.

"You should pay me a visit," the Irish girl said softly. "Just yourself and meself. I'm still at the hotel." She leaned toward him and kissed the tip of his nose.

Masel felt his blush intensifying. Perhaps she's trying to transfer her pimple to me, he thought. He took his change and lifted the bottles and bread in his arms. Although he knew it was grotesque, he turned to the Irish girl and, then, as if something horrible, twisted, had happened to his face, he winked. She complacently looked at him, like a sheep.

Masel staggered to the door - a soft swishing noise slowly rising then subsiding in his ears - and, after catching his sleeve on the handle, pushed through it without looking back. It dawned on him that he hadn't said a word to her.

The embarrassment broke him up. He returned to the car. Was any of this possible?

* * *

"Well?" Katy asked, a little impatient, her eyes shifting between his nose and the wine and the bread on his lap. "Where's the nappies?"

"Nappies?" he said, nervously. As if by magic, his head cleared, though the recollection of the hallucination remained sharp. "Er - they were all out. I bought these instead." He nodded at the bottles, grateful for her company. "I thought it would be nice. For our wedding night."

Katy's expression softened dramatically. "What's that stuff on your nose?" she asked.

"Er - red wine," he said, quickly, at first not knowing exactly what she was talking about, then half-realising. He was still jumpy. "That's it," he said, "I was tasting some red wine. It was an offer they had."

She looked at him in bafflement, as if for one moment he might be somebody else completely. "And so you decided to stick your head in it?"

Masel shrugged, and felt his heartbeat steady itself.

Katy turned to the wheel and gunned the engine. She shook her head slightly and took off. A smile on her face suggested inner contentment. It calmed Masel. He looked furtively at his nose in the vanity mirror of the sun visor, although by now he knew it was a red smudge from the Irish girl's lipstick. Pretending to have an itch while looking out the window, he cleaned his nose with his forefinger, and spit. He felt his back sizzle with sweat against the seat. When he looked again into the mirror, he was surprised to find that he was smiling.

With good humour, Katy said, "I want you to be happy." Masel, moved, said he loved her.

"My gentle American," she said, touching his hand.

He whispered to himself. "I have arrived."

* * *

Late that night, their wedding night, they made love generously and with pleasure. She gave intrinsically, and he gave with relaxed ease in return. His heart tapped in his ears. She touched, caressed, kissed in an intimate way with her tongue, her bare legs on his thighs. Masel loved her, aroused, sensed her sensuality. He felt himself a gifted man, expanded, an excellent musician, confident lover, a god. The profundity of pleasure was all but unbearable. She let go in surprise, he gratefully with a whisper.

"Ell-ee-ot," she sang warmly.

Afterwards, he rose restfully, satisfied, from the bed and crossed the room to the wide window, the curtain drawn open.

He peered through the sharp darkness into the skeletal trees in the gardens across the street. He felt somehow stronger, a feeling he attributed to the fact that something good and positive had happened to him. He was married again. It would be better this time. He didn't know why, but this positive feeling also made him feel alone. Can this be possible? he wondered. Can this be happening to, of all people, me? Katy, sensing his movement, rose, too. Marriage had bequeathed her the gift of closeness. She put her arms around her American husband, embraced him closely, passionately, and tenderly kissed his bare shoulders, a gesture that emotionally stirred him. Her warmth pressed softly against his back. He half-turned and nudged her head against his chest, kissed her hair. He smelled her sex-scented body. Not many men had it this good, he contemplated. It was the truth. Masel having a honeymoon. He was as happy now as he could remember ever being. She had become the guardian of his solitude.

■ Three

Masel discovered a disturbing connection between sex and his Gizmo. He found that the more he played and the harder he practiced for the GBH, the more Katy exercised physical affections on him. The opposite, he soon realized, was also true, and as Katy busied herself more and more with her work - she stayed late at her district council office nearly every second night - Masel's enthusiasm for his instrument drained away. His eye bandage now removed, he felt her absence deeply and for weeks brooded. He experienced faint melancholy, had doubts about himself and generally wasted valuable practising time. He played with Sam and Jenny, but mostly refused to play his new Gizmo. Consequently, the honeymoon was brief; Katy would have little to do with him and, for weeks, he slept under a hairy, woollen blanket on the couch, receiving nothing in the way of marital affection except scorn.

"Men," she said, one evening, blowing air through her nostrils like a mare, "Every man gets what he deserves."

Honeymoon for a day, he thought, trouble for life.

"Who's got?" he asked.

"Exactly," Katy called back, storming into her bedroom, the door slamming behind her, the lock turning.

He consoled himself with Sam and Jenny and enjoyed their company. Sometimes in the early evenings, Masel stretched out on the floor and played cards with them - it was the only time he could get the pair under control: otherwise, they slapped, teased and taunted one another. Sometimes, he played Jenny Puff The Magic Dragon or Chadgadyo, an old Jewish folk song about a baby goat, after tucking her in for the night, but he played it quietly, without Katy knowing. Masel the dad, the surreptitious guitar player. Masel the middle man.

After Jenny was asleep, Sam often wanted to wrestle. In response, Masel put him in the bath, although the warm water was usually too much for the boy's weak bladder. With his little penis in his hand, laughing, he would hose down his plethora of tub toys, seemingly fascinated with his ability to pee. The bathroom looked like an abandoned playground, and Masel often crunched plastic dripping ducks and rubber hippos under his feet beneath the bath mat. On more than one occasion, he stubbed his toe. Whatever maturing influence he was supposed to have on the boy, he wasn't sure. I've never been a dad before, he reminded himself with faint satisfaction.

Katy, on the other hand, gave him little peace of mind. Most of the time - when she wasn't at work - she moved stealthily from the kids to the kitchen to the bedroom to the bathroom and back, never once even glancing at her husband.

"What's the matter with mummy," Jenny asked, while crawling aimlessly over Masel's chest. Sam had him pinned to the floor in a vicious headlock.

"How should I know?" he replied, shrugging his shoulders instinctively, his face as red as a tomato, struggling for breath in Sam's grip.

The truth was he did know. He worried profoundly: Am I worthy of Katy if I don't perform the next show? Am I worthy of myself if I do? Do I really need the GBH. It was the same old story over and over again, and the same old arguments - love versus responsibility: but love and responsibility versus what? he wondered. He worried about the future of his family.

The cold wind clattered through the streets, made draughty tunnels in the old, wooden windows. During the night, Masel sneezed from prurience. Gevalt, itchy pants.

"There are no monasteries for Jews," Masel, frustrated, called to her locked bedroom door.

Before dawn, Yehwah, like some lunatic prophet of doom, came at him in swirling dreams.

He had a despotic look about him. Yet his eyebrow was cocked in a way that made him look quizzical. "I apologize, Masel," he called, winding a lock of his wiry silver hair around his index finger, tightly curling it into ringlets. His voice was raised; he always seemed to be shouting. "Believe me, it's as

hard to create a good marriage as it was to part the Red Sea."
Yehwah swirled dizzily into a black hole of night. It caused the American sea-sickness. Masel awoke with a start and sat bolt upright, desire dripping into him. He was suddenly aware of a pulsating organ. Don't start what you can't finish, he warned himself.

Four

The next morning, after Katy had taken Sam to school and Jenny to her nursery class, winter gave herself full expression. It began to slowly snow. Big, light flakes fell onto branches and hung there as more flakes fell, mounding up until it toppled like sugar. The sky was grey and still. Not even a sparrow moved. The snow began to build on the icy ground, oozing dull shadows against the bare trees. Masel left the window and gloomily went back to his blanket on the floor, momentarily baffled at how cold it was. He closed his eyes and lost himself in a reverie of San Francisco - the nights of half-rain, half-fog, foghorns belching out in the harbour, like robot-speak and lamenting cosmic sighs. His mind floated free until a strange uneasiness creeped up on him bringing him back, spinning, to the floor of this old Victorian tenement flat. He held his breath and confirmed what part of his brain seemed to already know: he was not the only one breathing in the room. He half-rolled slowly around and felt icy fingers on his belly.
"Fegghgghhhghaghhhhhhhhh!" he screamed in fright, snapping open his eyes, recoiling. It was Katy. She was kneeling close beside him, passively smiling.
"See the effect you have on me," she said.
"You nearly gave me a heart attack."
"You know, Elliot, I've been thinking. If you really don't want to do this show, you don't have to."
Masel lay on the floor, unmoving yet moved.
With one hand, she fiddled with the zipper on her leather jacket; with the other, she clasped his member in her palm. He

wanted to tell her that sex wouldn't work on him as a persuasion strategy, and that he knew better. But he feared he might set a precedent for future encounters, so he let her carry on. He grew swiftly excited. She pretended she was changing gear in a racing car.

"Vroom, vroom," she said, laughing air out of the corners of her mouth and nose. Her free hand, tightly gripping mid air, held an imaginary steering wheel; the other, clasping a nervous, quivering stick-shift. "Nyeeeeeow. Vroom. Nyeeeeeeow."

Masel appreciated her playful mood; he lay back and enjoyed it. She was pretending to be in the Grand Prix, and was driving at break-neck speed, screeching around corners, over bumps, through tunnels and under low bridges. She was gripping him as if for dear life, her thumb pressed over the slanted eye of his penis, four fingers clenched tightly around the shaft. Masel shuddered when she tried to twist him into reverse. Now she was cranking him.

"Do you want to do it?" she asked him matter of factly,

With little hesitation, Masel admitted he did.

"Not here." She stood up. Breathless, she said she only had a few minutes. She was late for work as it was, but if they hurried, twenty minutes didn't matter. "I want you, Elliot."

Masel, serious, said he wanted her, too.

Katy grinned and beckoned him silently to the bedroom. Masel, too long frustrated, rose and followed. What have I done to deserve this? he wondered. In the back of his mind there were umpteen objections to this, but now they were as meaningless as fog. Gevalt, he thought, like a lamb to the slaughter.

Masel gazed at the bed hungrily, then at Katy. She undressed quickly, removing first her blouse and bra then a long, flowery skirt, stockings and pants, and lay gently over him on the cool sheets. Her sharp breasts prodded him excitedly, her lips kissing his cheeks, his forehead, his chest, suddenly so sweetly and tentatively, as though the slightest error would make him draw away, feeling foolish and rejected. He was somewhat reticent after having been stuck on the floor for two weeks, but her body was extraordinarily lovely, and his mind, with all its doubts and fears, switched off. His heart, on the other hand, hastened to activity, and began to labour with momentum.

"I've missed you," he said.

She raised a finger to his lips. And when he kissed her hand, she pulled it away and lowered her fingers from his throat to his belly. He had forgotten how tender she could be. Katy's beauty seemed to him at this moment beyond his wildest fantasies. His heart was drowning in pleasure. Her eyes widened when he touched her perfect nipples. She bit her lip and drew breath.

"Wow," she crooned into his ear.

When she had to go, she kissed him, as if magically, three times on the nose. He was repaired.

* * *

Masel, now persuaded otherwise, planned the show and practiced his impersonations - old ones and new ones - almost every waking moment. It was less than five weeks to the GBH deadline. Katy - she had worked late only once in the last week - performed her usual routine, her brow lowered, her mind concentrated. She telephoned Longman, arranged ticket promotions, did deals with the GBH, organized seating, lights, not to mention the complicated business of the holograms.

"That's what the public want," she said. "And that's exactly what they'll get." She was in her element.

He guessed he agreed, yet couldn't entirely stave from his mind the feeling of impending torture; those damned holographic helmets. Yet he psyched himself into dangerous delusions of greatness; he found it a method that worked, a good way of tricking the self into activity. Masel the positive thinker. He developed a habit of constantly checking his wristwatch, as if tonight were the night.

"Stay relaxed," Katy begged him. "You're doing fine. Don't spoil it now. Only four weeks to go."

"I'm worried about my mental state," he confessed.

"Nobody will notice."

Masel rubbed his perspiring hands together in trepidation

and gulped. He would notice and probably wouldn't be able to do anything about it. His anxiety was relieved only by Katy's emotion and sexual expertise, her open enjoyment of carnal pleasure, usually at night, but sometimes during the afternoon, if she decided to leave work early and come home.

Gevalt, now he was Masel the stud. He wondered if he was a sex slave or a slave for sex.

* * *

Late one chilly night, Masel, after discovering an empty place beside him in the bed, rose to find Katy weeping at the kitchen table, looking miserable in his red checkered bathrobe. Her hair was stacked like a golden tower on top of her head.

"I don't want you to leave me, Elliot."

Masel sleepily pulled up a chair and sat beside her. "I won't." He leaned over and took her in his arms, but she drew back to dry her eyes with the sleeve of the robe.

She frowned thoughtfully, as though her mind were struggling for control.

"My father left my mother," she began, still weeping. "She used to cry all the time when I was young. Then she remarried, but that didn't last long either. She was miserable then, too, during and after her second marriage. It was the worst time in my life. I don't want us to be like that, Elliot. I don't want us to be miserable."

Masel said he understood and took her in his arms.

"Promise you won't leave me."

Masel promised.

"I love you," she said. "I really do."

He told her not to worry.

They made love passionately on Sunday morning, while Sam and Jenny were building a lop-sided snowman in the wooded gardens across the street. Masel felt vast, magnanimous, generous. Afterwards, as they embraced in the warm double bed, Katy fell asleep on his arm. He gently moved her. Her face was peaceful, very pretty, her skin glowing in the white, morning light, her hair glorious on the soft bluish pillowslip. Masel was glad to observe that his wife was satisfied, happy. He felt pleasure at being able to give pleasure.

 Five

Masel was struck by an idea. It came to him one evening, like some joke brainwave, while munching a bowl of crunchy nut cornflakes at a seat in front of the livingroom window. Sam and Jenny were asleep, and Katy was working late again, although for the first time in a while. Masel crunched his cereal and took measure of himself, happy to discover more than he had expected. His life had somehow been nudged on to an even keel and the whole experience had lent him the feeling of inner peace and contentment. For some reason, at that moment, he remembered the hallucination he'd had in the supermarket, the visions of his father, Zelda, the headless body of his mother, and the rest of them. He looked back on it like some kind of exorcism. He had his doubts about the power of psychological symbols; nevertheless his memory of that incident, as if it were the finale of some great cosmic transformation, was strong. He couldn't deny the fact that it was the phantoms, with all their dark fear visible, real or not, who had fled, and not him. He was rebuilding himself, letting in light, when it came to him that the experience could be used to his advantage, not only spiritually but also professionally. The idea - at first shocking to him - was to make a concert out of it, holographic ghosts, back from the dead, howling silently behind him from a haunted house, a kind of silent, phantom rock opera cum weird fantasy.

He saw his reflection in the window; for a moment he appeared like a child not yet touched by shadows. Outside, nothing moved. Snow lay deep all around the tenement block, boxing it in. Inspired by his thoughts, excited, he considered telephoning Longman at once, but a moment later, lost his nerve. What if he thinks it's a stupid idea? He paced restlessly around the living room, the bowl of cornflakes in his hand. After another moment, he said to himself, "Just pick up the God-damned phone."

Longman's telephone rang and rang. Masel glanced at the clock on the mantelpiece: it was just after eight. Abruptly, there was a click. "Aldous Longman here." The line sputtered. It was his answering machine. "I'm not available at this particular moment," he said - there was righteous indignation in his voice - "and as I'm far too busy to indulge in idle banter, please leave your name and number after the pleep and I'll decide if I want to get back to you or not, as the case may be." Masel nervously waited for the pleep. "Er - it's Masel." Unintentionally, he interjected a dead pause. Silence. Then he spoke to the machine as if he were talking to a foreigner or a very stupid child. "Please phone back when you can. I have something very - well, ghoulish - to tell you. Ha ha! It might be a good idea for the GBH. "

He hung up and continued pacing the living room, the bowl of cornflakes still in his hand. He had a fleeting thought - what if he were to perform this concert, not just for Katy, but for himself? He would have the best of both worlds, success and Katy, in harmony with one another. The jangling of the telephone, a moment later, startled him. He snapped it up, excitedly crunching cornflakes into the receiver.

"My God, what's that?" Longman bellowed down the crackling line. "My boy, are you all right?"

Masel apologized. "I'm chewing. You caught me by surprise." Panic rushed into his chest.

Longman coughed phlegmatically."You sounded like you were about to lay an egg. What's this about something ghoulish?"

In his mind, Masel saw the professor's bloated, red face, darkly blotched under his eyes, his big hand, like a bear paw, around the receiver, his eyebrows arched.

"Well it's like this," he began, "most of the people I imitate are dead, right?" He waited a moment for a response.

"Right." Longman sounded wary.

He hesitated, suddenly unsure of himself and the idea. "Well, suppose the stage is set up like a haunted house."

"Excuse me?"

The American sucked in air and felt himself disheartened.

"Haunted house," Masel repeated nervously. He was now convinced Longman was laughing at him. There was silence. He wiped his forehead with his fingers and, caution shot to the sky, he went on, "Well, you've heard of rock opera, what about a one man and his acoustic guitar opera, but with all the atmosphere and razzamatazz of the big thing? I thought about a haunted house as a back drop, with me and the holographic musicians appearing as ghosts. There could be other sound effects, like howls and wind and rain and thunder and rattling chains, etc. And fog, too."

There was a long, terrifying pause. The line was silent for a long time, and Masel wondered if Longman hadn't dropped off to sleep. He imagined him closing his fat eyelids, shaking his big head. Then he heard what sounded like sad laughter. Masel's heart dropped.

"It was just a thought," Masel added meekly. "I - "

Longman interrupted loudly, booming, "A stupendous idea, my boy, a truly stupendous idea!"

"Really?"

"Really," Longman answered, mocking Masel's accent - it sounded more like "relly" - in a good-humoured way. "Why don't you come over to my house right away, and we can work it out. Sounds like you may have stumbled upon something, my boy." After a moment, in deep baritone, he added, "Seriously."

"I can't," Masel said. "Katy's working late, and Sam and Jenny are here. I can't leave them alone."

"Bring them with you. I'm their old Uncle Aldous. They love me. You've got the car, don't you? It's not that late."

Masel confessed, "I've never driven in snow before. I don't think I can make it."

"Don't be absurd. Of course you can make it. There's no question of it. It's a matter of absolute necessity. You simply have to. It's only down the road. Look out your window. The snow's stopped. You want to be a success, don't you?"

Masel, questioning himself, was unable to deny it. He smiled hopelessly to himself.

"Then do as I say. Come over to my house immediately. The concert is only a few weeks away. I won't hear of this. There is absolutely not a moment to waste," his voice was correct, like an over-zealous army officer. "See you in half an hour, and be snappy."

Longman hung up the phone. The line went dead.

Masel went to the closet and slipped on Katy's big, brown duffel coat. His thoughts made him jump.

* * *

The clouds cracked open and the temperature plummetted. There was a luminous, ghostly aura down the street that seemed to stretch upwards. Masel emerged from the tenement hall, a hooded figure in a white wilderness, to check first that the car would start; no point in waking Sam and Jenny for nothing. There were small bluish-grey drifts of snow about the street, blue under the cold moonlight away from the glow of street lamps. He looked up. A circular pool of clear, starry sky between the low clouds twinkled at him. He thought for a moment what it would be like to be a huge success, a hit, to put on a magnificent show. That was truly what he wanted. But that dream gave way to another. Now he saw himself as stout Scott of the Antarctic ploughing through the white wasteland, a first for the California Kid.

No big deal, he thought, trying to psyche himself up. He was relieved to observe the road had been gritted. He fumbled ham-handedly with the keys in his pocket and then tried the lock. Damn it, the thing was frozen. He couldn't even get the key in. What now? He tried it again, frantically jerking the key back and forth over the icy groove, trying to force it forward. It was frozen solid.

According to his watch, it was now eight-thirty. He was going to be late, not that it mattered. Then he tried the frozen lock once more, without success. "Typical," he said aloud, smiling at himself. He bent down and, rubbing his gloved hands together, breathed a hefty waft of warm breath into the lock in an attempt to thaw it.

A surge of panic shot through him. When he tried to pull

back, he found his lips had iced to the door, as if welded to metal. He was stuck.

He struggled further, but after a moment realised it was pointless. Masel worried he might detach his kisser permanently from his face. I could die here, bleed to death in the snow. His muscles tightened, producing involuntary shivering - so much so his whole body shook. Even that did not free him. A tear froze below his right eye. He tried to call for help, but was only able to call out, "Fegghgghhhhghgghhhhhhhhh!"

A cold wind whipped around his neck.

"Fegghgghhhhghgghhhhhhhhh!" he cried again.

Minutes went by, his heart thumping, his gloved hands braced against the car, his lips severely pained. The air was bitterly cold and thin, as though he were on a high, snow-capped peak. His lips grew colder, icier. It seemed to him, as his frosty nerves pricked through his skin, that he had been stuck to the car for hours. For a moment, he lost track of reality, felt as though he were in the midst of a nightmare, but it came to him harshly that this was no dream. He breathed heftily, attempting to warm the air as it huffed from his mouth on to the lock.

His cold nose half-dripped an icicle. Keep up the blowing, he warned himself. Either that, or wait for spring, or Katy, or morning, or the trappers, which ever came first. How long could a man survive with his face stuck to a frozen car door? God's irony? His own irony? His toes, too, prickled numbly, frost-bitten. He was getting paranoid. He heard the telephone ring, but there was nothing he could do about it. Am I destined to die here? After living through so much, and with so many plans? Like this? Gevalt, why me?

At last he unstuck himself, after pulling and breathing out hot breath for twenty minutes. Because he had had to pull back with such force, some of his skin remained frozen to the lock. Dizzily out of breath, his chest whamming, warm tears began to drip from his eyes. Sensation slowly and painfully came back to his mouth and cheeks. He sprinted up the stairs and into the warm apartment, pained, and lay his head in front of the electric heater for ten minutes.

When Masel looked at himself in the bathroom mirror, he gasped, a tear of pain in his eye. He had ripped off an entire layer of skin. His mouth looked like a raspberry, split and oozing blood. Numbness fell away as pain increased. He squeaked and moaned, sterilising the wounds with alcohol and some ointment he found in the bathroom cabinet.

With a crisscross of band-aids attached to his upper and lower lips, he went down and tried the car again. He thawed the lock this time with hot water. Good thinking, Mr PhD. Careful not to let it freeze again, he quickly stuck the key in and turned it. Thank God, it worked. He turned over the engine and let it idle while he went back in the house to rouse Sam and Jenny. His tongue rubbing stretching band-aids, he dressed the sleeping children in the warmest clothes he could find.

"Where are we going?" asked Jenny, half asleep as Masel lifted her in his arms.

"We're going to see Uncle Aldous," he answered.

"Oh," she said, sniffling twice, then fell asleep on Masel's shoulder, uncaring.

"Whaaah," cried Sam. "I don't want to go."

"Stop whining," Masel told him.

Miraculously, intense at the wheel, Masel was on the icy road. He glanced circumspectly to his right and left, then cagily back at the tenement in the rear-view mirror. Sam slept soundly beneath a mountain of blankets in the back seat. Jenny, strapped in and wrapped in a puffy baby jacket, sweater and Masel's scarf, was conked out in the safety seat beside the boy. The streets were empty.

 Six

He crossed University Avenue against the lights, feeling the frozen slush under his tyres. God help me. There was sheet-ice all over the road and up the concrete pathway to Longman's house - an old black-stoned university house. He bundled himself and the two children up to the front door and knocked.

He was extra careful not to slip with Jenny in his arms. He couldn't quite believe how cold it was. Sam knocked on the door, too, as if for good measure, thumping it hard with his little booted foot.

"Come on, Sam," he asked, smiling nervously, "give me a break, will you? Behave yourself."

Sam giggled and pointed at Masel's aching lips. "Plaster man," he said, laughing good-naturedly. Sam was fully awake now. Who could blame him?

Masel was tensely aware of the silence. No reply. He rang the bell this time. A thin, glass-flute light went on over his head, and Longman, at last, opened the door.

"My boy, you're late, but it's bloody wonderful to see you." The professor moved his hand in the just perceptible suggestion of a wave. He smiled like a frumpish spinster, unexpectedly complimented. He seemed animated tonight. "What happened to your mouth?" His voice had such refinement, Masel didn't quite register the question as a question.

"Er - shaving trouble," Masel answered after a moment. His lips felt puffed-out. Longman either didn't hear him or showed no interest. "Mmm, goodness," he said, his mind otherwise occupied, his hands in mid-air with his own thoughts. He seemed much fatter than the last time Masel had seen him. His face was a drunken wreck of blotches and broken veins. "Come in. Come in," he said, as if just realizing that a man and two children were standing in the bitter cold. "I've been waiting for you. I've got it all worked out." His face jerked in and out of a smile, not quite meeting Masel's eyes.

Masel edged himself and the children into the doorway, and Longman swiftly led them into his study, a disorderly room with an open fireplace, scattered books and an old desk, on which sat his computer. The machine was switched on. Masel was sorry he had come, and berated himself for dragging the kids out on such an unholy night.

"Have a seat," said Longman, indicating the couch with a dismissive-type wave. "Sit by the fire, where it's warm."

"Thanks," Masel said. He was shivering. "Good."

Then, abruptly, before Masel had a chance to move, Longman jerked his attention to the children. "And how are my little cherubs tonight." He pinched at Jenny's cheek enthusiastically and the little girl winced, moodily drawing her head back. With a laugh, he slapped his hand on Sam's head and ruffled his hair. The boy stood passive, oddly well-behaved, probably too tired for anything else.

Masel smiled uncomfortably and put Jenny down at the other end of the couch, where she immediately fell asleep. Sam sat on an adjacent easy chair and also went down easily. Masel put Katy's duffel coat over the boy. The fire was dying. Masel obediently sat on the couch.

"Sure is a wild night out there," he said, as if he were desperately trying to get some stranger's attention.

"So," said Longman, drawing up his wooden desk chair and placing his bulk squarely before the fire, blocking what little heat there was. In one hand he held a large yellow notepad; the other hand moved as if it were under water. "I'm going to make it as simple as possible for you." His eyes flicked onto the yellow pad, referring to it. "It'll involve only an electronic foot switch or two in your department, just to keep some of the sound effects in synchronization with the music. I can control all the other sounds, laser projections and holograms, etcetera, with my computer. The biggest problem is to stage the haunted-house set in such a way that the holograms appear to be freely moving - but I'm working on it."

Longman laughed explosively. He showed Masel a diagram he'd drawn on the pad; it looked like the Allied invasion of the Normandy beaches, long penciled arrows here and there sweeping around from opposite sides, meeting and crossing each other.

"That's the way it works. I've got it all worked out. Piece of cake, my boy," Longman said. Masel bent forward to take a look and pulled his lower lip in puzzlement. He remained shtume.

A cat appeared through the door, its white head tipped towards its ginger body, and decided to settle sulkily not far from Masel, by the lowly-burning fire. Longman ignored it, sucking furiously on his pipe. Masel waited, his heart thumping. "What do you think?" Longman asked eventually. "Are you fit for it?"

Masel, playing with his ponytail, put on an expression of unconcern. He saw himself triumphant amid billowing blasts of dry ice, his holographic ghost band behind him, Masel himself a holographic ghost, a dead rock star back for a visit with heavenly chums. Behind him, a haunted house creaked and rattled to the sound of cracking whips and twisting chains.

"Did you hear me?" Longman asked.

"I heard you. You can do this?"

Longman shuffled his feet together, slowly. He laughed faintly to himself. "The big question is: can you? I've been hearing one or two disturbing things about your state of mind lately." He rolled his eyes between Masel and Sam, who was still asleep in the chair, "Put it this way," he said, his eyes suddenly concentrating on some point above Masel's head, like the double-barrel of a shotgun aimed at geese. "We don't want another episode like the EPI Centre, do we now? It was a good thing that Katy got us good press, or I would have had to pay the university back for all the holographic film that was destroyed. I would have lost a fortune."

Masel slightly reddened. He stood up, needing to pace, but sat back down. His mind snagged on Longman's laugh.

"It wasn't my fault."

"Come, come, my boy, let's not dwell on the past. Bygones must bebygones. I'm much more interested in the future."

"Me, too ," Masel said, flatly. "I know it was my idea, but now that you describe it in practical terms, maybe...well, maybe it's just too complicated. It sounds like too many things can go wrong. It sounds like I mifgt get electrocuted. Maybe I should stick to just playing my guitar."

"Nonsense," Longman bellowed sharply, suddenly excited, his voice abruptly a notch higher. "This will be the most stupendous and tremendous thing you've ever seen. Nobody will have ever seen anything like it before." Blood stung Masel's cheeks. Longman went on, "Your name will be remembered along with those in the annals of performance history, forever. It'll be one of those classic concerts. I'm even going to arrange to have it filmed."

Longman chuckled heartily. Then, solemnly, he looked down at his big hands, as though he were just noticing they were empty. He went to the table, where he had left a half-drunk bottle of beer and took a large, greedy swallow, the cords of his neck pumping as if he were about to retch. "Think big, my boy, that's the secret," he said. "This is on a grand scale. You'll be famous. Just remember to sing Auld Lang Syne when the clock strikes twelve and press a couple of foot-switches, and everything will be just fine and dandy."

Masel forcefully blew out a breath, as if he had been holding it for the last half hour. Neither Sam nor Jenny had moved a muscle since closing their eyes just after arriving. The cat was now scratching at the door, its head lowered contemplatively, like a man who had just been sentenced to death.

Masel reflected solemnly for a moment, his fingers lightly rubbing the band-aids on his pained lips. It would be a good thing to do, he thought, even a great thing to do. My one chance, he thought. Take a risk. A nervous reverie of stardom hovered trickily in his mind.

"I guess that's it ,then," he said.

"Wonderful, my boy," said Longman. He coughed, finishing off the dregs of the beer in his glass. "Now perhaps you might do me a small favour, just on your way home."

"Depends," said Masel.

Longman stood up and nimbly manoeuvred his weight from one toe to the other, like some joke-ballerina. "I was hoping you could drop me at Strathclyde University, just so I can get the ball rolling right away. Difficult to get a taxi on a night like this, you understand." Longman briefly closed his eyes then snapped them open again. He was grinning. "I'm going to run the haunted house past a friend of mine there, and see if we can't iron out a few technical points."

Masel gathered the sleepy children.

***

Snow began to fall again, and it swept wildly into the headlights of the car, making it difficult for Masel to see exactly where he was going. Longman sat bulkily in the passenger seat, lazily sucking his pipe, his eyes reflectively lost. The streets were deserted and white. Masel watched his own clownish reflection in the windshield and lost himself in a fantasy. He saw the ghost show in his mind, he, triumphant at the front of the stage. The image was as clear as one of those dread-filled moments in a dream. The expectant stage set in dim mist, shining in sudden light, then a scream, a dead rock idol rising, his own living voice...as if back from the grave...the cheers...He suddenly remembered Longman in the passenger seat.

Masel shivered. "I can't quite come to grips with how cold it gets here. It feels like I'm in the middle of an ice age. I don't think I've warmed up in the past six months."

"I thought you were trapped inside a sleeping bag last August. How about that for starters? It must have been bloody warm in there, and during that heat wave, too."

Masel frowned. "Well, lately, I mean."

"Try it at seven-am," Longman said, sticking his chin out. "It was so cold walking down University Avenue this morning I didn't know whether to hold on to my hat or hold on to my bloody ears. I blame global warming, myself, pollution, weather patterns completely cock-eyed. I can't remember when we last had a winter this early or this bloody severe."

"Weird," said Masel. For a moment, he feared for the future of the planet, for Sam and Jenny and for the children he might himself someday have.

Longman cranked around in the seat. "Tell me this, does Katy know about your ghosts?"

"She's working late tonight."

"That's handy."

The snow now seemed to be coming at the car from every direction. "What do you mean by that?"

"Well, my boy, you've been here so long, I keep forgetting you're not a local. The district council building is just around the corner from the University of Strathclyde. I presume you'll be collecting her. It's most unlikely she'll get a hackney at this time of night and in this weather. Piece of nonsense really."

"I'm not even sure she'll still be there at this time. She's probably gone home by now. Anyway how would I get in. The place will be all locked up."

Longman shook his head sadly, as if depressed by the difficulty. Then, abruptly, he said, "I have a key to the back door. Katy gave me her spare in case of emergency, rather fortuitous, wouldn't you say?" Longman held the key in front of Masel's nose.

Masel smiled. "Thanks." He took the key and slipped it into his coat pocket.

"Just here will do nicely," Longman said, pushing his open hands forward in the air, in a braking motion.

He let Longman out at the Strathclyde student union bar and did a U-turn on the snowy street. In his mirror, he saw the professor, like an old hippopotamus, clump through the snow.

At George Square, the headquarters of Glasgow District Council rose up through the blizzard like an ice palace, glistening magically like some multi-edged diamond against the Christmas lights across the street. He parked the car, and feeling in his pocket for Longman's key, entered the building quickly at the rear.

"Hurry up, kids," he said, guiltily. "It's time to go see mommy."

* * *

The place smelled pungently of cleaning fluid. Nothing stirred. It was as dark as a tomb. Masel bit his lip. He climbed the empty stairs, Sam clinging to his right hand, passive from exhaustion. Jenny was asleep in his other arm. When they reached the third floor, the lights were off in Katy's office.

I knew it, he thought, I've missed her. He was about to turn and leave, when, along the corridor, he saw a yellow streak of light under the door of another office. He looked down at his watch - nearly ten-thirty. For some reason, his heart thumped in alarm. He scratched his beard.

"Hurry it up," he whispered to Sam, but Sam was lagging behind. He moved Jenny from his left to his right arm without disturbing her, and she breathed gently into his hot ear. Masel crept silently along the corridor, until he stood half in and half out of a dark, glass reception area. He had been here before, but only once, several months ago. He barely recognized it. He looked again at the yellow streak of light; it seemed alien to him, as if from another planet. Masel's heart raced. Then he looked at the metal nameplate on the wooden door. Gevalt, it was George MacGregor's office - the last person in the world he wanted to see at this moment.

He was ready to retreat when, suddenly, he heard something. What was that? Then he heard it again; it was the faintest hint of a woman's voice. For some reason, panic fired up in him. He froze where he stood, then moved slowly, without a sound, towards MacGregor's door, all his senses jangling. He felt his pounding heart through his whiskered cheek.

Masel stood crooked forward; he couldn't decide whether to knock or just ignore it and walk away. What did MacGregor's business have to do with him anyway? He looked back at Sam, leaning against the wall, ten feet behind him, his eyes closed. Jenny was sound asleep, her head flopped on Masel's shoulder. Masel stood immobile, stiff, his fingers frozen around the door knob, his head close to the cold wood. The stillness came to him like a drowning sensation.

He looked behind him again, but saw nothing unusual. Why should there be? His constricted throat throbbed.

Then, from behind the door, he heard the voice again, like a hushed whisper. Masel felt a tingling sensation, like rising fear, in his chest. At the same instant, impulsively, he turned the door handle and, nudging the door open just a crack, peered in.

His pounding heart beat the breath out of him. With a gasp, he grabbed Sam by the arm, and, his heart whamming, galloped wildly from the building, his face twisted, his head shaking almost spasmodically.

* * *

Jenny began to cry when Masel put her in the car. He yelled at her through his constricted throat, but apologized a moment later. There was enough ill-feeling in this world without him adding to it, he informed her. She looked at him and salivated from the side of her mouth. Masel, his head spinning, gunned the engine and took off.

Then, as if from some sudden whirlpool in the forepart of his brain, he cringed and winced, nearly crying, at the recollection of Katy looking into his dark eyes, past MacGregor's greasy head, over his bare, dandfruffed shoulder. Her eyes had been passive. Momentarily, he struggled to keep the car on the white, snowy road. Perhaps she had been too shocked herself in that moment to show alarm. The image seared itself, like some burning, intricate photograph, in his mind; he had observed her on the couch, half laying over MacGregor's chest, buffering him, her arm around his hairy neck, his nose in her bosom. What was this web he had spun, apparently by accident? How can such a thing be? What fish had he hooked? Himself? Them? You're a complete jerk, Masel. God help me.

Both Sam and Jenny were crying now. He didn't notice. Nor did he notice Longman's light on, or the professor's fat, sullen face at the window as he skidded over the lumpy mounds of fresh snow past his house. Sam began to cry and, in all his anger and embarrassment, he realized Katy couldn't have possibly recognized him, stooped as he was in the dark hallway, more or less invisible through a half-an-inch crack of light.

The Farewell

One

CUCKOLDED, grieving, punishingly hungover, Masel endured well but suffered badly. He lay half-unconscious on the bed of a hotel room - which particular hotel, he had at this point no idea - his hands clinging to his face in misery, so sunk in despair he could hardly take a breath. It was snowing again, and its bloom lighted up the wall paper with silvery glints and dull greyish lines, chillingly sharpening the room's angles and curves. A fog had pounced in the street below him, the wallowing, lowly-hunched ghost of an old woman, extending itself like tentacles, the long, white arms of a blind man, seemed to seep into the room. Lost weekend on a Tuesday night, eh Masel? he berated himself not without sarcasm. Another one. He shook his head, as if straining to pierce the room's silence, its mask, and found with not exactly much surprise his tongue amiss. A church bell peeled very faintly, far away. In his ears rang a grinding hum, a kind of grating, sickening sound that seemed to come from inside his own head. "Gevalt! What the hell is that?" He turned sharply as if there might be someone else in the room. He knew he was alone. My life will end in disaster. Masel, you old devil, who are you kidding? My life already is a disaster. He felt more alone than he could remember ever having been. It seemed, for an instant, as if time had halted and all the misery on earth was just one great illusion. The roof of his mouth felt like the rear end of a vulture - his own analogy. The snow turned to thick, dirty rain, pelting the window like a veil. He shut his eyes, saw Katy, her collar open, low, saw the dark curve of her breasts beneath her white blouse. When she glanced up and saw she was being watched, a paleness came to her cheeks and she raised one hand instinctively to her throat. Masel shifted his gaze, snapped open his eyelids, pushed to the final humiliation, abruptly died.

The failed husband and performer cheerlessly blew his nose and felt the aftermath of a dyspeptic headache he must have had while he was asleep. He cursed the gassy Scottish beer, rose from the bed and, stomping on an empty whisky bottle, tumbled head over heels into his Gizmo D25. He was still slightly drunk. The instrument thudded on to his crown, clanging horribly out of tune as it assaulted him. The guitar is a Jewish animal, he moaned to himself. Clawing at the telephone wire, he raised himself, and carefully placed the Gizmo in its case, then on the bed, as if to sleep, before hastening to the bathroom to relieve himself. The nagging noise in his ears continued and caused him to vomit after he had urinated, the crushing weight of self-disgust upon him. Blood bolted to his face. The bump on his head didn't help.

He closed his eyes again and leaned back against the bathroom wall; none of it could be true. Are you trying to kill yourself? He felt as though he were at the top of some isolated mountain, waiting for an unknown visitor. Struggling against thought, memories flushedthrough him. He thought of Zelda, of Katy, of his own lonely childhood, of his father, widowed at thirty years with the birth of his only son, him, Elliot, then dead eight years later; a Talmudic scholar, paralysed by sorrow, turned to excessive quantities of wine, then, near the end, Scotch whisky. Masel's first connection with Scotland. Had his father hated him for the death of his mother? Was that why he had come here? Some ridiculous perversion in his subconscious that in the end could only result in sorrow. Can a son be blamed for the actions of his father, the death of his mother? Masel remembered how, through the barely perceptible crack in his ajar bedroom door, he would look into the kitchen to observe late at night a sad figure hunched at the table, mixing the Scoth poison with milk. Tears smarted in his eyes. He punched himself in the forehead to break the reverie. A car crept through the snowy street below his window, crushing and smashing the frozen slush beneath its tyres. Then shame - life's only enduring sentiment - came at him, bursting inside him, like a mushroom cloud. He put his hands to his face, fighting his own urge to break things, smash free from this horrifying circle of sorrow and failure. What did it all amount to? What did any of it mean? Where was he ever going? It was a cruel delusion, nothing more than a pipe dream, so ridiculous it was comical. What is life? He had fought entropy, but in the end, he knew, entropy must win. Chaos must inevitably triumph over order. That's the nature of life. But it was the struggle that counted, and the struggle was everything, the essence of life itself; there was no time for anything else; beginnings and endings were of no consequence, goals and aspirations useless, except as a reason for the struggle. Masel didn't exactly feel heroic at that moment, but then there was that absurd half-buzzing, half-melodic noise in his mind. He flushed the toilet and went back to bed. He felt old, like his father, sick.

"Now I've done it," he groaned, coughing feebly, his mind beclouded.

Because Masel listened, he heard. It wasn't exactly the symphony of the spheres; it was more like someone had poured a whirring wind into his ears, a toilet flushing in his forehead. Delerium tremens? It began to torment him, was now all around him, seemed to enter the room by way of himself. Through the thrumming, he recollected jumbled thoughts, vague memories confused with fantasy, terrifying revelations he at first refused to acknowledge. He went over and over them in his mind. A man can do terrifying things to this world, he thought, but the world can also do terrifying things to him.

Masel lay very still on the bed. He recalled checking into the hotel. He also recalled the blue-white curve of the receptionist's breasts, her pale stomach. Then he stopped himself, his eyelids trembling. What did he do to the receptionist? Perhaps he had imagined it. Oh, God, he hoped so. Then it came to him how he had sat with the lights out, waiting for Katy, feeling sorry for himself, not knowing what to do, dreading the moment he would hear her key scrape in the lock, breaking the spell. Traffic rumbled lowly in the street and his courage waned. He carefully packed his Gizmo D25 in its case, took with him a few items of clothing, including Katy's duffel coat, and wrote her a shaky note. He told her he was leaving Sam and Jenny with the next door neighbour, and that he needed to be alone the two weeks before the concert. He signed off "Love, Elliot", but then crossed out "Love".

His black ponytail and beard brilliant against the snowy street, Katy's duffel coat on his back, he left for the nearest hotel. What the hell, he could afford to spend money now. And what did he have to lose? Now, as then, as hard as he tried, Masel was unable to subtract nothing from nothing. Flashes of memory continued to pound his insides.

That Jews had always lived under emergency conditions gave him small consolation. When you're hungry, sing, he advised himself; when you're in pain, laugh. I'm too young to live on memories; too old for a leather jacket, too young for a cardigan. He blamed love for his pain, but laughed badly. He rose again and went to the bathroom. He tried to throw up, but this time could only retch. He peered at his face in the bathroom mirror, gazing into his befuddled eyes; that they were open to the self anguished him. No masks; Masel was wide open.

Beneath the wretched, irritating sound, Masel thought he heard a faint, surprising melody. He returned to bed and threw his face into the pillow. He listened until his ears ached. The whine renewed itself as the melody diminished. He punished himself with Yiddish insults, was pained to discover that after all he was still deeply in love with Katy, in spite of everything, including the fact that he was no longer sure she loved him.

"What a fool I am, if only...if only."

Then the noise began to transform itself; or the underlying melody, if that was what it was, began to override it. In the midst of his suffering, while dragging on an old half-smoked butt, Masel discovered a moment of freedom. Ach! it was the aspiration of slaves. Yet, while trying to unleash what refused to let go, to put out of his mind what was apparently riveted to his cranium, Masel's pain nervously gave way to inspiration. In his mind, there lay, like slowly cracking ice, a foggy, wavering, sixteen-bar blues.

Masel lifted his Gizmo out of its case, as though he was

lifting a little girl out of her crib. He embraced the instrument, caressing it, its delicate curved shell against his heart. With a shock, he remembered the sight of Katy and MacGregor sprawled majestically on the office couch. He saw it clearer than it was, slowed down, like an old movie. He saw the look on Katy's face. His ears burned as he recalled the sweating holographic helmets. Perched on the edge of the bed, he strummed out his pain to a sad, passionate rhythm, picking out notes, his fingers fluttering as if singing. Masel felt the Gizmo's vibration rise through his flesh to his head. It was as if the instrument he played, played him. It rang with shocking clarity.

Hurriedly, his blood rising again and again to his brain, like a grey-black sea monster, he began to scribble notes on a brown paper bag. The words came every which way. At first it was jumbled poetry, garbled grunts, cliches, things that almost took wing - a title like Why Am I So Stupid - but not quite. Then the ugly noise began to rise again, reverberating in his head like steel wires. He scribbled furiously, doubt lingering, constantly thinking yes then no then yes again. In desperation, Masel wondered if he should have taken up the flute or the tuba.

He crouched over the instrument, playing somberly, passionately, as if drawing a sexual melody from it. This world is an illusion. The real world is hidden behind veils and masks of symptoms. In elongated staccato bursts of rhythm, he continued strumming and the noise subsided, struggled upwards, became articulated, simplified, directed and then, at last, transmogrified itself into song:

My baby, she don't love me/ Oy oy oyoyoyoy-yoy.../ My baby, she don't love me/ Oy oy oyoyoyoy-yoy.../ Because I've got the oy gevalt blues/ Oy gevalt, what am I going to do?

Katy's blatant rejection of him weighed like a sick, dying animal around his neck, as did his pip-squeak cowardice. In truth, what he really wanted was to forgive her, but he had seen her with his own eyes. Yet, on the other hand, he already had one ex-wife; he didn't need another. He pushed himself from within to extract another verse, but instead he produced a strained bridge to the song. He suffered physically the Oy

Gevalt Blues, took it personally.

I've been sleeping in the park, baby/ Because of my love for you/ and I feel like a shlemasel/ Probably 'cause you're a shiksa, too/ I've got the oy gevalt blues/ And it's the worst blues you can use.
Exasperated, suffering heftily for having shovelled punishment upon punishment, he gave it up, crumpling his lyric sheet and pitching it at the wall. I'm a useless prick.

He put down his guitar with agitation, sucked in air and head-butted the mattress. Groaning, Masel cursed his weak, half-hearted, half-assed talent, his face engulfed in a pillowfull of suffering. The noise roared up like a tornado, hissing like a giant lizard in his ears, increased in volume, grew unbearable. It helped only when he strummed and, as he slowly strummed, the melody ascended. With bowed head, Masel, as if famished for the very notes themselves, listened to himself and played on, obliterating the whine, transforming it into harmony. He played as though he were conversing with God. To his favourite flat minor ninth, he forced out a crooning cadenza:

My name is Masel/ Not Shlemasel/ Oh yeah!/ My name is Masel/ Not Shlemasel/ Oh yeah!
He scribbled furiously, vigorously, until, by mid morning, the Oy Gevalt Blues was at last complete. He lay back on the bed, his guitar at his side. Abruptly, a vast rush of cosmic feedback assailed his ears and fell away into a hushing quietness. Masel passed out.

* * *

The blizzard continued and stung his anguish. The snow stopped, and turned itself into a thick, grey rain. Christmas Eve came and went, and then Christmas Day. Never in his life had he experienced anything so terrible. "So be it," he said to himself, shuddering through a shaky version of Dylan's Love Is Just a Four-Letter Word, "Not long to the GBH now." Although his heart told him to get on the first plane out, the promise of fame continued to beckon him, as did his sorrow over Katy. What choices did he have?

By December 26, Masel, feeling boxed in in the small

hotel room, had given up his repertoire rehearsals for the GBH. The very act of playing the guitar had become a constant reminder of Katy and all his troubles. Instead, he sipped whisky alone and walked the winter west end, collecting butts and, with hyperbolic zeal, avoiding Bowmont Terrace. The temperature plummetted and more snow fell. It came down like a curtain. Gizmoless, Masel found he could go hours without thinking about her. Other things occupied his mind: the grey, winter fog in San Francisco Bay, escape. Then he thought of Zelda, depressed. Watch out, he warned himself, you've still got to live in this world. Therefore, one afternoon, while standing at the hotel cocktail bar, when he saw Katy swoop through the revolving doors with MacGregor, Masel hastily took flight through the kitchen. Knocking over a cauldron of soup de jour and a waiter with trays, he left by the back. A cook shook an angry meat cleaver in the air, but Masel was gone.

He trembled, panting. "Oy gevalt," he murmured, his heart hammering. I've got to get out of here. As he hurried on to Byres Road, he slipped on his ass in a frozen puddle. His tail bone and spirit equally bruised, Masel hailed a black hackney.

"Where to?" the driver asked.

Because he could think of nowhere else, he gave Aldous Longman's address. The haunted house concert at the GBH was looming and was a legitimate enough excuse for a visit. It was also possible that Longman might know something about Katy, or at least of Katy's reaction to his running out, if that's what it was. Did she see him that night? Did she even miss him? He shook it from his mind. He had had enough of wandering aimlessly around the neighbourhood.

The driver nodded. "Do I know your face?"

"I doubt it."

The driver eyed him in the mirror. "That's not a Glasgow accent. Where do you come from?"

"San Francisco."

The driver gazed at him intently. After a moment, he asked, "Are you not Elliot Masel?"

Masel denied it. "Just a tourist."

The snow lay deep on the streets and the cab sludged carefully through it, as if blind.

"He's a real nutter, eh?"

"Who?"

"That Masel fellow."

"I'm sorry. I don't know him."

"Well, anyone who roams about the Botanic Gardens half-naked for weeks on end needs a check up from the neck up in my book." The driver eyed him warily. "You know you're his spitting image."

Masel smiled nervously. I'm a prisoner of my own history. For good or ill, flight from oppression was his only answer, the only problem was that it was he who oppressed himself. Where do you run to now, Masel, eh?

The cab felt it's way slowly along University Avenue. Masel battled to lift himself above his unhappiness but, failing, began to weep. Get a grip of yourself, he thought, his teeth clenched determinedly. The show must go on, and so must I. A man has to construct his own freedom. He based this point of view on revelation and tradition.

The taxi drew up before Longman's house. He considered opening his heart to Longman about Katy, but after inventing and discarding several strategies, decided to keep to the business at hand. In his excitement, he slipped the driver a ten-pound note. The fare was one-seventy.

■ Two

"Come in. It's open," Longman called from a distance. His voice was thin and resonantly high.

Masel opened the front door, and through the dimness of the professor's cluttered hallway, made his way through another door, which he remembered from the last time, passed into the livingroom. Masel's mind was in turmoil. He was surprised to discover he had walked into a cupboard. He knocked his head on an ironing board, and found the right door across the hall.

Longman turned sideways at his desk, his computer before him, adjacent to a half-drunk bottle of Scotch and some crushed beer cans, his greying, red hair unkempt. He was dressed in his shabby, black teaching suit, and the legs of his steel-rimmed glasses cut into the sides of his big face. The room was ice-cold. Suddenly, Longman shot his head upright, his eyes bloodshot, yellow, dead-looking flecks at the edges.

"Masel," he said, surprised to see him. "It's you." An expression of pain came to his face that, a moment later, eased, save square, clenched teeth that might have suggested distaste.

"You all right?" Masel asked.

Longman laughed, as if disgusted by the question. The colour of the room was golden with lamplight and the reflection of snow; Masel's own colour heightened. The place was full of sounds - the ticking clock on the mantelpiece, the airy buzz of his computer, the hiss of an almost-dead wood fire, Longman's deep intakes of breath, like monstrous dignity. Masel waited for him to speak, bent forward, off balance, but nothing.

"I thought I'd drop by," Masel broke in, dipping his hands into the duffel coat pockets and then pulling them out again. "Just to see how things are going." He shrugged warily.

Longman still said nothing, save a hiccough, his eyes sliding up toward Masel, then away.

"The haunted house?" Masel feared the worst; everything he'd hoped for was down the stank.

Longman poured more whisky into a glass and drank it. His legs shuffled uneasily under the desk. "Have a Milwaulkee beer," he said at last.

"No thanks."

"A goldy?" He pointed to the whisky.

"Nothing. I can't stay."

"Suit yourself," he said, curtly, with irritation, and quickly tapped something into the computer. "That's the trouble with Americans."

For some reason, Masel got the impression of the lion without courage in the Wizard of Oz. He cleared his throat, "So how are the holograms working out?"

"Everything's set," he said.

Masel's chest fluttered. "And the haunted house?"

"Everything's set. I told you." His eyes darted up at Masel. "So where have you been hiding? I thought you were Katy."

Masel's face flushed. "Have you seen Katy?"

Longman's face darkened and he pointed to an old wooden chair opposite him. "Sit."

Obedient, Masel sat, slightly shivering in the cold room. Longman's eyes flashed as he poured himself another drink. "I saw her this morning," he said. "She's been looking for you. You're making a habit of this disappearing business. Once, I would say, is bad luck; twice looks like a pattern."

All at once he was awash with guilt. It took him several seconds to breath. "I've left her," he blurted out, unable to help himself. He could hardly believe the words. I'm in for it now, he thought. He searched his pockets for a butt, but found none. He remembered he was wearing Katy's coat. Her perfumed scent had remained on the collar and was now assailing Masel's nostrils.

Longman looked away. He took a handkerchief from the breast pocket of his black jacket and wiped sweat droplets from his forehead. "It's the whisky," he said.

Masel noticed a painting of small naked children in green grass, on the alcoved wall askance from the fireplace. "It's my nature," he said after a moment. "These things never work out for me. I'm the sort of guy who falls on his back and breaks his nose, remember?" He laughed enthusiastically, but then stopped.

Longman nodded solemnly, drinking the whisky in one gulp and warily stood up and sat back down. His big-pupiled eyes were staring now. He drew in a breath and his expression became deathly.

"I know why you've come," Longman said, suddenly.

"Eh?" Masel uncurled a smile, pulling nervously at his bottom lip. "Has Katy said something to you?"

Longman gave no reply, his eyes remained transfixed on

Masel. He took another gulp of whisky, finishing it, and hung his head, his huge chin doubling. A groan came from deep in his throat. He pounded his fist on the desk. A sad chortle made his feet jerk. Abruptly, he knocked his empty glass from the table with the back of his hand, and it smashed.

"Crazy bastard," he said, shaking his head.

"Excuse me?" asked Masel. His face stung with colour. He feared violence. He sat motionless, his heart thudding.

Longman continued shaking his head, slowly lowering it. With a gasp, his eyes looking up, bulging like boiled eggs, his huge face purple, he grabbed Masel by the wrist.

"I set you up, my boy." Masel gently tried to pull back, but Longman had him in a grip. "I'm deeply sorry." Big tears filled Longman's eyes. "Please. I have to tell you. Listen to me."

A pain shot into Masel's shoulder and he jerked his arm free. Longman, his chest heaving, drew back in fright. Masel gazed at him in terror, not exactly sure what was going on. "Gevalt," he whispered. "I'm a pacifist."

Tears began to fill Longman's big eyes. "That night when you brought Sam and Jenny, I set you up. I knew Katy was up there with MacGregor." Longman's lips trembled, twisted. "I can't tell you how thoroughly ashamed I am."

Adrenalin crackled in Masel's brain. He jumped up from his seat, knocking it back behind him. "Son of a bitch." He wanted to flee, to hide somewhere, but remained rooted. In a rare rage, he glared at Longman in hatred, wishing on him terrifying punishment.

Longman spoke in a solemn, yet almost-theatrical way. "She seduces you, doesn't she?"

Masel hadn't the courage to deny it. "What's it got to do with you?"

"It's all my fault." Longman's eyes squeezed out tears that rolled down his fat cheeks.

"Oy vey," said Masel. "Bullshit."

Longman spoke determinedly. "You don't understand. I am her step-father, her mother's second husband. One night, Katy was thirteen, I'd come back from a university conference.

I was drunk, you understand, and it was late, and I was alone in the house with her." He stopped, momentarily. His hands shook; otherwise, his large frame was motionless. "Let's say I...interfered with her." He wept dramatically, almost howling.

Masel couldn't at once comprehend what he was hearing. Yet, as he reflected, he began to believe. He looked again at the painting on the wall and felt the urge to strike out. But looking at Longman's huge visage, blotchy and red, he found himself fighting the impulse to violence, almost pitying him.

"I paid for it," Longman went on, coughing and loosening his collar, his eyes miserably darting around the room, then back at Masel. "I was in prison for sixteen months. Believe me when I tell you I lost everything. My job and my family."

"You deserved worse."

"I don't deny it. When I got out, I didn't see Katy for ten years. Then when I did, I told her I would do anything to make up to her for what I had done. The guilt, you understand, is overwhelming." He was holding his chest now, breathing heavily, as if he were about to have a heart attack. A sad, horrifying groan, a sustained lament, rose up from the base of his gut. "You see, she uses me the same way she uses you. She prays on our weaknesses. But Katy, Sam and Jenny are all I have left. That's the worst of it."

"What do you mean by that?"

Longman hung his big head, sunk in gloom. "Sam and Jenny are my children."

Masel felt a knot grip his stomach. He almost rushed the man, but checked it. "I don't believe it."

"I'm afraid it's the truth. It hurts me that they don't know. That's the reason I set you up, I know that after this concert you'll take them to California with you. How could I let you take them away from me? I was against you from the very beginning; you were a stupid San Francisco Jewboy."

"I don't have to stand here and listen to this." Masel half-turned to exit.

"Do you know Katy picked the wrong Masel on purpose." He turned back. "What?"

"The real Masel, or Madel, I think his name was, was too expensive. You came cheap, my boy. But I was tied to Katy. I had to do my best for her at the EPI Centre. Otherwise, I would have finished you off there and then. I saw how attracted to you she was that morning. It broke my heart. You were the wrong man in the wrong place from every point of view."

Masel glared at him in hatred, his fists clenched. Moving the family to California was news to him. Poor Sam, he thought, poor Jenny, even a bad match can beget good children. Sadly, he thought also of Katy. What future did they have now? All hope was gone.

Masel went to the door. "I'm getting out of here."

Sea-grey streaks lined Longman's cheeks. "You don't understand, I'm telling you all this because I'm to blame. I made Katy the way she is, I raped her when she was a child. I made her grow up ruthless and manipulative. I supplied her with a lifetime of misery, and much more. Think for a moment. What life has she had?"

"I don't believe a word of this. You're a liar."

"Sadly, my boy, it's the truth."

"Don't 'my boy' me." Masel slowly became aware of dry lips. "I can't think of one good reason why I should believe a word you're saying. For instance, why this sudden reversal?"

"Because I'm guilty. Can't you understand that? I can't carry it with me any longer. That's the bloody irony of the whole sordid business."

Masel glared at him with disgust. He licked his lips. "What's that supposed to mean?"

"It means the GBH concert must be a success. It's the only chance any of us have for happiness. Take Katy and the children to California with you. You can do it. Take them away to be happy and free of me. It'll be my exorcism."

"You don't deserve an exorcism," Masel said. Everybody wants an exorcism, he thought. He felt shipwrecked, confused. He hurried dizzily from the house, not knowing what to think or do, his hot breath clinging to him like a cloud of insects.

"What about the GBH, my haunted house?" Longman

called after him, wiping his bulbous eyes.

Five minutes later, after marching angrily around the snowy block, it came to Masel he was chopping off his nose to spite his face. His heart banging, he returned, kicking open the livingroom door as though he were entering a cowboy saloon.

Masel stood, a shadowed figure in the door frame. "Be there on the night," he warned.

Longman promised faithfully, weeping. Masel wanted never to see him again.

He fled through the snow.

■Three

Large, wet snow flakes fell lazily about the street lamps, casting a pale, powdery orange aura in the darkness. The shadows seemed to rise up around him. The air was bitterly cold. No moon. Hogmanay revellers appeared, drunken, loud, and then disappeared like ghosts in the snow and mist. With a wavering voice, his Gizmo upright in its case by his side, Masel telephoned Katy at the GBH by way of a call box around the corner - fifteen minutes before he was due to appear on stage.

"Elliot," she demanded. "Where the hell have you been?" Then she said, "Don't dare do this to me tonight. You know how important this night is to us."

"Who's doing?" Masel asked, suppressing terror. He blew white breath on to his hands.

"You," she said.

"Not me." He stabbed his shoulder accidently, by leaning over into a sharp icicle that hung inside the telephone box. "I'm doing my best. I'll be there as soon as I can."

"Well hurry," she hissed. Her voice echoed in his head, and he felt himself giving in. Was he going mad? He considered the question carefully. It was a distinct possibility.

"Got to go," he said quickly and, conscious of his chattering, trembling teeth, hung up.

Now I'm going to give her a taste of her own medicine.

Masel attempted to use delay tactics. He sauntered across the street into a crowded, windowless bistro. In the corner, a folk band were strumming out Van Morrison's Brown Eyed Girl - nearly a three-decade-old song. Masel wondered if the Oy Gevalt Blues would be around thirty years from now. He doubted it would last thirty days. He stood at the end of the bar and sipped a beer as slowly as he could, but succeeded only in exacerbating his nervousness.

Broken up, he wept into his glass, surprising himself.

The bartender gravely nodded. "Out."

Masel rose without finishing his beer. He heard someone behind him call, " Isn't that Elliot Masel?" He hurried into the street, miserable.

After a moment, he found his bearings and jogged around the corner to the GBH. The eerie winter street light stalked him closely. He squeaked under his breath, "Now I'm in for it." Deep, black cloud bellies deposited powdery snow flakes on his head and whiskers. "Gevalt," he groaned. He didn't want to see anyone; just wanted to do the show, get paid and get out. No complications, please God, he pleaded.

* * *

At the back entrance to the concert hall, after a minor altercation with a security guard, who didn't recognize him, Masel ascended the dark stairway. It was warm inside. He hastened in sneakers along a short, dimly-lit, timber corridor, one arm extended a little, and knocked his head on the glass casing around a fire axe. Damn it, he thought, holding a throbbing temple, a bad omen. He could smell new paint on the walls. Mentally, he was hyped up, but he was physically exhausted. He felt as though he hadn't slept for days. He remembered with disgust the painting on Longman's wall. Then he remembered Longman's words: It's the only chance any of us have for happiness. What chance do I have? he asked himself. What good could possibly come from any of this.

It was strangely quiet back stage. Everyone was in position. The heat was intense. He made his way to a thick sweating curtain and, pulling it to the side slightly, gaped in terror.

Longman's dramatic set was in clear view; black windows, grey boards, a picket fence; the home of rock music's living dead. At the front of the stage, he nervously observed the holographic helmets on a black table, each one name-tagged. Then he saw the flashing red lights of Longman's foot-switches.

He could see the crowd now; a huge mass of people, packed into a place three or four times the size of the EPI Centre. This was it; no way back now, only forward. The king of the hill on top of the heap. He removed Katy's duffel coat, revealing tight black trousers and the tattered jacket of his blue flannel suit. Then he unpacked his guitar, slipped on his old Californian sun-glasses and, briskly putting his hand through his hair, walked onto the stage.

Rapturous applause rushed at him, like the roar of a dragon, stunned him. He made his way to a microphone stand and, looking above and behind him, saw Katy at the light controls. She gave him a nervous wave and Masel, in reply, nodded, his throat on fire. He felt like a clown, a buffoonish imitation, but remembered that that was what the crowd had come for. He rested his hand on the microphone, and the silence thickened heavily. He tried to speak into it, but there was no sound. Gevalt, what now? The attentiveness of the crowd astounded him. He remembered after a moment to switch it on.

"Hi," he called, coolly smiling. Katy's spotlight bathed him. His voice echoed through the speakers and bounced from the black walls.

More applause came at him. Ping! The spotlight went off. Masel staggered in the darkness. He wound his way to the table, nearly falling off the stage at one point, but not, and picked out the John Lennon helmet, his ears burning almost immediately. Cautiously, he placed it over his head. He closed his eyes and strummed to a slow, steady, almost dirge-like, four-four rhythm.

Ping! The light flipped on again, flooding him in a white waterfall. The haunted house remained blackened behind him.

Someone in the crowd whistled; another one shouted.

Then he began to sing. It was a slow and soulful version, a perfect, honest Lennon in every aspect, almost sacrilegiously so, a version the man himself might have approved:

"When I was younger, so much younger than today," he crooned from his gut, a tear in his eye. "I never needed anybody's help in any way."

Masel nervously touched a foot-switch with his toe, his heartbeat hard, erratic. Longman's lasers began to dance around him, twirling, like flying ballerinas.

The audience were riveted, mesmerised.

Suddenly, a blast of white light flooded onto the haunted house behind him. There was a clap of thunder in time with Masel's instrumental break, and Keith Moon appeared, his holographic ghost drumming silently and ghoulishly in mid air.

The audience sucked in breath with one simultaneous gasp. They seemed to draw back then forward.

Soulful Otis Redding began to glow and move, as if in exquisite pain, in one of the windows. Then, in another window, Brian Jones, his hair hippyish, his eyes drugged, shook his head wildly and ran his fingers up and down the fretboard of his ghostly electric guitar.

Buddy Holly leaped from a window into nothingness, then back into the window. Several people in the crowd shrieked. The old wooden house creaked loudly and gruesomely.

A giant laser flash cracked to the sound of booming thunder. Thick chains, with horrific torture clamps at their ends, rattled and jumped eerily beside the house, and then moved across the face of Keith Moon. The laser beams shimmered snake-like, bent and sparkled as if in magnificent, heavenly exaltation.

"HELP!" Masel cried, red laser light refracting boldly against his guitar and then into the audience like space-gun fire. "I need somebody. Help! Not just anybody. Help!"

Screams now came at him from the crowd. Most of the audience were on their feet, except for a few at the front of the balcony. Masel played on, rocked steadily with his silent, ghostly rock band.

The heat in the place was becoming intense. Masel attempted to ignore it. But by his third song (Jim Morrison's When the Music's Over), sweat soaked his back, legs, and slippery palms.

With soul and feeling, he sang "...Music is your only friend...until the end...until the end..."

Beneath the helmet, his head was like an oil-soaked mop ablaze. Then, Katy began to appear in his mind, deviously. It was a thin, abstract image at first, but it grew quickly more vivid, trailing like a smoke-cloud across the front of his brain.

"...People are strange when you're a stranger..."

Masel's love for her simultaneously anguished and angered him. He shook his head to see if it would help. It did at first, but then not. He grew angrier and by the time he reached Jimi Hendrix's Purple Haze he was furious.

"Purple haze is in my brain," he cried out. "Lately things don't seem the same."

The crowd were completely in his hands now. They were jumping to the music, swelling with song, dancing, beating the floor with their feet, agog at the visual wonders before them. They sang with Masel, as if in anthem, pointed in the air, swayed with each other in the motion of a wave. The auditorium shook. Masel thought the floor would crack and give way.

By the time he reached Janis Joplin, Masel's tormented cries became embittered with fury and heartache. He sang about loneliness, fear, betrayal, psychic desolation and emotional barriers, and somehow all this pain made him feel good.

Otis Redding howled silently, chillingly, did a twirl. The ghostly holographic band behind him seemed to be going crazy, moving and twisting in every which direction.

"Baby, when you ain't got nobody," Masel screamed, even his tongue sweating now. "Ain't nobody wants you."

Chord by enraged chord, he battered out his repertoir, the intense heat wrinkling every inch of his slippery body.

Fearing he was about to hyperventilate, Masel whipped off his Paul Kossoff head, his face blotchy and shocked by the sudden rush of oxygen, and pitched it into the audience. As he wrung the sweat from his beard, he saw a girl with a mountain-

ously-deep cleavage, freckles, and dark plum-pit eyes catch the
head and kiss it. The audience applauded, yelled uproariously
in celebration.

"It's too hot in there," he told them, his voice raspy. "I'll
do one of my own."

The audience cheered thunderously, like surf, whistled in
ecstatic approval, arms raised in the air, their heads moving
back and forth, circling, arching. They seemed to be dancing
some mystical dance, half-frenzied, as if with the Master of the
Universe.

Brimming with confidence now - he didn't know what
had come over him, or them - Masel launched straight into a fast
funky version of The Oy Gevalt Blues.

"My baby don't love me," he bellowed from his heart.
"Oyoyoyoyoyoy-oy."

He stomped angrily on another foot-switch. Lightning
cracked. The air heated with the tumultuous press of bodies.
Laser beams shot around him like machine gun fireflies. Then
there was a bellowing clap of thunder, and the house behind
him began to flash and glow, as if in a boiling hellfire or perhaps
it was the omnipresence of God. Masel's eyes sweated. He felt
that he was in the presence of the uncanny or the supernatural,
for then, suddenly before his eyes, Yahweh appeared. He came
out of the crowd from the front row, bearded, his mouth open
as if in anticipation, white smoke billowing round him.

"My God. What are you doing here?"

Yahweh responded in thunder, but Masel understood
him. "You have seen how I bore you on eagles' wings to arrive
at this place. Now, then, if you obey me and keep my covenant
you shall be my treasured possession among all the peoples."

"But I'm just a folk singer."

"Not anymore you're not. You're a man."

"Oh no, here we go again. In that case, what do you wish?"

"You must use what you have created," said Yahweh. His
eyes were white and burning.

"What have I achieved?"

"You have created your own freedom, whether you know

it or not. Truly great men can create freedom for others, in the process of creating their own."

"But what have I, in fact, achieved?"

"Me. I am your greatest creation, because I am everything that is good."

The crowd chanted, "All the Lord has spoken we shall do."

Yahweh, whistling faintly to the tune of California Here I Come, vanished in a puffy cloud of bright-white smoke.

Masel strained for concentration. "Because I've got the oy gevalt blues..." he sang on.

He snapped out of it, still strumming, shaking his head. What was happening to him?

Astonished, Masel played for the turmoil and confusion of his life and the weird way it seemed to fit together. He played for San Francisco fog. He played, heart-laden, for Zelda and the children he never had. He played for space, for freedom and for escape, for poor Sam, poor Jenny, poor Katy. He played for creation. Then the images in his mind of Katy and MacGregor again and again began to drive at him.

He closed his eyes and breathed lightly. To forestall possible disaster, struggling against the weirdness in his head, he finished the song and took a half-time intermission.

* * *

Backstage, in the semi-darkness, he could only make out shapes. The place, he saw, was teeming with life, chaos. Masel, profusely dripping sweat onto the black wooden floor, his vision blurred, stumbled behind a hot curtain in a soggy trance.

The people around him seemed oddly distant, as if lost in time, like ghosts, moving silhouettes. Masel's breathing remained heavy, almost forced. Clutching his guitar to his breast, as though it were a living person to whose soul he was forever bound, he gazed around him and felt like a stranger looking in. Who were all these people? Through the steamy air, the light of someone's cigarette near him brightened then dimmed. He could smell its noxious odour. He now saw that most of the people were wearing work overalls, although there were also a couple of policemen and roadies among them.

"What's going on in this place?" Masel asked a teenager in dirty blue overalls.

"Heating system's jammed on full, can you not feel it?"

Masel's eyebrows dripped irritably. "You think I was born on the sun? Of course I can feel it."

Abruptly, a little man with a houndstooth suit and wrinkled pear-shaped face appeared before him, as if conjured out of thin air. He clasped Masel hard on the shoulder then let go. "The name's Heinrich Shnazelberg."

"Huh?" Masel looked past him, uncertain as to whether he was actually there.

Everything around him was like a bleary, old, black-and-white movie. For a moment, he thought he was dead. He felt as though he were seeing from beyond the grave. He raised his left hand, like a general ordering the charge, testing the air.

"Oy vey."

"Dr Masel," said Shnazelberg, his voice chiseled like a New Jersey cab driver. Masel, half-listening, looked around in petrifaction. Shnazelberg went on, "I'm from Chutzpa Music Incorporated in New York City. I know you're busy, so I'll make this brief. The bottom line is I like your show and I want to do business."

All Masel could say was "Huh?"

"I also hear through the grapevine that you're not exactly prosperous these days," said Shnazelberg. "This sort of show is one thing, but real success is another."

Masel stared at him in bafflement.

"That song," Shnazelberg said, coughing badly, "The Oy Gevalt Blues, I can make it a big hit. There's an enormous Jewish market back in the States. Believe me, a great deal is at stake here. And with your talent, sir, need I say more."

Masel, blushing radiantly, guffawed. He was now convinced that Shnazelberg was a figment of his imagination. Nightmare or dream, he thought, I might as well enjoy it.

But in the same instant, he saw Katy coming toward him. Her face was like a heart, luminous as the moon, her head lifted in a frozen smile. With a shock, he remembered making love to her. Why must I torment myself? he wondered. He thought of Longman raping her. How could she have two children by him, after that? What kind of person was she? In his mind, Masel pitied her, saw her life as tragic. He tried to look away, but she was staring at him, still smiling. He flicked a glance at Shnazelberg to see if he was still there, but his eyes were forced back. The other people around him were like the ghostly holograms in Longman's haunted house.

Shnazelberg dropped a card into Masel's jacket pocket. "Call me at a better time. But make it soon. As I said, a great deal could be gained for both of us. Business is business."

Katy dismissed Shnazelberg with a hiss. She seemed somehow older, thinner.

Then Masel caught her hand with both of his. "Listen, Katy, I know this isn't the time..." He laughed and, sweating, nervously looked past her out to the audience, then back into her face. It took considerable self-control for him to stop tears flooding. "Come to California with me," he said, beseechingly, rambling like a madman, the light of desperation in both eyes. "I'm leaving after the show. To cut a long story short, I love you. Let's forget everything before. Let's just get this show over with and leave. What do you say? Please say yes."

She looked at him in amazement. A wince fixed itself around her mouth, and she threw a look back to the workmen. At last, apparently by an act of will, she forced a smile. "We'll talk about this later," she said, putting her fingers up to his whiskers. Then her smile turned to a pout. And as if in slow motion she brought her lips up to his and kissed him, her tongue trapping his like a snare.

Masel jumped miserably to her embrace. Groping for his self-control he felt himself melting. Yet, suddenly, the secret of what afflicted him became clear; in the same moment her kiss enraged him.

"I won't have it," he heard himself saying out loud. "No, I won't have it. I won't be a party to any of this anymore." How many times must a man be trapped by the same tongue?

The answer blew in the wind. Katy pushed him away.

* * *

Before Masel knew where he was, he was back on stage, the crowd once again applauding, anxious for more of whatever he had done previously. He stared out at the darkness before he moved, his fists uncontrollably clenched.

Breathing heavily, Masel hurried, almost ran, to the piano. He contemplated putting on the John Lennon head, but shied from it; the heat was too much for him to bear.

The audience clapped excitedly. They were on their feet again. Longman fired a beam. It spun magically through the air, leaving dappled light trails before Masel's eyes.

For the first time ever, Masel launched into Imagine, not as John Lennon but as Elliot Masel. He played it in G, his favourite key.

A mellow harmony of colours began to flow before his eyes.

He began gently, deeply, almost hypnotically, chord after steady chord, forcing most of his anger into a strange sublimated self-restraint. Yet, he was still partly lost in it by the middle of the opening instrumental, and didn't at first notice that the humidity had stuck fast the middle G key.

When he did notice, he said, "Gevalt. Holy shit," by accident into the microphone.

The heat got hotter.

A murmur rose up from the audience. He shrewdly moved down to F-sharp. His chords began to sound like weird clinking, tavern-piano glissando. What the hell was going on? The heat and humidity also affected the PVC piano stool; it was now greased with sweat. He was sliding every which way, breathing hard, like a cowboy trying to stay on a furiously bucking bronco.

He groaned to himself, almost sliding completely off the seat. Then, while pouncing energetically onto a high F-sharp-minor chord, he found that, against his will, he had swivelled on his ass around to face the audience in mid verse. The chord he made was not of the piano, but of the squeaking, glistening stool.

Snickering laughter rose after silence. Masel's heart raced. He feared the audience slipping away from him.

He slid back on the seat and continued to sing raspily, as if gasping for water.

He sucked on his lips. God save me, he said to himself, in between the verses. When two F-sharps and three B-majors stuck, Masel, ever the professional, still refused to abandon the tune. Instead, he tried to free the note by furtively kicking the sustain pedal. It did him no good. A foolish idea. A renewed rage rose in him and, with his heel, he booted the piano's ornate wooden leg. Then, all at once, it gave way and the instrument thudded heavily to a tilt, hunched to one side, at a thirty-five degree angle, like a sad, old wounded elephant dying on its hunkers.

"Holy shit," he yelled into the microphone. "God damn it. Son of a bitch, God damn it. Holy shit. Gevalt. Son of a bitch."

He would gladly have cremated the thing if he had a match to do the trick.

He thought of Katy. We might have made it together. A gloom descended on him. Fuck it, he thought. It occurred to him his destiny was no longer in his hands. Laughter and wolf whistles echoed in his head and throughout the hall.

He hesitated for a moment, before rising from the stool. As he fled the stage, sweat flew from him in every direction, his beard rabbinical, his hair, wild, like a mathematician.

Midnight struck in then out. The New Year bells rang through the auditorium, but Masel was oblivious, only heard them faintly, as if from within his own head.

A moment later, he returned, a metal fire axe in his hand. The audience were riotous with laughter. Blow by blow, he hacked the piano to pieces.

Some of the audience began to scream after being hit by stray, flying blocks of ivory and wood. His blows made thudding sounds, and he insanely chopped the instrument until it was mangled firewood. He stomped on the remains, furiously jumping up and down on them, until the last of his energy had at last deserted him. My first Gizmo for this piano, he thought, his heart swollen with rage. A fair exchange. Their piano for my ruined marriages. They both deserved death for not living.

In that moment, Masel felt extraordinary relief. He stood motionless, exhausted, puffing, attempting to regain his breath. He was terrified, felt weak as water all over. He would have cried out, but his voice was frozen in his throat.

He relaxed his fingers, and let the axe fall from his hand with a deep clunk on the wooden stage. Several ushers and police came to restrain him. He raised his hands to cover his eyes and a policeman conked him on the head with his baton.

Masel was carried off the stage unconscious.

Four

A few days into the New Year, wearing Katy's duffel coat and his Californian shades, a bearded fugitive escaped from British police custody on a charge of inciting a riot and malicious damage to a grand piano, Masel furtively entered the flat at Bowmont Terrace, while Katy was at the laundry. He had been watching the house all morning and then followed her before slipping back. He looked dishevelled, desperate.

Masel the Jewish bandit.

The house was strangely quiet, yet somehow alive, sun-bright. There was a distant feeling about the place, something not quite belonging, perhaps him. Familiar things seemed tainted with strangeness: the flowered wallpaper in the hall, a child's crayon on the floor, the black and white tiles in the bathroom. In the living room, he found Sam playing with his toy dumper truck; Jenny was building a tower with plastic red bricks. They looked up, as if in glee, when Masel appeared.

"Daddy," Sam called. "You're home."

"Da..." said Jenny, salivating as she giggled.

Masel had to fight to hold back weeping. "Put your coat on Sam, we're going out."

"Where?"

"To see the planes."

He put Jenny's tiny ski jacket on . As he was lifting her, he accidently knocked over her tower of bricks. She began to cry.

"You can build hundreds of others later," he said to her, hugging her close, pacifying her, almost tearful again.

He scribbled a note to Katy and left it on the kitchen table, propped up against a carton of orange juice.

* * *

They left the apartment - Masel, his Gizmo in one hand and Jenny in the other; Sam, as usual, lagged a few feet behind, good-natured. They made their way to Glasgow Airport by bus. Rubbing the bump on his head where the policeman had clobbered him, Masel took a slow look out of the window as they crossed the Clyde. The snow clouds had cleared, revealing a big, frosty, blue sky.

"I want my mummy," said Sam, becoming restless in the seat beside Masel.

"So do I," said Masel, Jenny on his lap. "Don't worry. Everything will be all right."

Over a quick beer in the airport cocktail lounge, twenty minutes before he was due to board, he bought Sam a diet coke and Jenny a small can of orange juice with a looped straw. Although he was expecting her, Masel, in a mirror behind the bar was panicked to see Katy running toward him. Tears were streaming down her face. His heart beat racing, he held on tightly to the kids.

Katy came bolting up, her breasts pointing accusingly at him, and stopped just in front of him, her hair wild. Her mouth was angry, but her green eyes were soft, emotional. "What the hell do you think you're doing? Give me my children."

Masel smiled wanely. "I had to get you here somehow," he said as heartily as he could.

"Give me my children." she demanded. "Now." Her voice was husky. He noticed dark circles around her eyes.

Masel let them go and they ran to their mother, weeping because she was now weeping. Katy put her hand desperately through her hair, pushing it back from her face.

She spoke rapidly."What's going on, Elliot? What are you doing? I should have called the police after I saw your note. How did you get away from them? Where have you been for the last two days?"

"Hiding." He smiled ironically.

"Where?"

"Where else? In the Botanic Gardens - well, the Botanic Hotel, which overlooks the gardens. I woke up after the concert in the back of a police car. I saw two cops standing outside having a cigarette, so I just slipped out the other side."

Katy shook her head, incredulous. "You're totally crazy, do you know that? "

"Come to California with me."

"Now? You must be crazy."

"Maybe," he said, "but I'm serious. The plane leaves in forty minutes."

She was smiling at him, her green eyes on him. "It's not too late to change your mind. You were in all the papers again."

"As a piano killer? An escaped fugitive?"

"You are crazy."

"I'm not, I'm just scared." He smelled her perfume, his nose ravished. For good or ill, he still loved her; he couldn't help himself. He noticed her firm calf muscles and the way her skirt clung to her beautiful hips. He always liked that.

"I forgive you," she said.

When Masel looked at her, he found her wanting; then he found himself wanting. "I forgive you."

Katy pushed her hair back again, and slammed a smile at the eavesdropping barman. Masel looked but didn't see him.

"It was you, wasn't it?" she said, quietly, her lips half way to Masel's ear. "That night at George MacGregor's door?" When Masel said nothing, his heart pounding, she went on. "You forget, Elliot, I've had to survive on my own, with two children, for a long time. It's difficult to get out of the habit. I treat people the way they've always treated me. I'm sorry if I hurt you - I never actually wanted to hurt you; I always felt for you. To tell the truth, I did love you and still do - but sometimes it's hard to resist an opportunity when it comes along."

"I spoke to Longman," he said, his heartbeat gaining momentum as he spoke, his mouth dry. "I think I know everything."

Katy looked at him, at first shocked, then not. She took a deep breath. "So now you know. So what?"

"I don't know what to do," he said, shaking his head in confusion. His mind snagged on the thought that even the most terrible betrayals and mistakes might be forgiven. Why did he bring her here? he asked himself. Because she was sinking in her own past, as he had been? Because together they could make it, and with love and trust they would rise above all that fettered them? With a shock, he remembered Yahweh at the GBH. "I don't know how to end this," he said, feebly. "All I know is I want you, Sam and Jenny to come with me."

Her eyes shot up into his face. "My life is here. Now that I have your two concerts under my belt, I can't just throw them away. I worked hard to achieve what I have."

He glanced at the children. "But who will love you? Longman? MacGregor?"

Her eyes were abruptly lightless. "Longman's dead," she said. "He drowned himself in the bath yesterday morning. I thought you knew."

Masel's own heart stopped for a moment, then it recovered. He thought for a second: suppose she killed him. No. He erased the idea. He paused to wipe the sweat from his eyebrows, recomposing himself. "I didn't know. I'm sorry. But what did he or MacGregor ever do for you? They only used you. You must know that."

Katy slowly shook her head. She was quiet for a moment. "You're wrong. I used them." Jenny began to cry again and Katy bent down to hug her. She looked up, distracted. "It was you at that door, wasn't it?"

"In that case, stop using people. It can only end in disaster. Look at it this way: when I came here eight months ago, you were my ticket to freedom. Now I'm yours. Even though I know now that you tricked me. But I don't care about that, because I love you."

Katy bit her bottom lip pensively; Jenny stood watching her, her pout drooping slightly. "In all honesty, I don't believe anybody could love me, truly, except my children. That's why I had them, if you want psycho-analysis, even with a fucking bastard like Longman."

"You're wrong, Katy, I love you. I'm also your freedom. I want you to see that. You have to break free from those terrible things that hold you down. This is your chance, Katy, take it. I'm offering it to you. I must be crazy, but I do love you."

"Longman is dead." she said. "I am free. I think we should try it again here." She was smiling a little now. "Just to see if you can make it to the end of a show."

He grinned at her comment, but said, "Come with me."

"You're special, Elliot. You're like something from another world, a curiosity, something from the past. Let's face it, you're exclusive. We could be a wonderful team if you stayed here."

As exclusive as leprosy, he thought. Masel the performing leper. "That's it?"

She looked into his eyes. "Sex," she said, flatly. "We have good sex, don't we?"

Gulping, he thought of MacGregor. "Spare me."

"Well, we had good sex, whether you want to admit it or not. Stay. I feel lonely."

His cheek twitched emotionally. "I can't stay, " he said, "because I can see what will happen if I do. You're too caught up in a life that's guaranteed to destroy you, and me along with you. I've been down there, Katy, and I never want to go back. If I've learned anything in this country, it's that opportunities are few and so you have to invent your own freedom. But to do it, you have to break free from the past and your failures. I know about your past. Besides, I'm a wanted man, remember?" He was sweating profusely now in the bright yellow airport light and wiped his forehead with the sleeve of her duffel coat. She stared at him, her neck strained, said nothing. He went on. "I know what Longman did to you. I'm just now beginning to understand your needs and what you must feel. This is really the beginning for us. Don't kill it before it starts. Break free, Katy. I can make you free, because I love you."

Now she looked at him angrily, but her eyes were tearful. "You're so obsessed with your stinking failures, you make me sick. You ruin everything with them."

Masel saw the justice of her remark. "It's success I have the problem with," he confessed. "What can I say to you?"

"You can say you'll stay."

"I can't."

"It sounds like yes."

Masel said he was sorry.

"Elliot," she said, suddenly crooning. Then she seized his hand as if he were Sam. Masel shook loose, so she held his head by the cheeks, gripping his whiskers in her fingers, and tried to kiss him, but his head nuzzled down to her breasts until her embrace loosened, and he slipped free. He could hardly breathe.

They stared at each other, wanting, hurting.

Masel handed her a deeply hued, though somewhat faded, half petalless, plastic red rose from the bar counter. It was the colour of her hair. She looked at it, incredulously, leaving him to hold it helplessly in the air. He awkwardly withdrew his arm, the plastic rose drooping sadly in his hand at his side.

"I want my duffel coat back," she said, wiping her cheek.

He took it off and threw it at her in anger. It lay on the floor. He tossed the rose on top of it.

"Stay," Katy said. Light came from her skin.

"Come to California with me. Be truthful with yourself. If we can be together here, we can be together in California."

Katy screamed, throwing a fist down abruptly at her side. "Oh God, Elliot. Enough of this. You want the truth, okay, let's have it out. If I went to California, we'd drive each other crazy. It would be the same if you stayed. You'd never trust me and I'd never know. It would be like our own private nightmare, like some secret murder." Tears welled up in her eyes, sadly magnifying them. She spoke as if with sorrowful admission, her lip gently quivering. "I couldn't bear to live like that. It's no good, Elliot, I can see it would never work." She was crying now. "That's the truth."

"We'll never know unless we give it a shot."

"Elliot, you're not listening to me. I'd rather you remembered me when I loved you. Don't you see. The only way we can be in love is to be apart. I can't explain this very well." Katy took a handkerchief out of her coat pocket and wiped her eyes. Then she blew her nose. "One side of me wants you to stay, needs you to stay; the other side of me knows that we can only love each other if you go."

"That's not love."

Her eyes were wide, as if she were terrified. He felt his heart beat with momentary fright. Jenny was sobbing and Katy picked her up and held her. "Try to understand that I'm choosing love above everything else. And I don't think I'll ever be the same, but it's a risk I'm taking. I'm only just realizing this myself, but I have to let you go."

The air around him seemed oppressively still and bright. His flight number came over the loudspeaker. "Come to California with me," he said. It was his final offer.

"Go fuck yourself, Elliot" she said, her breasts pointing westward. Turning sharply on her heels,weeping, she left in a hurry, Jenny held fast in her arms. Sam, quietly sobbing, jumped to Masel and hugged him around the leg, then ran after his mother and sister.

Masel, a large tear in his eye, picked up the duffel coat and went home. He left the rose.